The frog and the scorpion

Steevan Glover

Find out more about the author and his work at
www.steevanglover.com

Steevan Glover was born in the Seychelles, but lived with his family in Malawi before they eventually settled in Bedfordshire, England. A former drama student and rugby player Steevan lives with his wife and son in a village near Windsor. The frog and the scorpion is his first novel.

This book owes its existence to the support of many people. Special thanks must go to Kay, Rob, Martin, Annie and my father. To the various family and friends that have read and re-read manuscripts, offered advice, encouragement and support I proffer my heartfelt thanks.

For you and moo

Prologue

The naked, pallid body meandered its way through the murky water. The morning summer sun had risen over the Essex lowlands and begun to burn the lingering mist from the banks of the river. Sunlight dazzled off the aluminium-clad Thames Barrier towers, Gregor Bartok's final obstacle before the tide tried to pull his lifeless body to the freedom of the choppy seas of the English Channel.

His obese frame had provided an early morning feeding frenzy for many of the estuary's scavengers as it drifted aimlessly and unnoticed past the Millennium Dome, Greenwich and towards the iconic Barrier. The water cleansed him of any trace evidence as to who had killed and mutilated him before setting him off on this final scenic journey.

The river narrowed towards the Barrier, the funnelled water sped up and moved towards the giant towers with greater force. The body spun and pitched in the eddies and faster flowing current as it silently floated towards the driftwood and debris-cluttered at the base of the central tower.

Gregor's outstretched foot reached the tower and debris first, snagging amongst the river detritus anchoring the body to the tower. The fast current pushed at his rotund frame, dragging it round and leaving the body trailing in the water. The body rose out of the water, pushed up onto the debris by the fast flowing river. Lying exposed at the base of the tower the dead man now revealed the full extent of his grisly demise.

Chapter One

"Find her! I don't care what you do or how long it takes…
track her with a sodding sniffer dog for all I care! But fucking *find*
her!" Barry yelled.

At the other end of the line, Ramon heard only the
unemotional click of the dial tone. He didn't hear the receiver
being slammed down with a reverberating bang, he didn't witness
Barry pick up the phone and hurl it against the wall. He didn't hear
Barry's unnecessarily loud yell of "useless fucker," nor the
multiple kicks aimed at the unarmed and innocent wastepaper
basket.

It had been a bad day for Barry. Actually it had been a bad
week and you could even go so far as to say, that on balance it had
been a bad year. Business had slumped, there had been mistakes,
mostly just small ones, but one or two big ones – they all added up.

Barry Hunt could feel the pressure mount each day,
weighing down on his narrow shoulders. When he looked at the
sad tired face that greeted him in the mirror each morning, he
realised he wasn't the man he hoped he would become, the
gnawing realisation that what little he had achieved would soon be
destroyed only made his mood worse. His manor, his piece of the
South London underworld, had many rivals and now they were
moving in for the kill. He doubted he had the muscle or belief left
to fight them off.

Barry wasn't desperate, but he was down the road to desperate. The scruffy third floor of the Duke of Bedford pub served as his office. Not flash, never mind trendy or smart, merely functional. The Duke was the archetypal East End pub, although it was south of the river in Putney, where it stuck out like an American theme pub in downtown Baghdad.

Barry had bucked the trend of taking his organisations into respectable modern office-like premises. At fifty five Barry had settled into the 'old dog' stereotype, his compact frame supported an easy living gut, and a penchant for Merlot and single malt whisky had given his jowly face a crimson hue. He didn't have the capacity nor inclination for change.

"Mickey…Mickey…" Barry barked out in the direction of the corridor outside his office; he knew his oldest ally would have heard the commotion.

"Yeah?" came a gruff muffled reply.

"Get your arse in here…I've got a job for you."

Barry remained seated as Mickey eased himself into the room. At forty five, he was a little slower than he had been. But with greying temples and a maturing body came an experienced mind. Massive, that's how people thought of Mickey Finn. A truly massive, scary man. He'd boxed as a professional but the rules and discipline had never suited him. He had the physical attributes to succeed, six foot five and close to nineteen stone, some fat now, but still a whole lot of muscle. His square head sat on a tree trunk neck, no matter from what angle you looked there was no discernible division from one to the other. It was as if he had swallowed a Welsh dresser: shoulders, waist and hips formed an almost perfect rectangle.

Mickey sat down in the chair across from Barry's desk. It groaned in protest. He had worked with Barry Hunt for twenty years. He had always liked him. Barry had funded some of his fights and had always found him work. Occasionally he'd given Mickey money when he'd needed it and he'd even kept in touch when Mickey went inside. Not that Barry had had any real obligation. Mickey had been working for another firm at the time, but the job he was on had gone tits up, a stupid and unnecessary balls-up that had left Mickey holding the money when the shit came down. He'd taken the fall, of course, and done the time. That was what you did. And he'd expected to be looked after – that *used* to be how it was done. But it hadn't happened that way. That had really pissed Mickey off. Barry and Mickey were old school, and it was Barry who'd looked out for him, stood by him.

Mickey Finn *liked* that.

Barry paced around behind his desk, nibbling at his fingernails like someone picking at a tasteless appetiser. He hadn't been like this for a long time. Not since the Brazilian whore incident of '95. Mickey had cleaned that mess up as well.

"It's Melissa…I can't find her. I know what you think," he put his hands up to stop any comeback, "No surprise… but she hasn't gone alone this time."

11

Mickey nodded slowly, knowing that only a woman had this effect on him. Barry had taken a shine to Melissa...he always fell for the wrong ones. Melissa was a whore. Literally and metaphorically always on the take. She did nothing, said nothing or even acted without calculating what was in it for her.

Mickey had a sneaking admiration for the girl. She looked like butter wouldn't melt, nice tits too.

"What she take?" Mickey asked.

"The Bartok fund."

"Oh fuck…" said Mickey.

Chapter Two

Adam sat in his car. The air con hummed out its icy tune, the windows shutting out the world as well as the stifling heat of the day. His car thermometer read that it had hit 30 degrees outside, day three of a mini heatwave. As usual, the complaints poured in, "too hot, can't work". These, the same people that a week before had bemoaned the week of light irritating showers and grey skies. "What kind of summer is this, I hate our summers." Adam disliked the hypocrisy and seemingly addictive habit of people to moan and complain. He liked it hot, it felt good to feel the sun on your skin, to have that desire to strip and leap into rivers or lakes. Kids would do it, he had, leaping into the river Itchen by the water meadows at the St. Cross Monastery, but as an adult you hold back, you become so conservative.

He looked at the map. Croydon to Winchester, no matter which way he went, it would be slow. He revved up the Renault Megane – the diesel engine apologetically simpered into life as he indicated and pulled out from his parking space and onto the main road. He did a lot of driving, the Megane had proved to be a sensible car, he could get nearly 600 miles out of a tank and he didn't need to impress anyone with the look of his car. If anything, a modest car made him more likeable to his financial clients. He understood that as an independent financial advisor a stereotyped image followed him, but he wasn't from an accounting or banking background, he was different.

The car suited Adam Warriner physically, like it, he was compact and efficient. His long body and short legs made him appear shorter than his near six foot, his midriff had that familiar lazy paunch of an idle twenty something and it came not from excessive drinking or overindulging, but more from a case of relaxed muscle. It would be safe to say that Adam had not entered into physical activity or even run in anger for a good ten years.

As he drove he flicked on the Bluetooth earpiece and waited for the beep. "Messages" he said, activating his mobile to retrieve his voicemails. He had two. One from his mum and one from Jake. He called his mum.

At fifty, Mrs Kathleen Warriner devoted herself to her two pride and joys, the first, her garden, continuing the green fingered vision of her late husband; the second of course was her only child, Adam.

She answered on the third ring.

"Hello"

"Hi mum"

She called him every day. He didn't always answer, he rarely answered in fact, but that didn't matter. She liked to call; she liked to let him know all was well.

"Hello sweetheart," she replied in faintly mock surprise. "How has your day been?"

"Same as always. Talking to desperately dull people, about dull things they don't understand and earning money for filling in forms." Adam had delivered the speech before. He liked to be sardonic about his job.

"Glad you're still loving it."

Adam had always been something of a loner, his job suited this, what few friends he had she rarely saw. Girlfriends proved rarer still.

"Now, your birthday is only a month away. I need to plan for the dinner, I presume you are coming?"

Adam smiled, another year and another birthday meal.

"Yes I'll be there. Steak and chips as usual please!"

"Well God forbid we should try anything new, hey? Anyone else you want to invite?"

She always asked and he always said no. As a supposedly joyous occasion his birthday meal lacked any real fun. They toasted his father, the only joint active moment of mourning they performed each year.

One year they had met in his friend Jake's bar before going out to eat, changing the tradition. It hadn't worked out as planned. Adam had wanted, selfishly he later realised, to take the situation away from the family home, away from the memories and try to make it a happy occasion. He misread the importance, for his mum, of having it at home, surrounded by those memories.

"Funny mum, real funny. You'll be the first to know if I meet someone special, promise," Adam paused, bit his bottom lip before starting again – "Look I wanted to tell you that I won't be round tonight as I promised. I know you need the light sorting out in the bathroom, but I have only just left Croydon and, well, there's something I need to take care of..." He trailed off.

He could almost hear the disappointment in his mother's breathing. He hated letting her down, he knew how much his little but often visits meant to her. It also made up for only one extended Sunday visit each month.

"I know you're busy. It can wait until Sunday darling."

"Cheers Mum, I have to go as I'm driving. I'll see you at 12.00 on Sunday."

With that they exchanged their customary sign off and the phone went dead. He hadn't lied to his mother, he really did have something to take care of, but he still felt guilty.

Adam's father passed away shortly after his 21st birthday. Adam had spent the six years since the funeral trying to remember his face without the need to be reminded by a picture; it became harder with each passing year.

He called Jake using speed dial one.

Jake answered in two rings. "Hello sir?" he said in his customary manner.

"You rang me?" said Adam – both clearly not used to indulging in small talk.

"I did. I have considered your dilemma and after careful consideration I have reached a conclusion."

"Please articulate," Adam replied.

"With pleasure. I think you should tell the silly bitch to fuck off!"

"Just like that?"

"Well you could punch her as you throw her out, but I rather think that would be overkill. She's trouble, always was and always will be … do you need that back in your life again?" Jake, as usual offered his opinion bluntly.

"Well I'll take your point of view into consideration. But I think a more diplomatic approach may prove more fruitful."

"Really."

"Yes Jake... we can't all adopt your blunt militaristic approach to life," Adam said.

"I suppose... but Adam, be warned. The damsel in distress routine is simply a load of bollocks. Don't get suckered in, she probably wants money again and maybe even a place to hole up while she sets up the next loser to rip off. My worry, my friend is that you're the next loser in her sights."

Adam smiled to himself. Jake always looked out for him. He didn't need reminding about her, trouble followed her, and it always would. But when someone you loved needs your help, you help.

"You don't know her Jake… you judge her on what my mum says about her."

"..and the stories you have regaled me with. I remember her from the bar as well… if nothing else I know the type. I appreciate

Adam, that you shouldn't judge based upon the opinions of others…"

Adam sighed, "If you knew her…well look anyway it's my life isn't it…"

"That it is… be careful though. Have you finalised on the house?"

"Don't worry I know what I'm doing. The house..? Nearly… need to set a date for exchange that's all."

There was a moment's silence, neither man felt the need to speak, Jake had offered Adam a way to terminate the increasingly uncomfortable conversation.

"She'll be gone by Saturday," Adam said wearily, ".. and we can all forget about her. Melissa Henderson isn't getting back into my life."

Jake let out a faint ironic chuckle, "Adam we're discussing her, she's coming to stay… she's therefore, already back in your life".

Chapter Three

Mickey walked out of the office and shut the door slowly and calmly. No histrionics. Boxing had taught Mickey many valuable lessons, the most important being patience, never rush at a challenge, think it through. There'd be plenty of time to panic later. By and large, he had been a successful fighter, mostly in the no-holds barred and bare knuckle format, where the less limiting rules suited his more brutal style. Mickey won not just because of his immense size and power, but also because he was never intimidated. Still, he knew that, sooner or later, you always meet a better man.

He pulled out the mobile phone and pressed speed dial three. It rang for two rings; then, predictably – voice mail.

"Jonno…it's Mickey. TURN YOUR BLOODY PHONE ON, Muppet! Please tell me you had someone on Melissa this week. Tell me what you know. Also prise Ramon off whatever girl he's on and tell him if he wants to hang onto his Spanish balls he needs to call me in the next ten minutes!"

He clicked the phone shut and strode into the pub's main bar. The pub served as the legit cover for much of Barry's and the manor's business, but with the sponsored boxing gym down the road, it was a bit too Lock Stock for Mickey's taste, but Barry thought he had an image to uphold. He sat at the bar and caught the barmaid's eye. She ignored the other punters and brought him an orange juice and lemonade. He took a sip and the phone rang.

"Ramon! ....Button it you greasy little ponce. Just answer *my* questions - When did Melissa go? ...Right, so that was the *last* night she worked? ... Why didn't *you* tell *me* she had "gone to visit her mum"...You what? You told Barry? You fuckwit...just answer the questions and stop fucking *thinking*. Got it? Good. Now listen carefully...check her room for any personal stuff, picture, letters whatever. Collect everything you can and have it ready in an hour."

He put the phone down and subconsciously wiped his hand on the bar towel. The phone rang again. Jonno this time.

"Spill the beans," Mickey said curtly.

"I didn't have a regular tail on her – but luckily I did that day." A nervous tinge of fear ran under what he said. "She left The Palace at about six p.m. She went straight to The Duke, went upstairs to see Barry, stayed mebbe ten minutes and then she headed off to Waterloo Station – no other stops. Got on the train to Bournemouth, with stops at Basingstoke, Winchester, Eastleigh, Southampton ...I think that's the lot."

"And..."

"And what?...My man didn't get on the fucking train with her, my task was to report activity, we weren't on fucking protection duty, sorry if we screwed up Mickey, but if I'd put one of the boys on the train we would've been one man down on the doors and Barry would've gone spare..." The voice wavered, confident in its rationale but fearful of the consequences.

"Fair enough. Get over to The Palace, Ramon is sorting through her gear, go through it with him, we need to find out where she may have gone. Have a word with the dizzy blonde bint, you know the one?"

Jonno didn't respond, unsure which dizzy blonde bint at The Palace Mickey meant. Mickey screwed his eyes shut, trying to recall the girl's name. "The one with the big tits and saggy arse…nice face…what's her bloody name?…Gemma!…yeah that's her. Always good mates those two…she may know something… and Jonno…*be nice!*"

Mickey didn't move from the bar. He finished the remains of his drink in one swift glug, and then banged the glass onto the bar and when the barmaid looked up at the sound, he nodded for another. Mickey didn't run about anymore. That's what you had monkeys for.

"Were you working Monday night?" he asked the barmaid.

Judy moved down the bar and focused on Mickey. She gave him her best 'I'm game if you are' smile.

"Yeah, I was on the back bar."

She leaned forward over the real ale pumps hoping mighty Mickey Finn would notice her ample cleavage. Mickey's eyes never strayed from her face.

"Did you see Melissa come in and visit Barry – would've been about 6.15pm."

Admitting failure Judy stood upright and answered.

"Yeah I saw her go up, but she didn't see Barry."

"What do you mean she didn't see Barry?"

"Not Monday night, Barry wasn't in Monday. He switched his meet with the Turks. Met them Monday night instead of Wednesday. I guess he left at five mebbe earlier".

"Who the fuck was upstairs minding the office?"

"No one really – Anton was minding the back bar door and minding the stairs as well I suppose. But you know Anton Fat Cock, could'a been there, could'a been in anything."

"Oh yes I know fucking Anton, where's the useless prick tonight?"

* * *

Adam signed off his final call and removed the Bluetooth ear piece. He hated the way it made his ear burn. He pondered the microwaves cooking his brain. He wondered about the health repercussions that would be played out on 'Watchdog' in twenty years time. The new cigarettes scare of the 21st century. Would mobile phones have to carry health warnings in the future?

Adam loved that Melissa inspired opinion and debate. She always had. She had been out of his life for a long time now, and no matter what people said of the girl, no matter what she had put him through, they hadn't shared the moments with her that he had. For a long time now he had survived only on his memories.

Adam rubbed his hands over his face, those same memories taking his mind off the slow journey home. The traffic began moving in spurts; at times like this he wished he had an automatic. He had managed to go three years without hearing anything from Melissa, no calls, no demands for money. Then out of the blue, via Friends Reunited, six years after she had walked out of his life, he got an email.

> *Hey babe...*
>
> *Long time no see. How are you? I have started to get myself sorted, this time for real. Been clean for over three months. Trying to break out of the life. It's hard when it's all you know.*
>
> *Did you mean what you said? I know it was a long time ago... but did you mean it?*
>
> *M. x*

He responded. The reply short, polite and non-committal.

She asked if he was in Winchester. He said yes.

She asked if he was single. He said yes.

She asked if she could see him. He said yes.

Three days later she turned up on his doorstep, at midnight.

That was last night.

Chapter Four

An hour after demanding where the fuck Anton was, Mickey had hold of him several inches off the floor against the wall of The Duke's back bar, supported by his bollocks.

"Tell me again...tell me it all again, Anton. Do not fucking lie, do not fucking edit it, I want the unabridged version or so help me you'll never get wood again...understand?"

Anton nodded. A big man himself, the ease with which Mickey lifted him clear off the floor proved to be an unnerving and painful experience. He wanted it to be over.

"Melissa came in on the Sunday" Anton spluttered the words out, "she said she would be popping in on Monday night, she said she knew Barry would be out but she wanted to set up "a surprise" for when he got back. Something he would love. I thought nothing of it; she was always popping in to see Barry..."

Mickey tightened his grip – "Tell me about Monday." Anton grimaced and mumbled through gritted teeth, "She came through the back, just waved and walked straight on up, two minutes later she came back down and out, that's it I swear..."

"Was she carrying anything with her when she went up Anton?"

"Yeah she had a shoulder bag, you know like an overnight thing."

"Did it look full on both trips?"

Mickey's grip tightened and Anton rose up another inch.

"Yeah Mickey, it seemed so anyway…"

"You are a proper fucking cunt Anton…do you think I'm stupid? Do you?

Anton had no idea what to say, he knew that when Mickey lost it with someone, it usually ended only one way.

"Course not Mickey."

"Why the fuck are you lying to me...?"

"I'm not…Mickey…"

Mickey thrust his hand up, launching Anton up the wall, his head colliding with the ceiling, Mickey used his supporting arm to grasp Anton by the lapels and throw him across the room, landing him, with a resonating thud, on top of the pool table, the balls scattering to the four corners of the room. Anton groaned, his head and back had smashed hard onto the beize covered slate.

Mickey picked up the nearest cue and thrashed it down across Anton's prostrate and infamous groin, snapping the cue in half. Anton doubled over in pain and rolled off the table clutching his now much abused bollocks, yelling.

"You, my son, should have prayed for a blameless fucking life!" Mickey stood high over the sprawled figure, his features blurred by the bright light from behind his head, "Think fucking hard on what I am about to say and just nod to confirm, do you understand?" Anton nodded, his hands thrust between his legs cradling his damaged groin.

"Melissa! She came in here for at least 15 minutes Anton. Judy said you weren't down here on the door, and I trust Judy. Melissa comes in and you and she aren't seen for at least fifteen minutes...see what I'm getting at? Where did she suck your cock Anton? In the bogs, the kitchen? Or did you just bang the slut on Barry's desk?"

Anton just groaned shaking his head. Mickey grabbed him by the lapels once more and pulled Anton's face to meet his. "You are a stupid man. After all the pussy you have had and could have, you decide to stick that big black cock of yours into the boss man's favourite skank!" Anton groaned, no discernible trace of agreement or contention on his face.

"You owe Barry £100 fucking grand Anton... now am I right?"

Anton wept, the tears collecting in the grimaced folds of skin around his eyes, finally he nodded. Mickey dropped him back to the floor. Straightening up, and buttoning his jacket, Mickey levelled his giant, size 13 foot and swung it hard across Anton's face. Anton's moaning ceased with a crack.

* * *

Mickey sat in front of Barry. He had just explained that Anton would not be working tonight nor any night soon.

Mickey didn't revel in imparting bad news, but he had a job to do.

"Melissa?"

Mickey nodded and knew that Anton would not be mentioned again. He understood Barry's gratitude for what he had done and for the efficiency of the process.

"She's in Winchester. She caught the 6.45pm train on Monday night. Turns out she used to live down there. Went to college there or something. She has two sets of bank accounts, the one she used up here, created by the ponce Ramon when she came off the streets. The others seem to be a hangover from her student life."

"So Ramon didn't have total control of her finances?"

Mickey shook his head. It was a primary part of a pimp's job to keep control, total control, of the girls' lives.

Barry looked at the letter.

"She left this in her room?" he asked.

"That and a few other scraps, no actual statements, the letter is asking her to call in and discuss the accounts, it had slipped behind the back of one of the drawers."

"How can we be certain she went to Winchester?"

"We can't be one hundred per cent. But it adds up. It's where she has gone before, apparently, although never more than an overnighter. We found some old train tickets to there as well…small details…anyway, one of the girls…Gemma …you remember her? ..popular with the Ayatollahs?"

"I know who you mean." Barry's face broke into a smile of recognition. Gemma was another former favourite, prior to his infatuation with Melissa. Gemma was a nice girl he remembered, she had educated him about the process of mannequin shopping. That is to say he simply went from store to store and if the outfit on the display mannequin took his fancy he bought the whole lot, size permitting. Barry enjoyed his odd claim to fame, he had never worn, let alone bought, a pair of jeans and anyway he felt more comfortable in his black suit and t-shirt combinations.

"Well Gemma became quite friendly with Melissa and apparently there's some ex-trick that lives down there, Melissa has talked of him, the falling in love type. Apparently Melissa has fleeced him before, in her street days. We're not sure of the address but we found a printout of a map under her bed, it's from streetmap.com, it's for a place called the Peninsular Barracks, off a Romsey Road. Only one place matched that on Google, a housing development in Winchester in the old Barracks, near the town centre." He pushed the map across to Barry, who glanced at it without much enthusiasm.

"When you combine the map and letter with the accounts, her doing a runner etc, we figure Winchester is the spot. We'll start with this street and see if she shows her face…"

Barry nodded. He was focused on the view out of the window and had stopped looking at Mickey.

"We've a picture of the trick, or who we think the trick is." Mickey, proud of the find, handed it to Barry. "It's Melissa and a guy, if you look in the background you can see the Statue of King Alfred, it's a Winchester landmark apparently. Gemma thinks he

29

might be the guy, the ex trick, but we can't be sure. I'll send Jonno down with a couple of lads to scope it out and locate her."

"Gemma offer up all this info voluntarily?"

"No. I provided her with an incentive."

Barry raised his eyebrows questioningly.

"I simply said if she helped find Melissa she would never have to shag you again." His big body shuddered slightly as he let out a little giggle. Barry managed a smile.

"I want you to deal with this personally Mickey. I want it done right…you know what I mean…no silliness!"

"I'll bring her back boss, I'll bring it all back."

Chapter Five

Adam pulled the Megane into his allocated space in front of the small town house and stayed in the car; it had been a tiring stop start journey. Melissa's email and subsequent return churned up so many memories, so many emotions; she framed so much of his past and defined how he felt about the present. He still had not come to terms with how he felt about her. Adam peered out of his car and through the main window into his kitchen. He was taken aback to see Melissa boogying while chopping vegetables. Melissa, it seemed, had not flogged all his worldly possessions, she hadn't trashed his house. In fact Adam came home to find Melissa singing along to Radio Two and preparing dinner.

This carefree dancing beauty was a far cry from the sheepish girl clutching her black bag to her chest when she had arrived the previous evening. She had arrived tired and agitated, but her mood had lightened a little after the ubiquitous cup of tea. Adam hadn't known what to say to her. They had sat and made small talk – Melissa, for once avoiding talking about herself, Adam nervously filling the gulf, telling her his news about his career.

"I'm pleased you're happy Adam… settled. It's a lovely house."

"How much do you want?" Adam had asked her, deciding to get to the point sooner rather than later. "What do you mean?" she asked, a bemused look on her weary face.

"Money! How much do you need this time?" Melissa nodded, put her tea down and looked as if she was readying herself for a difficult speech.

"I don't need your money, in fact I may be able to pay you back…"

The news had surprised Adam. She had wanted to go to bed, to tell him about it in the morning. "You owe me an explanation Mel, why should I let you into my house, with your track record?"

"Fair enough" was her reply.

"I'm still expecting some pimp or pusher to knock on the door, ready to play the heavy. I'm not in the mood anymore." There was more steel in his voice than he truly felt, but no one knocked on the door and Adam felt this time was different.

"Tell me Mel, or you're out …..right now! I'm off to work in the morning and I need to know what I have let into my house," he'd demanded.

"I'm escaping, Adam. It's in some people's interest for me not to escape. But it's in mine to get away. No one from my recent world knows anything about my life here. I can rest, think and decide where to go next."

"Where do I come in?"

"I had nowhere else to go Adam. I won't be in your hair for long I promise… but you have always been there for me, no matter what I did, you always answered…I need you one last time."

"No money this time Mel, not a penny, you understand that?" said Adam, wrinkling his nose and fidgeting uncomfortably.

"I don't expect you to trust me Adam – I don't blame for you for that either. I've been a shit to a lot of people, some, like you, didn't deserve it. All I can say is sorry. This time I mean it Adam. I also mean it when I say I don't need your money, I have severance money…". She had let statement hang like bait, but he hadn't bitten.

"In fact I may need your help investing it, it's not enough for life or anything like it but if I use it wisely I can start again."

Adam shuffled the dilemma over in his mind, he should kick her out. That is what he should do, he knew that. He looked at her tired face, a face that still had something of the Melissa he remembered and not just the shadow that had ghosted in and out of his life in the last few years.

"In the few times we've spoken Mel, the odd occasion we've met…you have never once asked about it…not once."

Mel pulled the bag closer to her and shrugged.

"I don't know what you want me to say."

"I don't want you to say anything…I want you to care, to show some understanding that the actions you took had repercussions…" he trailed off. He'd been searching for answers from Mel for a long time, he was so desperate for them that he felt he could even beat them out of her.

"My father had died and I needed you…you left me to be investigated by the police…you owe me," his voice was no more than a whimper and the stony silence that followed chilled both of them.

Adam gathered himself together and got to his feet.

"Look, you can sleep in the box room," he said.

Melissa didn't answer. She simply nodded. She looked afraid and alone. Adam thought about how vulnerable she looked, as if the cocky bravado had been drained from her. She didn't repeatedly sniff and track marks didn't litter her forearms, in fact she looked reasonably healthy – he figured with his limited knowledge he hadn't opened his door to a junky.

Adam stared through the car window watching the former love of his life dancing in the house and felt a twinge of guilt. He'd been hard on her last night, aggressive even, but seeing her now made his heart flutter. He was nervous about going in and starting the conversation they both knew they had to have.

She hadn't mentioned her email last night and that bothered him. She didn't mention her stealing from work which got him fired from the Westgate Hotel, which pissed him off. She said sorry, but he didn't think she knew what she was sorry about. Was she sorry for getting hooked on smack and turning tricks on the streets? Was she sorry that police stations always called him when they picked her up and she was out of it? It was always him she called to bail her out.

Adam shook himself out of the memories, collected his trappings and climbed out of the car, counting the twenty steps to his front door.

Melissa looked great. The music was turned up loud enough so she hadn't heard him enter and close the front door. He stood, framed by the door and stared at her, dressed in what Adam's mother would refer to as 'softies', a pair of tight cotton/lycra trousers and a vest top. No bra. They revealed all the natural beauty she still possessed, the vest top emphasised her pert breasts, the nipples slightly erect and the trousers hugged her cute round arse. She had aged for certain, and life had taken its toll, especially when you looked at her eyes, but she still had a hell of body and Adam still wanted it.

He realised he was staring, fantasising, so he looked up and away from the dancing buttocks, it was hard to do because they bobbed in time to Shaggy's "It wasn't me". He focused instead on the back of her head. Her hair was tied up and she didn't appear to be wearing make up. She looked fresh and she looked good.

He put his bag on the table with a thump; she turned at the noise and caught sight of Adam. A sudden pang of self consciousness surged through her, and she hurried to the radio to turn it down.

"Blimey you were quiet...sorry, I love that song, I haven't heard it for a while. You're home early!"

"Yeah" replied Adam softly, "I got away sooner than expected and so headed straight home."

Melissa raised an eyebrow and put her hands on her hips.

"Came home early to check up on me did you?"

Adam flushed slightly with embarrassment, but managed to hold it back, retorting, "no, well yeah… it's my house, not rented…so, I'm nervous, that's all."

"Well, that I can understand. Wish I'd known when you'd be back. I was going to tidy the house up, but then remembered it was you. I would make things look messier, so I stopped."

Adam smiled a little; he enjoyed the banter and liked the playful flirting undertone.

"I wanted to cook dinner for you, maybe glam up…you know to say - thank you."

Adam moved to the fridge and pulled out a bottle of Villa Maria Chardonnay and then rooted in the adjacent drawer looking for the corkscrew.

"You don't need to glam up – you look lovely." He liked the fact he wasn't lying, she wouldn't believe him of course, but meaning it sent a shot of adrenalin through his heart.

"Hardly! I don't have many clothes with me. Didn't have time for a comprehensive pack. Kind of scooted out under the radar!"

Adam handed her a glass of wine. She paused, held out her hand, then she pulled it back, almost scared it may burn her.

"No… no thanks. I am staying off everything. I'm serious about making a new start."

"It wasn't a test," Adam offered. "What's for dinner?"

She broke into a tired smile, rubbed her hands over her forehead and sighed. "Well there wasn't too much in, but I'm doing a Spag Bol. Missing the bacon but hey lots of garlic. I just need to cook the pasta…"

Adam took a big sniff, made his best satisfied and encouraging smile and said "I should've opened a bottle of red! I had no idea you could cook…"

Twenty minutes later, the meal had been served and consumed, they had eaten in relative silence. Adam knew the meal and the effort were nothing more than the appetiser; the main course would come now. Adam had stared across at her throughout the meal, trying to understand what he was doing, why had she really come back? There were the marks and scars, real and emotional, that her life had given her. But she wore them well. Adam wished he still didn't feel horny when he looked at her, he hated the control she had over him, even after all this time.

Adam had changed over the years, he'd watched his cheeky boyish face fade into a harder more lined and mature look. He had probably improved with age, but most notably, he had so much more confidence. They moved from the dining area which linked the kitchen area with the lounge and into the sofa defined section of the room. Adam flopped into his favourite brown leather armchair, Melissa sat on the sofa under the window opposite Adam.

They sat in silence for a few minutes and then Melissa gathered herself together and began.

"I guess you know by now that I'm running away Adam, story of my life. You need to know that I fucked up. I fucked up big style…I know what you think, nothing new there. But I need to try again."

Adam sat quietly. He had drunk most of the wine and was feeling a little numb.

"I'm sorry for what I did to you. I'm so sorry that I've taken and taken and abused people's trust and love. I am sorry for what I turned into… for what I allowed myself to become."

Adam carried on looking towards Melissa but not at her. She had no real idea how much she had hurt him, how long it had taken for him to get over her and move on. He still hadn't had a serious girlfriend since she left six years ago.

"You know bits of my life since I was here… you know I was an addict…you know I worked the streets… a lot has changed… but not all of it. I've been fucking for a living, not working the streets though, more an escort and brothel scenario."

Adam said nothing, no flicker of emotion on his face.

"It paid well Adam." She threw the words out, hopeful they might offer Adam a justification he valued.

"I can't explain how I spiralled into it but it all seemed like logical steps, I suppose I always used sex to get what I wanted from men, maybe I 'd done it for years. The leap is then only one of pride, you convince yourself that sex for money is simply pragmatic. I willingly allowed myself to be used...it was a sad way to live life."

38

"And the drugs…" Adam offered. "You slept with the people who supplied you drugs."

Melissa nodded. "It robbed me of my soul Adam. I didn't know who I was, I became someone else. I existed… I didn't live as such, just existed. When you get trapped in that particular cycle you can't get out… you try but you lack the will, the strength. There are always people who wanted to keep me in it as well, to keep me down."

Adam watched her carefully. She was balled up on the chair, her knees pulled to her chest. Her blonde hair hung in front of her face. She looked at him as she spoke, but Adam couldn't make out her features or see her eyes through the hair hanging in front of her face.

"I don't deserve trust… I can't ask for it, I don't expect it. I want you to understand that I am sorry. I want you to realise that I know why I am sorry and that I won't behave, no, CAN'T behave like that again."

Adam rested his wine glass on the arm of the chair, holding on to it at the base of the stem. He studied it for a moment, before realising she had stopped speaking and was now looking directly at him.

"How do I know that?"

"It's taken me years to realise what I am, what I have become. I used to like who I was, I thought I had control, I liked the power over people, especially over men. I thought men deserved what they got…but somewhere along the line, I stopped being in control…I started being used and I was the one being taken for the ride…"

"My heart bleeds Mel…"

"I know, I know – it all sounds really wank. This is no born again epiphany, no shining light of God. I haven't found Jesus… I just woke up to myself… I'd been in a trance for so long, in the rut…"

"So you're not still blaming your mum then?"

"No." Melissa tossed her head back and looked at the ceiling. "I haven't seen her in years… but it's not all her fault. Partially it is but not all."

Adam knew her back story, the single parent family, father walks out and the mother resents the daughter for the loss of her life. Melissa's mother had sought approval through men. She failed to register that as she aged, the men she wanted showed less interest in her. So she countered this and put out earlier, a stream of men and suitors were paraded through the Henderson home. A young Melissa knew when to stay out of sight, to keep away from mummy and her special friends.

"I blame my mum for a lot… she never taught me to how respect myself. I learnt a lot from her…but nothing I should have needed. I can't blame her for not changing sooner, I didn't have to become like her."

Adam watched her closely, he'd never seen Mel like this - vulnerable.

"I never listened to you…I didn't want to hear the nice things Adam, nice didn't last. Drugs worked, drugs were really fucking good. And you're right, I did use to shag the men for the drugs…you knew what I was long before I did."

"So how come within three years of leaving me to face the music at the hotel, you're arrested for vagrancy and prostitution in Kings Cross?" Adam never had been able to piece her life together.

"You need to feed a habit. As the dependency grows you quickly live only for the drug and nothing else. The guy I was with simply couldn't supply enough money to get the drugs…so I slept with the main dealer…that led to all the drugs I wanted…but then he wanted paying…and the sex wasn't enough…so he put me to work."

Adam sat stoically unemotional in his seat.

"You don't take care of yourself when you're an addict, the tricks get harder to come by, and the money gets squeezed. You become a liability not worth having around…you end up on the streets."

"And yet here you are a few years on looking healthy and full of tales of escape?"

"I was put into a police rehab programme…it cleaned me up, made me presentable, I got off the smack. Mum…well she didn't respond well to my pleas for help…she had remarried…anyway…I had some names, connections…I went to work. But off the streets, in London, Putney actually. I worked for this villain, a small time gangster in London. I started in his brothel, an English girl was a novelty. After a time I suppose I became his girlfriend and yet he happily sold me to fat Middle Eastern business men for £1000 a night... I never thought 'this is wrong,' I convinced myself it was my choice...."

"You enjoyed it for while though, didn't you?"

The comment surprised Melissa, her eyebrows rose at the accusation.

"Sometimes...Adam, yes. In the early days sure. It turned me on. But it didn't last. Trust me on this, I didn't enjoy it for long." She fiddled uncomfortably with her hair, reluctant to divulge any more details.

"Melissa, you walk back into my life after so many years and just say 'sorry'. You didn't ask last night, nothing again tonight, about the fallout after your final stunt at the Westgate. I get 'sorry.' I suppose this goes some way to help me understand that what you did, was just you. It wasn't a one off. I just kind of hoped I wasn't just part of the run... another in the sequence."

Melissa looked at him; he was the only one she allowed to call her Mel.

"I know what I did is as bad as it gets, I was high and the guy I was with saw an opportunity to make a quick buck. Sorry you got into trouble."

"Trouble – they thought I had organised the break in. When it was obvious I hadn't, they sacked me anyway for covering for you..."

The resentment was real but Adam struggled to still be angry.

"Before all of that we had fun, didn't we. I didn't steal or use you did I?"

"Not for money I suppose, well there wouldn't have been much point would there. I knew you weren't faithful Mel, I knew about a lot of it, maybe I shouldn't hear the rest...you used me to fill a void, I was a friend Mel, I wanted to be more than that..."

"We were lovers."

"I made love Mel, you didn't."

"That's not fair Adam, how do you know I wasn't making love?"

"You never referred to it that way, you bolted for the hills when I said it..."

Melissa was silent, thinking through her past actions and why she had freaked out when Adam had said the scariest three words she knew, "I love you." Adam had meant it, he thought her email proved she had always truly hoped he had.

"What do you really want with me Melissa?"

She took a deep breath, dropped her knees down and put her feet on the floor. She pushed her hair back, revealing her face. She looked directly at Adam. He noticed there had been no tears, no weeping behind the mask of hair.

"I need a place to stop for a few days. I won't be here long. I promise. Can I stay till Friday?"

Adam said nothing.

"I'm going abroad. I have some friends in Spain. I'm planning to go there and get away from here. I have some money, so I can chill for a while, then I can get a job or something...I just need to get my head together before I go, can I do it here?"

Adam gulped the last of the wine. He looked into the glass, disappointed it hadn't magically refilled. He moved forward on his seat and looked at her, his eyes met hers and he searched for the truth in her face. She held his gaze, smiling.

"You can stay a day or so. It's not that I don't want to help, it's because I can't...I can't have you back in my life...you need to understand that."

Melissa moved forward and put her hands on Adams knees and looked up at him.

"I won't hurt you again Adam."

He fell back into his chair as she moved closer.

"You can't help yourself Melissa. It's what you do, but this isn't about you, it's about me." He sighed.

"These people, you're running from, it's their money isn't it?"

"Yes...but it's nothing more than I'm owed...."

"And that's how they will see it, is it?"

"No...they'll want it back and Barry, the top man, he'd probably want me back as well...I made them a lot of money." She bit her bottom lip and shrugged. Adam sat back in the chair, keeping her hands in his.

"It's a chance for me to have something for myself," she said. Adam understood that motivation.

"You're sure they know nothing about me and here?"

"I can't be certain, no, but I never talked about this place and certainly never mentioned you...I didn't know exactly where you lived until we talked last night, did I?"

"True," Adam said, his brain moving into overdrive trying to work out all the permutations of her return.

"Where is the money?"

"Somewhere safe."

"I presume it's in cash...?"

Melissa nodded.

"If you're off to Spain then you'll want my help to get the money over there?"

Melissa nodded again.

"It's cash so the money is laundered already, none of it came from robberies or forging, did it?"

Melissa thought for a moment, "No... it's all cash that goes through their legitimate businesses, the covers, but you can't be certain about all of it."

"Well that means you can't really risk putting it into bank accounts..."

"Would I want to?"

"Well yeah, make deposits of no more than £3-5000 in several different accounts in different banks and then once in Spain

45

you simply start transferring it into a bank account in Jersey or similar. I don't know how much you have...?"

"Getting on for £100k?" She said.

Adam did some calculations and considered the amount.

"If I had a lot more, cash, how could I make sure that it was safe?"

Adam focused on the chance that she might have a lot more, but tried not to let his interest show.

"The safest but slowest route is to make big cash purchases and then sell the goods on somewhere else for cash…cars are good, medium car dealerships often deal in large sums of cash; buy a car from one and then sell it to another…slow but effective. You can also take a fair amount with you to Spain and do the same thing there, just avoid large money exchanges near to where you are going to stay."

"It's complicated, isn't it?"

"Not really...what you need to do is put at least one transaction between you and the notes going back into the official system, if you manage that then you'll never be linked to the money… if of course any of the notes are dodgy….better to be safe than sorry."

"Thanks for the advice."

She rested her head on his knees; he brought his hand up and placed it gently on her head, moving it with small deliberate strokes.

"You have to decide which is most important, getting away quickly or laundering the money properly…"

"It's worth nothing if I can't enjoy spending it… I need it to last a long time. Want to help me spend it?"

"I don't think I should get…well at least not any more involved." The statement seemed to snap Adam out of his daze, he stopped stroking her hair and eased her away from him. She moved back and allowed him to stand, following him up as she did so. She rested her hands on his chest and looked into his eyes.

"You haven't asked me about the email," she said.

"No… I figured you'd mention it if you wanted to."

"It's complicated…" She fiddled with his shirt button, "I don't want to say anything I don't mean Adam…I need to be sure of my feelings before I put us…" her words trailed off as she struggled to find the right meaning.

"Don't get ahead of yourself Mel…"

"No you're right…I suppose though, I need an answer, to help me through."

"An answer to what?"

"My question in the email…you remember?"

Adam certainly remembered. It had been all he had been thinking of since he received it. Did he mean it when he said he loved her? It had happened so long ago, Adam couldn't be sure if he meant it then, let alone now. He looked deep into her eyes, searching for the truth, then without warning he leant down and kissed her. He pushed his lips hard against hers and moved his hand behind her head and held her firm to his lips. She didn't resist, she relaxed a little as he kissed her, opening her mouth ever so slightly, but Adam released his hold and pulled away. It took her a little by surprise. She returned his gaze, the start of a wicked smile on her face,

"Do you want me stay in the spare room again?"

"Yes Melissa, I want you to stay in the spare room."

Adam turned and headed up the stairs, his pace deliberate and slow, Melissa, still at the bottom called after him.

"You haven't answered my question Adam."

He paused at the third step from the top and turned his head. "From the email, I need to know if you meant it?"

"Yes Melissa I meant it." The words washed over her and her face lit up with a bright smile, she started up the steps towards him, as if given an invitation to attend the biggest of summer balls. Adam watched as she came up close to him and put her arms around his neck.

"I knew you did, I knew it…I do...Adam I do too."

"You misunderstand me Mel, I MEANT it, past tense. I meant it when I said it then." He took hold of her arms at the wrist and gently pulled them away from his neck. He leaned down and planted a slow tender kiss on her cheek. Then he turned round and went into the bedroom, closing the door on Melissa.

She stood there staring at the closed door, alone, and for the first time in her life, a little scared. She went up the final few steps and waited a heartbeat on the landing, then moved to her right and went quietly into the spare room.

Thirty minutes passed, the door to Adam's bedroom creaked open, throwing a shaft of light across the landing. Adam moved into the light and across the landing, and without knocking, he eased the box room door open and stepped inside.

Chapter Six

The duvet heaved up and then down. The mass beneath it let out a short angry snore. A mobile phone chirped its seemingly cacophonous alert. The mass paused, rocked and finally flattened out. A skinny female arm poked out from beneath the cover and fumbled with the bedside light. A warm glow of orange helped guide the hand toward the chirping phone, as it grasped it the duvet fell back and a small bleached blonde head with flattened hair jutted out to meet the hand and phone.

"YES," the acidic East-European tone cut through the stale bedroom air.

The large, now disturbed mass still huddled under the duvet, rolled more towards the other side of the bed.

"Da! I'm glad it is done. What did you do with its balls?"

The muffled voice couldn't contain its excitement as it passed on the news.

"My sister will be happy. You have done well Yuri."

The thanks were genuine and the tone conciliatory, a tight smile played across her half lit face as she put the phone down. She straightened her silk nightie and sat up against the headboard. For the first time since waking she looked at the mass beneath the duvet.

"Stop pretending. I know you are awake." She forced a kick under the covers and connected with some soft part of the body that lay there.

"Get up… get up and get out of bed. You smell."

The mass moved, rolled and finally two tree trunk legs hit the floor. They were followed by the large hairy body of a well built young man.

"Go next door. Is my sisters turn. Tell her Yuri has finished the job."

The man shuffled around the bed toward the door, his semi-erect penis leading the way.

"What are you, animal?" the woman barked. Her words halted him mid-stride. "Go into bathroom and clean your teeth first."

Without a word, he turned and padded toward the en-suite.

* * *

Adam had woken at 3.00am. He wasn't certain if the phone had actually woken him or not, but he checked it anyway. The envelope icon blinked at him. A message from Jake waited for him in his inbox. He slid himself out of the bed and away from the slumbering Mel and headed into the bathroom across the landing.

Like most men, Adam was now in desperate need of a post sex piss. He read Jake's message as he took aim.

"Been thinking... if you can get a shag and have the chance to be the bastard. You should. It's your turn. Call me in the morning. J."

Adam smiled. Jake knew him well.

He and Jake could pinpoint when the fundamental shift in their relationship changed from that of acquaintances to becoming close friends. Usually relationships mutate, they evolve, but for Adam and Jake it happened because of a single event, a bonding that brought two independent spirits together in an odd alliance.

Jake had looked out for him that night and he had done so ever since.

In late 2001, after Melissa had deserted him, but a while after his father's death Adam left Jake's bar - Bar J, and began wandering up Winchester High Street. It had been close to 1.00am. A little merry, he had been celebrating the birthday of a friend, a lovely girl called Sarah. Adam had the drunken strut of a man pleased with himself; he had a girl's phone number.

As Adam passed the 'Butter Cross', the large medieval monument two thirds of the way up the High Street, a small group of loud and abusive lads wandered in from the street on Adam's left. Adam paid them no heed, but their path cut right behind his and they trailed him by no less than five paces.

They called out to the apparently diminutive man ahead, yelling various puerile comments. Adam noticed, stiffened a little and quickened his stride hoping to get up to the end of the High Street and across Jewry Street, where he knew there would be a few more people leaving the fun pubs found there. The lads behind had other ideas. In any pack, it only takes one to start something, then the others follow like mindless drones. One of the pack darted out, yelling at Adam,

"Oi faggot boy... nice shoes!" The lad raced round in front of Adam, trapping him between the wall of the bookshop on Adam's right and a fixed bench to his left. It gave him only a few yards of space to manoeuvre. Before he could really get a sense of the unfolding situation, two of the other lads moved in behind him and one shoulder-charged him in the back – he lurched forward, his hands coming slowly out of his coat pockets forcing him face first into the lad ahead. Who pushed Adam down on the floor yelling,

"Dirty little faggott, did you see him lunge at me, tried to kiss me...fucking arsehole."

With that he pulled his leg back, pointed his toes and swung his foot violently into Adam's chest. The foot impacted without any kind of block and pushed Adam clean off his hands and knees on to his back. Wheezing and clutching his chest in agony, he just had the presence of mind to close his legs as the same lad swung another kick aimed at his testicles.

The kick was mistimed and the kicker's shin bounced off Adam's shoe, the kicker hopped back yelping as he clutched his shin. The lad who had shoved Adam saw his mate pull back in pain and swiftly moved into a crouch over the still prostrate and wheezing Adam, and in the same movement he brought his fist down hard into his face. It connected with his open mouth, the fist ripping on Adam's exposed teeth, but not before his top lip had been split and his front teeth loosened.

Adam curled up into a ball, dazed from the punch, disorientated by the volume of blows coming his way, while the kicks and punches rained down on his back and sides. He vaguely heard shouting, but oddly found the whole process somewhat abstract. He had no idea how long he was down and how many times he had been kicked, but he slowly became aware that he was no longer being hit and yet the sounds of scuffling and fighting seemed to be continuing without him.

He risked opening his arms, and peaked out. Looking up from his prone position he saw a big man dispatch one his attackers with a punch to the midriff – actually it was the solar plexus, but he only found that out later. The guy fell to the floor gasping for breath and Adam noticed he had joined two of his former attackers, on the floor. Adam then realised that the big guy had dispatched the man with a punch while all the time he had another of his attackers, the lad that was in his face at the start, by the throat and held several inches off the floor against the wall.

Adam watched his face as his rescuer squeezed, the face turned red, then purple and then blue. The big man watched with mild interest the changing hue and then, as it seemed the guy was going to pass out, he dropped him.

Adam sat up, confident of his safety, and when the big man turned to him, he recognised the face. "You ok Adam?" said Jake Simons, the ex-special services landlord of Bar J.

"Yeah, I think so," mumbled Adam through his split swollen lips and throbbing chest.

"Cool. Let's just finish these little dicks off and we'll get you sorted."

Adam was about to protest that the little dicks seemed finished off already and that they would surely have learnt their lesson when he saw Jake pick up the hand of his already two thirds throttled former assailant. Jake twisted the hand round forcing pressure on the lad's shoulder, inverting the hand at the wrist, rendering the man helpless.

"Lads, getting pissed up - is fine, having a boisterous laugh - is fine. But getting pissed up and attacking some innocent as he walks home is out of order. I don't like unfair fights, I hate bullying. Now I think you have all probably learnt your lesson. But I just want to hammer my point home…" with that his short speech was over. He grabbed the little finger of the hand he held and twisted.

Adam heard the snap and then the yelp of pain. Jake released the hand and arm – the throttled lad stopped worrying about his throat and cradled his mangled finger.

Jake moved quickly and efficiently between each of the three lads on the floor and did the same thing. Adam looked on astonished at the speed and efficiency of the action. It seemed like only a second before Jake came over and helped him to his feet.

"My car is round the corner. I'll take you and get you fixed up." Adam didn't argue, he just surveyed the neat trail of destruction Jake had left behind. All four of his assailants sat on the floor behind the bench, leaning against the book store wall clutching their right hands to their chests.

"I'm taking you to my place," Jake said, "we can get you fixed up and see if there's anything permanent. Doubt it though. You covered up pretty well."

"Why can't I go to hospital," Adam said a little weakly. His lip was bleeding quite badly, his hand cupped under his chin trying to stop the blood dripping onto his shirt.

"On a Friday night, at this time? You'll be there for hours…best we stitch you up and sort you out at my place."

"Stitch me up…" said Adam even more weakly.

"Yeah, you'll need a couple to hold that lip together. I want to check you've not cracked any ribs as well. Don't worry I'm a trained medic, or at least I used to be. Stitched myself and others before now. Got all the kit at home."

"Triffic," said Adam.

As it turned out Adam hardly felt a thing, and was so impressed by his own bravery, he felt he should ask Jake for a lollipop. He got whisky instead.

"Thanks for the help by the way," Adam had mumbled rather sheepishly, "I am grateful ….for you stopping the fight."

"Ha ha…." Jake let out a belly laugh. "Is that what you call it? To be a fight you need to have active parties or sides fighting each other. In your case they were fighting, you were playing the role of target."

Adam smiled, "Yeah I suppose it was a bit crap of me, not fighting back."

"Toss mate. You did the best thing and the only thing you could. You were attacked and you defended yourself. Minimised the damage inflicted. It would've been worse if you'd stood up and had a go."

Ever since that night, Adam appreciated that Jake didn't think him a wuss and deep down was pleased his actions were deemed as right and proper by a man who knew about these things.

Adam waggled and wiped, before moving to the sink to wash his hands. He looked for the scar on his lip in the cabinet mirror. It was hard to spot now. Not really a war wound to match up to Jakes' genuine battle scarred body.

He dried his hands on the towel and stepped back from the mirror, it now revealed more of his reflected torso. He sucked in his gut and pumped himself up into a body building pose.

I might not be an ex Royal Marine, he thought. *But I definitely got the girl tonight.*

Jake had never had any trouble pulling women. They threw themselves at him. He never showed much interest mind you and certainly never dated girls he met at the bars he owned. To most he was a bit of an enigma. The ex-soldier hard man that had turned around the shittest pub in town. He'd then gone on to open two more bars and also run the biggest private security firm in the South. People got wrapped up in the image of what they expected Jake to be, they had no idea he'd been raised by his aunts or that despite all the horrors of war he had seen, they paled into insignificance beside a single moment of his childhood; the day he discovered the body of his father hanging in the family cellar.

To Adam though, he was just his friend. A man whom he would have hated had they met at school, but their shared tragedies and ambition linked them in a way other people couldn't fathom. Now they were joined through business as well, Jake was his most lucrative client.

Adam looked at his watch, still wired from his sexual conquest he knew he could never sleep even if he'd wanted to. The adrenalin seemed to be flowing non stop. Elation and confusion pumped through him in equal measure. Melissa was back and in a big way. Jake had sanctioned his actions, sort of. Why should Adam reproach himself for having a little fun.

No doubt he would have to reveal all to his friend when they met up. It would be good to be the teller for a change. He pulled on his bathrobe and crept downstairs to get himself a drink of water, he sipped it at the kitchen table as he rooted through his brief case and pulled out the financing documents he had sorted for Jake.

Big Mother security was the real financial force behind Jake's empire. A veritable army of former soldiers and servicemen, it had revolutionised commercial door work. Tough, disciplined and highly trained they had easily seen off the intimidation of the local gangs that had run the doors. They guaranteed a drug free environment and their presence had been welcomed and encouraged by the police. It took only a matter of months before the organisation expanded to cover virtually every major town between Basingstoke and Bournemouth. Jake had stuck to what he knew, and all of his businesses were run via a tight-knit military hierarchy. It was based on total trust. Adam remained the only civilian allowed into the inner circle.

Big Mother was now borrowing money to finance Jake's latest project, the purchase and refurbishment of The Stag, a boutique 5 star hotel in the small market town of Stockbridge, northwest of Winchester. He and Jake planned to meet there later that day with the surveyor Lee to ensure the capital valuation was accurate.

Adam had been instrumental in the deal, he'd seen Jake's chauffeur bodyguard service for the growing glitterati living in Hampshire really take off. So he advised that if the hotel fell into the right hands it could be a gold-mine. Jake didn't hesitate, he put in an offer based on his friend's recommendation and now looked for a quick purchase.

Re-checking the numbers and ordering the pages had the desired effect and Adam felt the dull ache of tiredness pull at his eyelids. He pushed the papers aside and crept back upstairs. He pushed the door open a few inches and poked his head around. Sitting on her knees in the middle of the bed was a naked Melissa.

"I wondered when you'd be back... don't think we've finished do you?"

Chapter Seven

Jonno sat hunched behind the wheel of the Lexus 4x4 and yawned. The silver 400h model had all the creature comforts you'd expect from a Lexus, but it didn't make up for a lack of sleep. They had set off from Putney at 6.00am, Mickey determined to beat the rush hour and be in place before Winchester folk headed off to work. Jonno hated the car, "it's not exactly 'gangsta' is it," he had moaned when Mickey had first started using it. It also couldn't be described as incognito; the tinted windows made it look like a silver-clad hearse.

Whenever Jonno got out, his six foot, well-muscled frame, clad head to toe in black with hair slicked back into a pony-tail, only compounded the problem. He looked every bit the London villain up to no good. Or as Mickey had described him, "you look like the backing saxophonist for some second rate country and western group." If Mickey then followed Jonno out of the car any doubt over their non legit profession was instantly removed.

Florists they were not.

They were crawling around Winchester's one way system, on their way to the Penninsular Barracks Estate. As usual, no matter what the time of the day, the one way system proved to be a nightmare. They had to turn left at the top of the hill and merge with Jewry Street – so called because it's where the Jews were imprisoned, persecuted and hung, Mickey informed Jonno, revelling in his Wikipedia research of the town. Mickey loved leaving London for old historic towns, so many Londoners have panic attacks or get nose bleeds if they get within three miles of the M25. Not Mickey, he liked his history and Winchester was packed with the stuff.

"This town was home to the first King of England…Alfred the Great, who merged the old Saxon and tribal areas to beat off the Vikings…"

Jonno nodded, he'd had enough of the history lesson on the M3, with Mickey telling him about the delights of the New Forest and its wild ponies. What the fuck did he care about wild ponies.

"Come on Jonno, I know you went to school, you must've learnt one thing about King Alfred…come on join in son."

Jonno sighed deeply, "Alfred, didn't he get an arrow in the eye?"

"NO – that was Harold, Battle of Hastings…no Alfred was the dude who burnt the cakes…"

Jonno glared out of the window, wishing Mickey would shut up, but wise enough not to say it. Anton had proved that upsetting Mickey was a poor long-term career decision.

He wasn't able to follow the Sat Nav – Mickey kept barking out directions, which would be repeated ten seconds later by the dulcet tones of the Sat Nav's computer voice. Jonno tried to blot Mickey out by imagining the Sat Nav lady. He saw her as a lovely blonde, older woman, sexy, but seen a bit of action, he nodded to himself as he conjured the image in his mind. He always visualised her in business wear, like the uptight suits from the city.

"Go straight on at the lights – ignore Southgate Street, we'll go into the Barracks via Romsey Road."

Jonno didn't answer he simply obeyed, he put his foot down and the Lexus pulled away up the hill. They went up round and past the Winchester West Gate and the hotel opposite and there on the left was the first major redeveloped section of the old Winchester Barracks. Jonno indicated left and pulled the Lexus into the inviting entrance way.

"Fucking hell...they have the Gurkhas museum here...be worth a look," growled Mickey. Jonno as instructed, pulled the car immediately into the first parking space on the left.

"You reckon?" he said in reply.

"Yeah," Mickey said looking at him. "Proper little hard bastards that lot. The stories of their bravery in battle is legendary. Any group of soldiers that collect ears as trophies has to be respected."

"Suppose you're right...my granddad served with the Gurkhas in Burma," Jonno added flippantly.

"Really," Mickey raised his eyebrows in surprise.

"Yeah – he was the Captain, no officers allowed amongst the colonial troops, or some such bollocks. He used to say that every time they got those fuck off knives out...what they called?"

Mickey raised his chin and shut his eyes in thought, "Kukri!"

"Yeah them…they had to draw blood – if not the enemies' then their own."

"Cool. Like I said, we should go in there…proper hard bastards," Mickey said with respect.

"Maybe later. Let's get this done shall we. What's the plan?" Jonno was keen to get this extended trip over and done with, he didn't feel as comfortable as Mickey with leaving the charms of the city.

"The map she had, showed that road." Mickey stubbed a giant digit towards the side road. "The one off left, that row of funny looking town houses. We sit here until we see either her or him" He handed Jonno the picture so he could ID the man in the picture.

"Any other roads or entrances?"

"Yeah there's a footpath in the middle there; it goes between the houses." Mickey squinted, hoping it would activate some imaginary zoom to enable him to see the alley more clearly.

"Doesn't look like any of the gardens have access from the rear. All cars have to come this way, only issue is if there's a back door to those two houses onto the alley…" Mickey had made the observation already, and seeing the road now, he knew that while their look-out point was the best they could get, it wasn't ideal.

"We might not see someone come and go if there are doors…but we don't know if either one on the path is the right house!"

"No worries I'll go and scope it out…" Mickey put an arm on the already exiting shoulder of Jonno.

"Easy tiger," he glanced at his watch, "if she's down there then she knows you and me a little too well, she'll bolt or go to ground… It's only 8 o'clock, I'd rather, for now, sit tight, wait and see who walks up and down. We might catch the trick walking to work or something; here's where we stay for the time being." Mickey knew it was weak.

"Maybe she'll get dumb and poke her head out the door as well…"

Mickey couldn't tell if Jonno was being sarcastic or not.

"Maybe," he offered.

Mickey doubted she would. The girl had planned this quite well, better than he would have given the druggy skank credit for. They only had this much info on her because he had been over-protective of Barry, and Ramon the ponce was a greasy spic control freak.

Mickey knew he needed a bit of luck. Melissa had bailed out Monday night, it was now Wednesday morning. They had moved quickly, but it might not be fast enough. She could have been down, blown the guy, found his wad and moved on by now. He rubbed his chin thoughtfully, he didn't know why, but he felt she hadn't moved on again…not yet. She would've banked on them not knowing where she'd gone or where she was. She would think she had some leeway, some time to sort things out.

Maybe that was her plan, settle back into life with this trick, get in his pocket, use him to kick-start her escape with the cash. Clearly this monkey wasn't loaded, not one hundred grand loaded anyway. Nice though the Barracks development looked, it was domesticated starter home non-entity bullshit…the poor little prick had no idea what was about to descend on him.

Mickey pondered the scenario, he had no idea why the hundred grand was so important. In the great scheme of things it wasn't a lot of money, they could pull a few jobs and replenish the funds within a week or two, no worries. But then, he had to accept, this was the Bartok fund.

Barry Hunt wasn't the biggest fish in the South London gangland pond. You always answer to someone. It's the way of things. In a South London pissing contest Barry Hunt had a big dick, but there are always bigger dicks out there and they are only too happy to see if they measure up.

Barry had been pissing with the best of them for over twenty years, you only do that if you know your place, know your friends and don't make too many enemies.

Gregor Bartok was a fuck up waiting to happen. A small time money launderer and deal broker between the East European gangs and established London firms, Bartok's business was not big and certainly not clever. He ran several bookmakers, laundrettes and scrap-yards, fine places to hide money in. They did have a habit of going bust and leaving a few debts, but hey, more fool you if you decide to invest with some iffy Ukrainian accountant with a penchant for Kentucky Fried Chicken.

Barry used to launder some of his illicit earnings via Gregor, only the overspill from good spells at his gambling pads, brothels and the odd drug deal. Barry needed to have some legitimate income, he could largely launder his own cash through the bars and clubs, but that might involve paying some tax. Gregor took care of reasonable sized lump sums, at a small percentage for himself; they were are after all, not barbarians.

Mickey had always thought of Gregor Bartok as a bit of a tit and had repeatedly cautioned Barry against using him too often. Gregor could bring down the heat on them at any time. Barry had largely listened to his old friend, but for the life of him Mickey had no idea why Barry, in his infinite wisdom, had decided to recommend and vouch for the services of Bartok to London's biggest underworld figure, Mr G.

The G-men saw no irony in their name; Mr G was not an easily amused man. In fact Mickey had never seen him smile, hell he hadn't seen his eyes. Mr G was always in a white Fila track suit, wearing white Nike sports socks with black sandals. Huge and some might say ludicrously ladylike Channel sunglasses covered his eyes. Laughing at his bizarre fashion sense wasn't an option if you wanted to keep your tongue. His massive six seven frame, shoulder-length dreadlocks and slow ambling gait, reminded you of a doped up Lennox Lewis. Mickey didn't feel uncomfortable around many men, but Mr G and his close quarter team were some of them.

Needless to say Bartok fucked up his transaction with Mr G. Mickey didn't know what it involved, but whatever Bartok did, it was stupid and the fat man knew it, he bolted, ran for the hills, as fast as his podgy little legs could carry him. That same day several premises in South London burnt to the ground in a series of seemingly unrelated but tragic accidents.

Mr G called Beano. Beano called Barry. Barry called Mickey.

Bartok had to die.

Mr G felt that while Barry was not responsible for Bartok's failure, his recommendation implicated him, his friendship tested by resolving the mess. Barry offered to carry out the hit, exterminate the error. The hit would be Barry's pleasure; the severing and serving of the head on a silver platter merely an added extra. Mr G insisted on it and would pay handsomely, £100k for the head of the Ukrainian.

The money arrived before Barry could protest or say anything to the contrary. The deal was done, Bartok's fate sealed, Barry placed firmly in Mr G's pocket. Mr G's message was clear, he wanted Barry Hunt's firm to put a high-profile ending to the Bartok issue. There could be no embarrassment for the G-Men, Barry had to sort it out. Mr G liked theatrics and once Bartok's fat balding bonce was on a silver platter he'd be satisfied. Failing to deliver was not an option.

Jonno looked up from his constant vigil on the cul-de-sac, they had been sitting in silence for over an hour. He didn't like silences, Mickey, exhausted of facts about Winchester was conversely very happy with the silence. Jonno moved to turn on the radio.

"Leave it..," Mickey growled.

"Come on Mickey mate," Jonno pleaded, his tone nasally and whining, "it's been an hour… where's the harm in having Radio 5 Live on?"

Mickey arched an eyebrow. He'd expected a demand for some tedious drum-n-base station or worse, Chris Moyles on Radio One. Five live demonstrated intelligence and a cultured streak that Jonno had not displayed before.

"While I applaud your taste – the radio stays off. No distractions."

Jonno conceded defeat. Once again he turned his head to face the road and continue his vigil.

He managed only ten minutes.

Jonno liked a good gossip, he wanted to chat about why they were so focused on this skank when the Bartok issue needed resolving.

"What you want?" Mickey asked, aware of Jonno's fidgeting and that he was looking for something to talk about.

"Well; I was wondering about the Bartok thing? I mean I hadn't had a lot of luck on it, but the boss seemed keen for it to be sorted quickly?"

"Well you fucked that then didn't you, fat cunt's been missing for over a week."

Jonno thought about that for a moment, but before he could conjure a retort, Mickey started again, "We're here to recover £100,000 and the thief that took it. It's not small change and liberty takers need to be taught a lesson. Otherwise, every skank crack head whore will think they can put their fucking hand in the cookie jar...can't have that, go down that road and what you get is fucking anarchy."

"Yeah but what about Bartok...?"

"Shut up and watch the road."

Mickey knew Jonno was right, Bartok and Mr G had to be the more pressing situation. Sure Melissa would blow a chunk of the cash but they would get most of it back. Why then had it taken precedence over Bartok? Mickey could only assume it was because Barry still had a big thing for the girl.

Chapter Eight

Adam rolled over in bed and pushed his arm out, and like a probing tentacle, it found the naked back of Melissa, lying to his right. A smile grew across his face.

The box room had proved far too small an arena for their second bout of passion, so leaving the room in a state of discarded clothing flux, they had barrelled intertwined across the landing, bursting into Adam's bedroom and hurled themselves bodily onto the bed. They ended up a tangled mass of sweaty limbs, panting heavily and repeatedly kissing each other in a frenzied attempt to re-charge their batteries before commencing once more.

At four am Melissa had silently disengaged herself from him and mounted the still slumbering Adam. She cupped his aching balls gently and stroked his inert penis, until, although still asleep, his penis powered into full potent life. Adam slept and murmured, caught in the most vivid and wonderful of dreams. Eventually he rose from the deep sleep to find a naked Melissa astride him, rocking herself back and forth. He signalled he was ready to participate by moving his hands up her lithe body and cupping her breasts, his fingers delicately squeezing her engorged nipples. She moaned and writhed a little harder, saying, "Now we make love baby." Adam could not recall how long it lasted; he simply remembered the unadulterated joy of each orgasm.

Now, as the morning summer sun blazed through the gap in the curtains bathing the naked pair in light, Melissa sleepily snuffled next to him. She stirred; lying face down on the bed she turned her face towards his and opened her eyes. She was greeted by a beaming Adam. She returned the smile, "morning" he said, "morning," she replied.

"Breakfast." Adam said it as a statement and got out of bed in a quick and unembarrassed naked flash.

"Just coffee."

"No problem!" and with that he leapt back onto the bed and planted a heavy kiss on her lips, before slipping off the bedside in a comedic heap. "Lunatic," she yelled at him. He rose, sucked in his belly, tensed his pecs and strode out of the room shouting, "woman want coffee... me get coffee."

He returned some ten minutes later, tray in hand, fresh coffee and thick cut lavishly buttered toast. Melissa sat up in bed and clapped her hands in mock glee. They devoured the toast, butter oozed down chins, coffee was slurped and spilt in gluttonous haste. Finally, feasted and sated, Melissa lent over and kissed Adam on the cheek.

"Thank you..." she said.

"For what."

"For being here for me one last time...thank you."

"No problem, it's what I do," he smiled and then sweetly kissed her forehead.

"Addy...I want to talk about something," she said.

He didn't reply, just waited for her to continue.

"I can't stay here indefinitely…there's a chance that they'll come looking for me. I was serious about needing to go abroad."

"I know Mel…but not just yet hey?"

"No… but you need to understand some of the circumstances. I wouldn't have needed to tell you, but last night, well it's complicated things, hasn't it?

"Maybe," he nodded his head to the side. Melissa sat up, back straight and legs crossed, it forced Adam to rejoin her on the bed and face her.

"Look, I wouldn't feel right if I didn't tell you some of what I know…"

"Ok … tell me."

Melissa bowed her head a moment, she had the look of someone ordering her thoughts, prioritising or even editing what she would say.

"Barry runs a manor, an area of criminal control, his manor stretches from Richmond to Wandsworth and then south all the way to Wimbledon, it's a big area, it takes a lot of policing." She paused again, then confident of what she would say next she resumed, "He runs brothels, pubs, a lot of bookmakers, snooker clubs, that kind of thing, there is some protection money but nothing like you'd expect. Then there are the drugs…"

Adam nodded, sage like, fascinated but scared of what he had invited into his life. "Drugs are bought into the area and a network of pushers and suppliers feed the manor. It's supposed to be controlled, managed. But it's getting more and more broken up, loads of small suppliers taking a share, ignoring Barry's threats, dismissing him as "The Man", trouble is though the more they creep in the more Barry loses face and money…his manor is breaking up."

"Nothing like stealing his money and kicking him when he's down, hey Mel?"

She ignored the comment.

"You need to understand that he's being squeezed, but he answers to *the* man of South London; Mr G. He really runs the show, he controls the manors, Barry and his like pay their dues…when their time comes, Mr G will swat them and replace them…"

"Law of the jungle."

"Exactly…Barry used to be feared and respected, he's old school, maybe the last of the archetypal London gangsters. He saw Mr G rise up through the ranks, running drugs, then a manor, before getting too big to be controlled."

Adam nodded. "So Mr G launched a coup and took over from the previous big boss?"

"Correct." Melissa watched Adam's reactions carefully.

"Mr G needed other manors allied to him, to show a united front. Barry spotted the opportunity, backed Mr G and rode on his coat tails."

"So does Mr G fear Barry?"

"Fear him. No. Mr G doesn't fear anything. He does respect Barry and the old ways and feels indebted to him for supporting his move for the top job."

"Can't Barry hit Mr G then?"

"Sure, Barry thought about it. He realised that with Mr G in the top spot he'd never get there. He could launch a takeover if they get big enough, powerful enough…but Mr G isn't dumb, and he doesn't allow any manor to get too big…" Melissa was earnest and her face a study of concentration.

"Mr G realigned the old boundaries, merged several smaller London manors and put them under new control, it happened slowly and without much fanfare. Barry hardly noticed the changes. He woke up one morning and realised he had no allies…Mr G had removed the possibility of a united attack."

"So is he happy to see Barry suffering?" Adam was intrigued if not a little bemused at the lesson.

"That's just it, he doesn't really know that Barry's in trouble, his payments to Mr G have always been on time and at the required level.

"So what's the problem? Mr G gets his cash…"

"The manor is a business Adam. It has overheads and an income. The payment to Mr G is simply gangland tax. But the manor needs to make money to survive. Barry has been skimming more than he should for himself, he's swallowing the bulk of what is left after Mr G takes his cut."

"He isn't sharing the wealth?"

"Spot on." She pointed a finger at him and winked. "His people aren't making enough through the manor…so…"

"So…" said Adam quizzically

"DAH" she pushed her tongue into her bottom lip, "If they aren't making money through Barry then they start doing their own thing, that's how the manor begins to break up, too many individuals start lining their pockets through extra curricular work…it leads to all hell breaking loose."

"Is that the background to your theft?"

"No that's the background to my life…Barry isn't fighting back. Once he saw he had no allies, that Mr G had effectively castrated him, the life, the energy drained from Barry. He's given up.

"He wants to retire?"

"Yeah - he's going to just run it down, skim what he can and head off into the sunset…now if he does that you have no idea who will take over. The smaller elements with ambition are already sniffing around the manor. Like any business going through change, you assess where you might fit in the new regime. Frankly I didn't like what I saw. So, I wanted out. I saw my chance…" she tailed off, aware her act of self preservation contradicted everything she had told Adam about how she had changed. Her fingers spread and she stroked the duvet, watching it flatten out one linen crevice and then form another further along.

She didn't feel guilty, Adam could never know everything she had been through. Adam understood money and he understood her. He'd help.

"Barry is trying to do a drug deal with a small London firm, some absolute nutters, the Petrovs."

"East Europeans?" Adam asked. Melissa nodded.

"They're not all here to fix pipes, lay floors and send money home."

Adam raised his eyebrows. Winchester's influx of migrants had centred on waitresses and agricultural workers. He cocked his head to one side and pondered the news. Melissa tried to hide the anxiety in her face, she tried to appear calm but the tension was obvious.

"If Barry pulls the deal off he hopes to push the drugs in provincial towns, well away from Mr G. He'll make a killing, as long as he manages to keep it quiet."

"Mr G wouldn't be happy about such a deal?"

"No he'd go mental."

"What's Barry's exposure?" Melissa could sense Adam's interest rising, slowly but surely the information was sucking him in.

"He's paid the Petrovs £100,000 already and owes them £100,000 more when they deliver the drugs. Barry hopes to find a buyer before he has to make the final payment." Melissa talked at a fast pace, regurgitating the words as if from a planned monologue.

"Sound financial planning, spreading the payments." Adam offered.

"Not really, he's spreading himself too thin, he has to pay over £200,000 to Mr G each month as well as financing the day-to-day costs of the manor…when I left I took a large part of what will fund it."

"Mmmm… what you're saying is, that if this guy, Mr G, finds you, he's going to hit you hard…right?" Adam had assumed her antics would have a consequence, but money has a strange way of blurring reason.

"Right…I thought you should know what you are involved with." She sat back pleased she delivered her lecture and that Adam hadn't erupted with self righteous condemnation.

"How do you know all this babe?"

"As I said… Barry kept me close, not quite the gangster moll, but you get the idea…"

Adam nodded. He didn't need or want to hear the details, he was struggling with it enough already. He had to hand it to Melissa though, she couldn't have chosen a better time to steal and run. This Barry would be in a world of trouble if word got out about his plans, maybe, just maybe he'd have too much on his plate to worry about Melissa.

"Hell, they may not even bother looking for you," he said optimistically.

"Well to be safe, I need to move on by the weekend…will you help me with the money?"

"Yeah I can help…"

Adam moved his hand across the duvet and rest it on her forearm. He studied it as it moved. He caressed her up and down her arm, lost in thought. "Will I see you again?"

Melissa looked at him silently; she sat back, "If you want to Adam…only if you want to."

He stopped caressing and fixed his eyes on the window and glorious blue sky that lay beyond. "I felt happy Melissa. Last night. Genuinely and totally happy…I haven't felt like that for a long long time. I liked it."

"I'm glad….so did I."

"Did you? Did you really? You say you've changed, you claim to be another person to one that ruined my life, ruined your own life."

"What are we talking about Adam?"

Adam rushed his gaze back from the window and his eyes fell on Melissa and the pair shared a moments silent contemplation of what the previous nights activities really meant.

"You can see me again Adam…I'd like that… but we don't need to worry about the context just yet…do we?"

"I suppose not."

"Over time we'll rediscover all of what we had, I'm sure of that. I don't want to hurry us. That's too important. I need to hurry when it comes to my current situation though."

Adam nodded again. "True. One thing at a time. We need to get you out of the country and safe."

81

"Great…a couple of days here, see how the land lies and then off to sunny Spain."

Adam nodded and then shook his head. "Is running the best way to do this? There is another way we can do this?"

"Explain?" She said biting her lip.

"Well Barry saw an opportunity when Mr G rose to power right?"

Melissa nodded.

"You saw an opportunity… and took the cash, right?" He continued.

"Yeah - what's your idea?"

"It's not an idea, more a thought, a concept that needs developing." He pursed his lips in thought. "Money is important to Mr G, but it's not as important as having trust in those that run his manors."

Melissa nodded.

"What if he found out about the mismanagement and more importantly about Barry's drug deal, he would be very grateful…right?"

"Go on…" said Melissa, delighted at how Adam had joined the dots.

"Barry's world will crumble, no matter what, it's simply a matter of time…so you say?"

"It will, he's doomed."

"That presents an opportunity." He raised his eyebrows.

Melissa decided to finish the thought, keeping her voice calm, as if it was only just occurring to her. "…maybe my actions are the crucial catalyst…if someone was in the right place at the right time, knowing the right things…they might be able make the situation work for them?" Her eyes were wide now, the excitement playing across her face.

Adam leant forward and kissed her, a firm closed lip kiss. As their lips parted he rested his forehead on hers. "Let's deal with the main problem first, getting you safe." She simply nodded. "Mel…if you see them, Mr G and his men, if they come for you, run…do you hear me… you just run."
Melissa nodded again.
"Good girl… let's have a shower?"

They skipped out of the room towards the bathroom, Melissa intent on not letting the conversation rest.

* * *

At the same moment across London, in the penthouse that Mr G called home, the man himself looked up at Beano, his most favoured consort and said,

"Say that the fuck again?"
"Bartok, the fat Ukrainian washed up in the Thames. He got caught up on one of the Thames Barrier islands – tide was taking the fat fuck out to sea."

Mr G wiped a giant hand over his dreadlocked covered head and contemplated the disappointing news.

"Let me guess, the cunt still had his fucking head…right?"

Beano, wasn't sure if he should smile, it was a funny question, not something you get asked everyday. It warranted a smile, but Mr G didn't seem to be in the mood for jokes. Beano opted for silence and simply nodded his head. Not an easy task for a man as fat as he. Beano had no discernible neck, his obese face and limbs merely protruded from his gargantuan torso like seal flippers. Beano couldn't move quickly, in fact moving at all proved a chore, wherever possible, he avoided standing if he could help it.

He shifted his thirty stone bulk back on his heels and rested his hands on his gut, the fingers only just meeting and locking together.

"I think that Barry Hunt owes you £100,000 Mr G…"

Mr G sneered, his gold capped teeth catching the morning sun. He clicked his tongue across the back of his teeth and reclined on the sofa unit.

"He owes more than money Beano, he owes me a fucking explanation. Get me a phone."

Chapter Nine

Melissa strode down through the graveyard off Sparkford Road. She had showered with Adam and they had talked some more, they fleshed out their plans and agreed a way forward. As he sat down to deal with some work, she decided to spend the morning mooching around her old college campus. She had swooped out of the house by the back door, and had turned straight down the little alley, away from the house, away and out of sight from the Lexus and the two large familiar men it contained.

It had been a long time since Melissa had called herself a student, but she couldn't hide her surprise at how different the campus now seemed.

The good memories of her time at the Student Union bar surprised her, not least by how many she actually had. The friends and incidents she had long forgotten, once again came alive, stirred by her ambling between the old buildings. She smiled to herself as she looked out over the graveyard – a regular cut through for students en route to the town and most of their digs... she'd had sex on several of those fallen headstones. Jamie Ellis…that cocky prick from the rugby team, who talked up his sexual prowess; when push came to shove, it lasted exactly that. Winchester is best in summer and now with the sun shining, she felt relaxed for the first time in an age, she could even feel herself smile, inside and out. Along with the feeling came the knowledge that she looked good, in her cropped jeans, midriff exposed, and she had received as many admiring glances around the campus as she had wanted.

She could still turn a head, and despite everything, it was still important to her.

She hadn't expected what had transpired the night before, it genuinely delighted her to feel the touch of a man that wanted her and not just her body. The feelings she hoped he still had were still evident. She knew that after their chat it was only a matter of time before she would have her Adam back.

Melissa sauntered out of the gates and crossed over St. James Lane and immediately cut left onto the Mews, a pedestrianised lane that linked it with Romsey Road . The lane was two thirds up the hill and ran along the side of the railway line, parallel to the barracks. It afforded some pleasant views of the barracks, and the town centre below. You could see through the topped out trees past the Gurkha museum and down the road to Adam's funny little house. She'd already decided to head to the Westgate Hotel and complete her nostalgic tour before hitting the High Street and doing some shopping.

That's when she saw the car. A silver Lexus 4 x 4. Tinted windows. A not uncommon vehicle in Winchester, but Melissa stopped dead in her tracks. She knew that car. She knew who would be in it. How the fuck had they found her so quickly?

Instinctively she dropped to her knees, her breathing laboured, it was as if she had just stopped after running a few miles. She began to sweat and panic.

'Fuck it...' she thought. 'Think Melissa, think. It's them, maybe it isn't but it must be, fuck it. Presume it is. What had you planned for this, it was going to happen, and this is just sooner than it should be. She didn't think Mr G would react to the trouble this quickly. 'They'll be watching the house, from all sides? NO. They don't know which house it is, they can't and they would have bashed the door in, surely?' She didn't even know which house it was until she called Adam. 'They're waiting for me to come back…is that right…maybe?'

Adam washed his hands. He looked at his reflection in his en-suite bathroom mirror, 'What are you doing?' he thought to himself. 'This is insanity, get this woman out of your life, let her take her money and just go.'

Adam had been having the debate ever since she had left that morning. He knew his actions were irrational, stupid even. He knew he shouldn't help Mel, he would be risking everything he had created. Was she worth it? Was the money worth it?

His mobile phone silently vibrated in his pocket. It made him jump, he stared at it as if it were an alien object.

It was Jake.

"Hello."

"Hello mate, fill me in on last night, has she gone with or without putting a smile on your face?"

Adam shut his eyes, unsure what to say. He thought about what Melissa had said before she left. He had to make a decision; did he want to be involved with this girl again? He expelled the air from his lungs with a puff of the cheeks as he conjured up his reply.

"Mate…you really aren't subtle are you?"

"Not my style, that's your department…I presume by the failure to answer my question that she's still around?"

"Yes… It's complicated Jake."

"Did you shag her?"

"No….Jake, I decided to rob her instead…"

Jake had readied his next witticism, but stopped, Adam's words halting his thoughts dead in their tracks.

"Say that again…"

"Erm…fuck it's a bit heavy mate." He sounded winded and his hands began to tremble. No faking it now, the full realisation of what he had begun dawned on him.

"Calm yourself Adam. Just take a deep breath…now what's going down? In fact stay put, I'm on my way over."

"NO," barked Adam. "I'll come to you, you're at the bar right? Yeah I'll come to you, I need to get out of here, get some air."

"Alright mate, I'll see you in five minutes, we'll get it sorted."

"Cheers, yeah, sure we will, see you in five minutes."

Adam clicked the phone off and looked at his reflection again. He was sweating. Jake would know what to do.

Adam nodded to himself, flushed the loo out of habit and strode out of the bathroom and down the stairs. Moments later, he came out his house, turned out onto the street and began walking away from the alley.

* * *

Melisssa composed herself; she knew they could see her from where they were. She needed to go back down St. James Lane – go into the barracks from the footpath, the houses would shield her from the car. What if they had another vehicle on St. James Lane? Wait - it was no parking on that road, at least not anywhere near the entrance to the barracks. She would see them before they could ID her…she could risk it, she knew the streets, they didn't. Adam's back door had access from the alleyway; she could, if the coast was clear, sneak into the house.

She started down St. James Lane, the road steep, she saw no cars parked on it at all, no people hanging about. She crossed to the other side where the road intersects with millionaire row – Christchurch Road. No one and nothing odd parked along there, from the corner she could see most of the way up the alley and footpath into the barracks. If someone was waiting they would need to be at the point where the paths crossed between the two sets of houses, no one there…

She surged forward focused on Adam's back door. She had travelled no more than five of the five hundred feet when she saw Adam, he was at the far end of the alley, at the front of the house. Turning away from her, eyes focused on his feet and the few inches ahead of them. She went to scream at him, but held herself back, pushing her fist to her mouth, paranoid and scared who she might alert with it. She tried to speed up, but within a few more strides Adam was gone, strolling up the street, away from her, towards the parked Lexus.

Melissa scooted up the pathway and kept herself pressed against the right-hand wall, she reached the end of the alley, missing Adam by moments.

Melissa watched horrified as Adam strode, undaunted, towards his fate. Mickey Finn, Barry's finisher and his apprentice Jonno leapt out of the car and surrounded Adam.

Adam would spill the beans, they'd make him talk. The plan would be dead in the water. She had to go, if she went and disappeared now she would live to fight another day. Her mind raced, she recalled what Adam had said only a few hours before, "if they come, RUN". The tears streamed down her cheeks, she looked at the door to the house, thought it through.

They could be here in a heartbeat. Did she have time to get into the house, retrieve the bag of money and get out before they saw her?

'NO', she shouted inside her head.

'No time…they could come round the corner at any moment.' Barry should have been able to hold on for longer, they shouldn't have caught up with her so soon.

She moved back along the alley, and leaned back against the wall, tears smeared across her face, she simply mouthed, "SHIT". She pushed herself away from the wall, turned her back on the money and Adam, and walked the first few steps before breaking into an uncoordinated run. She charged back down the alley towards St. James Lane and never once threw a backward glance.

Chapter Ten

Jonno looked up from the wheel at the little man walking towards them. He stooped at the shoulders, hands thrust deep into his pockets. Jonno watched as the man took self-conscious short steps – he flicked his eyes from him to the face of the man in the picture… It was him.

Jonno began opening the door before he said anything. Mickey, sensing Jonno's motion change, looked up and grasped the scenario; he too clambered out of the car a split second later.

The speed of the two men extricating themselves from the car halted Adam in his tracks. The first man, a huge lump with a square head stood directly in his path, his demeanour surly. His sheer size meant he took up the entire path. The other man moved quickly round the front of the car and came up behind him – blocking him between the railings and the Lexus.

"Hello sir - can you help us for a moment…" Mickey said in his most amiable tone.

Jonno moved in behind Adam, standing closer than was socially comfortable and while Jonno was not as big as Mickey, he still had a substantial presence. Adam subconsciously took a step back and made furtive glances around, checking to locate any easy escape route. Mickey put his massive hands up in a placatory gesture, seeing Adam's unease, conscious that he didn't need a scene or a lot of noise.

"We're looking for someone, we think she may be staying around here… we're not sure where… but we're you know, concerned. Concerned for her safety."

Adam shifted uneasily from foot to foot, his brain moving into overdrive. 'This couldn't be a coincidence', Adam knew coincidences don't happen. 'If they were connected to Melissa how had they turned up so quickly', thought Adam.

"Sure… who you looking for?"

Jonno answered, "A blonde girl, mid twenties, clever face, nice looking girl. Goes by the name of Melissa Henderson?"

Adam's heart skipped slightly on hearing her name confirmed, but he did his best to remove any trace of recognition from his face.

"Not a name I know…sorry fellas, can't help." Adam tried to confidently walk away, wanting to draw a line of resolution under the conversation. It lacked commitment and Mickey and Jonno didn't move.

Mickey just stared down at Adam, narrowing his eyes as if examining the minute details of his little face.

"Don't be in such a hurry, have a good think, Melissa Henderson. Are you certain you don't know anyone of that name?"

"Yeah, I'm certain. I mean it's not that common a name is it. I have known a Melissa, even a Henderson, but not a Melissa Henderson."

Adam stuffed his hands into his pockets and made another attempt at a forceful exit, he strode straight into the solid chest of

Mickey and comically bounced back - a powerful hand rested on his shoulder to steady him and stop him from attempting it again.

"She's a very pretty girl, striking even. She would turn heads, especially yours, if you saw her. SO - you sure you aint seen a girl like that around here?"

Adam chuckled a little, twisting against the paw on his shoulder, "Mate, this is Winchester, it's pretty girl heaven. It's something like an average of one man to seven women in this town…everywhere you turn there is a fit young thing bouncing around, noticing one in particular is tricky."

Mickey smiled – he liked this guy, he was scared for sure. Everyone that met Mickey for the first time was scared. Most didn't meet him in full threatening mode either. When Mickey got angry, grown men had been known to wet themselves. Mickey, like a lot of scary men, caused panic in people, not because of what they had done; rather because of what they were capable of doing. Even the mighty Mr G had nodded his respect for Mickey's intimidating presence. Mickey was operating at about ten percent of his scare capacity, but he admired how Adam had kept his sense of humour, it showed a depth of character he wouldn't have credited him with on first viewing.

"Fair enough. Maybe we could show you a picture of this girl, take a look, and see if you recognise her. Can't do any harm now can it?" Mickey let out an unpractised smile, he even stooped a little. He felt like a father cajoling an errant child.

Adam wobbled his head from side to side, neither really indicating yes or no. Finally his headed rested into the easy rhythm of a nod.

"Why do you want to find this girl? I mean what's it all about…is she in trouble?"

Mickey looked at Adam quizzically, "Nothing like that, she just isn't where she should be and that's worrying us. We need to be sure nothing's happened to her, to do that we've got to find her."

"Look, I'm late for an appointment, sorry I can't help, but I would like to go now please…" Adam flicked his head to get a view of the street beyond, hoping to see a familiar face.

Mickey sighed, held out his hand and Jonno handed him the picture, he glanced at it in front of Adam. With theatrical flamboyance he looked from the picture to Adam's face and back again, finally resting his eyes on Adam's, no joviality visible. His scare capacity was on the rise.

"It won't take a second to look at the picture now will it…sir." Mickey stressed the 'sir' all the while he carried on resting his left hand on Adam's shoulder. He thrust the picture in front of Adams face, about six inches from his nose.

"Recognise anyone?" he asked.

Adam looked at the picture and felt immediately a little sick, butterflies raced through his gut and a burst of dizziness wobbled him as he focused on Melissa's beaming face; she was looking great, arms draped around a man; and that man was Adam. He remembered when the photo had been taken, it was about six years ago, they had the Sunday off after a late shift at the hotel and had spent the whole day in bed together...before deciding to pretend to be tourists for the day.

Melissa had stood under the sword of the statue of King Alfred, testing the myth that it fell on unmarried women that had lost their virginity. Adam thought it funny she had kept the photo.

Adam snapped out of the memory when he felt a little jolt from behind; Jonno had prodded him in the back.

"Do you recognise anyone?"

"Yes," Adam mumbled.

"Shall we stop pissing about then? Why don't you tell me where she is?"

Mickey remained measured and calm, the scare capacity rose once more, he studied Adam carefully as the full realisation of his predicament began dawning on him. 'Now we'll see the strength of your character funny man', he thought.

"How the fuck should I know," blurted out Adam, finding a degree of courage that took both him and Mickey by surprise. "Yeah that's me in the picture, won't deny that. I haven't seen her though, not for at least, what, five years?"

"I don't believe you." Mickey grabbed a combination of flesh, shirt and chest hair as he pulled Adam up towards him, his voice still chillingly calm. "You lied and lied badly my little midget friend. You know where she is. You've seen her and you're going tell me about it, because odd as it may seem, I don't want to have to break your fingers one by one until you do… but know this – I will if I have to."

The scare capacity jumped to seventy five per cent.

Adam winced in pain as clumps of chest hair came away in Mickey's powerful grasp. It had taken 27 years to grow what little he had and in one aggressive grab this monster had set his chest wig growth back at least five years.

* * *

Barry Hunt rocked back in his armchair and stared blankly at his desk and the empty chair behind. A conversation with Mr G – one to one, was a rarity. He always avoided them where he could, happy to deal with Mr G's elephant seal of a bag man, Beano. Barry's phone had been buzzing all day with calls from him. Barry ignored it once again as it chirped its relentlessly optimistic tune.

Gregor Bartok had been found, Ramon the ponce had heard the news on the grapevine, a grapevine that began with two street walkers that had spent a night in the Paddington Green cells. They overheard that the fat man had been found, naked on the Thames Barrier, head at least, very much intact.

Mr G would want his money back. He had been quite clear, he would only pay for a head on a silver platter and Barry Hunt was responsible for the failure to deliver that service. Mr G did not have a benevolent nature.

'Times they were a changing', he mused.

Barry put his arms behind his head, twenty minutes ago he was down £100,000, now with Mr G wanting his £100,000 back, the debt had doubled to £200,000.

It was time for a re-think.

Chapter Eleven

Adam sat trapped on the back seat of the Lexus –
sandwiched between Jonno and Mickey, his nose bleeding and
Mickey and Jonno each holding one of his arms to his side.
Mickey spoke softly, leaning in towards him, "No point being a
hero son...so what's your fucking name?"

Adam sniffed gently, his head lolling forward, despite the
pinning of his arms, he did not want to snort blood into his mouth.

"Don't bleed on the upholstery," ordered Jonno. "It's a total
bitch to get out," he finished by way of explanation.

"My name is Adam, I really don't understand why you
punched me. If you wanted me to get into the car, you should have
just said. I would've got in quietly."

"That's nice to know Adam, but we don't to tend to take
chances in situations like this. We know what we're doing," said
Mickey.

Adam had to agree, albeit silently. The punch had
effectively demonstrated that they were serious people.

"So – with a bit of claret already flowing, you're now less
likely to do something heroic...know what I mean?"

Adam did. He nodded to show he did. His mind raced
though, how long had it been since he spoke to Jake? Fifteen
minutes? He'd been agitated, Jake was worried. The bar was only a

two minute walk away on Market Street. He'd be wondering where he was. He hoped.

"So Adam, let's start again, but this time be aware that Jonno's holding your pinkie. On my nod, he'll gladly snap the little fucker. Maybe pull it right off – it really depends if the mood takes him. Ok? So let's start with…oh something simple like…where the fuck is Melissa Henderson?"

Adam knew he needed to stall for time, the longer it took the more likely there'd be a chance to make some noise or draw attention to his situation. What was it Jake always said, "the captors are always too confident, use this, increase their false sense of security, act when they least expect it". Adam worried that he wouldn't know when the right time to act would be.

"Alright…alright, she was here. She did come to see me."

"Keep going."

"She came down Monday night …alone, looking happy. She stayed the night and then again last night. She got up and went this morning."

Adam kept the story close to the truth without any detail, he often told Jake it was the secret to effective lying.

"Really Adam…she just came and said hi, had a cup of tea, cuddled with you on the sofa and then fucked off…nice as bloody pie." Mickey's voice rose from threat to anger and finally to a shout.

"YOU TAKING THE PISS? You think I believe that fucking junky slag could appear and act like a fucking beauty queen, and not try to stiff you or anything?"

Mickey's scare capacity nudged maximum.

Adam flinched but took the cue and raised his voice right back.

"What do you want me say? She came in and said she had to change her life, needed to "escape" whatever the fuck that means. Said she had some cash, refused my offer to lend her a bit and said she was going to see a friend in Greece." Adam surprised himself with the intensity of his response and with the quality of his fibbing.

Mickey glared at him. "Had some fucking CASH? Going to Greece? Did she show you the cash Adam?"

"What the fuck are you on? No she didn't show me her cash. For chrissake is that what this is about? Has she ripped you off or something…"

Adam lurched into silence when Mickey rammed his giant paw into his gut. Adam coughed and spluttered, wheezing from the pain and force of the blow.

Mickey decided to personally break Adam's finger, but as he began his mobile chirped into life. 'The lion sleeps tonight' Mickey's novelty ring tone, wafted comically through the air.

"Fuck it…" yelled Mickey, as he fumbled in his pocket to pull the phone out, Caller ID showed 'Barry' calling. He began to open the door to take the call outside; he looked back at Jonno.

"Do me a favour and break the little prick's finger."

Adam saw his chance, and using his now free arm he swung an amateurish right arm punch and caught Jonno square on the chin. Whilst no Mike Tyson, the punch surprised Jonno, and startled him enough for Adam to pull his other arm free.

He pulled his arms to his chest and made a leap for the open door but he failed to get there, as Jonno grabbed him by his waist and pulled him back into the car. Adam landed on top of Jonno, both now sprawled across the back seat.

Adam kept his weight on his attacker, who tried grabbing at his hand still intent on breaking a finger.

As the fight developed into a comedy mud-free wrestle on the back seat of the car, Mickey began updating Barry.

"No Barry, we haven't found the money …no, nor Melissa… what… the noise?… oh that's Jonno scrapping with the civilian that Melissa was with last night…" Mickey cupped the receiver in his hand and bellowed at Jonno.

"Jonno, will you restrain that little weasel, now! Break his finger, for chrissake; can't you see I'm on the phone?"

He turned his back on the continuing mayhem and un-cupped the phone.

"Sorry Barry I missed that…what? No, the matter is in hand and will be resolved by end of play today…yes…"

Mickey didn't finish his sentence; before he could; his legs were swept from under him. He hadn't seen or heard the attacker. Despite his size and strength Mickey rose effortlessly into the air, phone still clasped to his ear. He landed with a heavy thud, squarely on his back, his head bouncing off the tarmac, the skin split on contact, and immediately began to expel blood. He had just realised what had happened when a fist rammed itself deep into his solar plexus. The air exploded out of Mickey's lungs, the pain instant and chronic. Mickey fought for breath as he writhed in agony on the floor, his giant feet flailing around.

Jake rose from the punch in one fluid movement, from one knee to standing and then moved off with a nerveless zeal around the car to the offside by the railings. Adam and Jonno's tussle continued inside; both men unaware that Jake had come round the corner and heard the commotion. He had seen Adam in the car as he arrived. Amateurs would have gone to him first. That would have been a mistake. A quick evaluation placed Mickey as a combatant and maybe a leader. Remove him and create a two on one. Jake liked to make the odds favour himself.

He yanked open the back door of the car and Jonno tumbled out holding onto Adam. The shock of falling backwards was the first thing Jonno noticed, the second, Jake's fist, smashing into his face three times in quick succession. Short and fast, using the heel of his hand, the first strike broke Jonno's nose and loosened his grip on Adam. The next two simply spread the nose and pain across his face.

It erupted in a geyser of blood and Jake side-stepped, only just dodging being drenched in the red fountain. He grasped Jonno's hair and pulled, dragging him clear of the car and dumping him against the railings, where he slumped, motionless and dazed. Jake was now confident he no longer posed a threat. He turned back to the car and grabbed Adam, who had by now righted himself and was surprised and relieved to see his friend.

As they quickly moved away from the car and the carnage of the two men writhing on the floor, neither noticed the mobile phone lying in the road, a lone voice issuing forth…

"Mickey…Mickey…what the fuck is going on… MICKEY!"

Chapter Twelve

Adam sat in the low-slung Eames leather armchair in the plush upstairs office of Bar J – headquarters for the Jake Simons empire. He had turned the whole of the two floors above the pub into an office space, and ran all elements of his business from here. The office was double aspect, directly above the bar space and the window behind Jake's desk looked out across the street to the cathedral lawn of the northern vista of the religious monolith.

Bar J had a long history as a public house. The Old Market Tavern had worn a lot of guises over the years, but the smart and contemporary bar design with gastro grub was by far the most successful. In addition to students, Winchester had a thriving thirty-something community, and being voted the best place in Britain to live had clearly helped. The pub stood on Market Street, which backed onto the cathedral grounds. The 1000 year old cathedral dominated the skyline and central Winchester landscape, a magnificent building, surrounded by a mismatch of others that bore the design, styles and construction techniques from the previous centuries. Bar J formed part of a large corner plot, elements dating back to the 17th Century, although the structure was now mostly 19th Century. One thing remained pretty consistent though, it had been an inn or pub since 1806.

Adam had stopped shaking a while ago. He had also finished his second whisky. While never one for histrionics, he wasn't used to professional thugs attacking him in the street. He had regaled the entire story to Jake who sat in silence and didn't interrupt once. He just sat behind his desk staring at the ceiling, concealing his own come-down from the adrenalin of the rescue. He'd missed the buzz of a fight.

Adam watched with interest and felt an increasing sense of being the naughty boy waiting to find out his punishment.

"So let me understand this," Jake said, his fingers steepled under his chin, "Melissa comes to visit… you chat… you eat…you shag…you wake to find she has gone, out, you say; as her stuff is still in the room."

"Correct."

"You leave the house and walk smack into Goliath's little brother…"

"Right."

"Go over the 'I'm thinking of robbing her' bit again, that's still a little hazy…" Jake furrowed his brow.

"Well I haven't robbed her yet…but…well she has £100,000 in cash which she's decided to 'borrow' from her former employer; she asked for my help to launder the money…to make sure that it's clean so she can skip off to Spain or somewhere..." Adam trailed off.

Jake shook his head in disbelief, "But you had every intention of simply laundering the money into your own hands?"

Adam nodded, a little ashamed.

"Where is this money?"

Adam readied himself, "You know the house over the alley, opposite mine..." Jake nodded. He and Adam had looked round the house a few weeks before and he had agreed that buying it as an investment might be a good idea.

"I still have the keys...because I acted so quickly no one else got a look in, so I hid the money in there," he lied.

"Well Adam mate, a fine old mess you've got yourself into."

Adam said nothing, intrigued as to why Jake was smiling.

"These two blokes, monster and co, they are heavies, you realise that? They are acting on orders. Any idea, any idea at all, who they work for?"

Adam shook his head.

"Melissa said nothing about who she worked for and who therefore might want this cash back?"

Adam shook his head. "She said the more I knew the more dangerous it would be... she said they'd never look for her here."

"Well she was a mile wide of the mark with that theory. We can plainly see that they are quite keen to get the money back, whether that or finding Melissa is the priority we can only guess at. I'll wager the money is more important though."

Adam nodded, intrigued by Jake's calculations.

"So me old mucker, we've two options. Firstly, we get the money from the house, try to locate the thugs and arrange for a handover and a deal to leave us, but mainly you, alone..."

Adam smiled to himself. Typical Jake, Adam had got into trouble, he was the one in the cross-hairs, but his problem became Jake's problem.

"Secondly... we could try and keep the money... offer up Melissa as bait and deny all knowledge of the cash. After all they never mentioned money to you did they? We've simply made that rather simple assumption…what do you think?"

Adam pursed his lips and thought for a moment. Rubbing his chin he said,

"With the second option, won't they hurt Melissa…?"

Jake raised his eyebrows, incredulity etched across his features. "Adam, no matter what path is taken by us, that silly cow is fucked. And by that I mean proper fucked. You do not rip off people like this and get away with it."

Adam nodded, wishing he hadn't said it.

"It's my considered opinion, and feel free to ignore me on this, that these guys are not going to be best pleased with the way I snatched you from their clutches. In my experience, they will want to hit back. I think we need to have both the cash and Melissa as bargaining chips. Best to cover all your options…I'd love to know who we're dealing with…"

"Why?"

"I hate not knowing the enemy."

Adam nodded out of habit rather than any real sense of affinity. He didn't share Jake's militaristic past.

"I like to understand my opponent, makes the strategy so much easier. It's good to feel the blood pumping once more."

Adam tossed his head gently from side to side as if weighting up the pros and cons of knowing the enemy.

"Yeah… I suppose they think the same thing."

Jake leant forward, putting his arms on the desk, and looked hard at Adam. "What did you say?"

"Well, it might be silly, but I weighed the facts up. They didn't know who I was… they just had a picture of me with Melissa."

Jake studied his little friend closely.

"I was trying to work out how they got to me... they didn't come to the house did they?"

"No, they accosted you in the street," Jake replied.

"Right. If they knew me or where I lived then they would have simply booted the door down. They want Melissa and had a vague idea she came to Winchester and might have come to see me."

Jake took his turn to nod agreement.

"Yeah, the picture was all they had. They couldn't be sure Melissa was even in the town."

Adam moved to the edge of his seat. "They still don't know who I am, not really, they just know I saw Melissa but nothing else."

"We know a bit more about our enemy." Jake said. "These guys are the search party, the full force is waiting in the wings.

They had to locate Melissa. They've done that…you said you saw her. It's what they do next that will be interesting."

"How do mean?" Adam said, genuinely confused.

"They came here not knowing anything for certain. They got hold of you and now know the girl is here or was here, at least. They have a fact. It's evidently more concrete than any other info they had before." Jake shut his eyes and concentrated.

"Now that they know her last whereabouts and have met the last person to see her, we've to ask ourselves, what would we do next?"

Adam understood.

"If it was me, and it seems this girl and or the money is crucial, then I would pile the big guns down here. Bang some heads until I got answers."

Adam shuffled on the edge of the Eames chair. It looked more comfortable than it really was.

"I was thinking," he said, "the way you came to my rescue… that would unnerve most people, right? Would it unnerve them?"

Jake pondered for a moment, and smiled. "I'd say it would unnerve them. They are used to intimidating people. The violence is often on the back of the intimidation, typical bullying. Me sorting them out like that would freak them out I think. Why'd you ask that?"

"Just a thought," said Adam. "You gave them a pasting. They're not used to that. It might make them think…who the fuck are you?"

Jake's face broke into a huge grin; Adam followed instinctively with a grin of his own and they sat looking at each other, a twinkle in their eyes.

"Adam Warriner, you are a fucking genius."

"I am?"

"Abso-fucking-lutely! They have no clue who we are, what we do, nothing."

Jake was up and pacing round his office. "For all they know they could have fucked around with the wrong guy…oh yes baby…I like this, I like this a lot." Jake stood in triumph.

"What's on your mind….exactly?" Adam interjected.

Jake moved to the front of his desk and crouched down to be on the same level as his friend. He did it with the athletic ease of a well trained man.

"Well I was all for revealing our hand, fessing up to the money and handing it and Melissa over…but, if we do that we play all our cards at once. We reveal our whole position and are open to retribution and attack generally."

Jake held his hand up to stop Adam saying anything.

"We need to be a little more certain of our position and the facts before we act. One thing is certain, these guys will be looking for us, but they will now be very, very nervous."

Adam nodded slowly.

"They don't know who we are. Do you see?"

Adam didn't nod, he simply stared.

"I think we should ascertain as much as we can, so that when they do come calling, and they will come calling, we're in the situation of holding the key cards."

"You keep saying *WE*, this isn't your mess Jake."

Jake looked down placing a hand on his friend's shoulder.

"I'm in it cos you're in it. Anyway, this is going to be too much fun to miss. I needed a bit of excitement."

He was up again and prowling around the office. Adam could picture him in his combat fatigues, camouflaged face, addressing some military problem with the same gusto.

"My primary concern," he said, "is to get you out of this with no bodily harm and no lingering threat. I don't think it will do us any harm to appear a little more 'of the street' than we really are.

"What do you mean?"

"I don't mean we engage these boys in some kind of turf war, it's no Godfather situation and going to the 'mattresses' - I just mean that we should present an image of being outside the law - like they are. Show we're not scared of these guys…act like we're from their world. They're probably likely to take a different tack if we act like we can handle ourselves, they've already had a taste of that… it simply means we've a more equal footing when we negotiate."

Adam's mouth dropped a touch at Jake's suggestion.

"See what I mean?"

Adam nodded, confused by the Godfather reference and perturbed that Jake wanted to pretend to be a gangster.

"It means bedding down for a big war…going to the mattresses" Jake recognised the confusion on Adam's face. "A film of another generation. Trust me Adam, if we still give them what they want but while doing it we present the right image, we can get you out of this with no comeback."

Adam gave him a boyish thumbs up.

"There'll be no escape for Melissa though…you realise this? She has to be fed to these guys to ensure no comeback." Jake stressed the point.

Adam nodded again, slowly. He knew Jake's position regarding Melissa, he couldn't be as certain, but he didn't want to lose focus on the plan.

"Ok first things first, we need to get Melissa. We presume she should either be back at the house or returning sometime soon, right?"

Adam nodded.

"I already have a guy standing watch over their car; he'll tail them or do whatever I ask as and when they come back."

"No messages," he checked his phone. "That means it hasn't moved since our little showdown, and David hasn't called in so there isn't anything new to know. I'm going to send another body round to your house to pick up Melissa and bring her back here and then I'll inform all my security staff about Goliath.

"Goliath?" offered Adam.

"The big bastard, hard but slow" said Jake. "No one knows about the other house so the money may as well stay in there. Once we know where we stand with Melissa we can re-think our strategy on contacting these monkeys and resolving the mess…Agree?"

Adam again nodded his consent, the speed of thought and decision taking him aback.

"Jake, I want to go back to the house, check on Mel myself."

Jake shrugged his shoulders in a 'if you want' gesture…

"Also, do you think, maybe, there's a chance we might resolve this so we don't have to give back the £100,000?"

Jake's expression didn't change. He just patted Adam on the shoulder as he walked past him and out the office door.

Chapter Thirteen

"Where the fuck are you...?"

Barry's voice yelled from the phone.

"Boss, please don't yell" pleaded Mickey, "you're upsetting the other patients..." He regretted saying it immediately.

"Other fucking patients..." Barry's voice spluttered to a halt, completely misunderstanding. Mickey switched the call from speaker to personal and moved towards the automatic doors.

"We're in casualty boss, in Winchester Hospital casualty. Jonno's nose is spread all over his face; it's a right fucking mess. Worst I have ever seen...you what? No, we got hit by this guy, he came from no where, so fucking fast boss. Professional."

He breathed deeply and listened for a moment, then battled on, "ambulance...yeah ambulance. No of course I didn't bloody call it! Some old dear had seen the scrap from over the road and called it in. Thankfully she didn't call the police...no she freaked at the blood from Jonno's nose...we were about one minute from the hospital it turns out. The ambulance arrived in seconds...it seemed best to go along and avoid drawing more attention to ourselves."

Barry was calming down; at least he had stopped shouting. Mickey began to update him on where they had got to.

"We had the Adam fella in the car, that's the name of the geezer in the photo, the ex squeeze of Melissa's, he had just started squawking about her and the cash when you rang. I took your call and half way through this big guy took me from behind… yeah bit coward like…but I cracked my head on the tarmac, winded meself and by the time I was up he'd smashed up Jonno and pulled the Adam bloke away.

"No boss I didn't give chase…coz I had no sodding clue where they went. Also Jonno was bleeding everywhere…the old dear was shouting.. it was tense boss."

Barry Hunt moved into full rant, Mickey held the phone a few inches from his ear and Barry still seemed loud, it was unlike any rant Mickey had heard before, it had an edge, a tinge of desperation about it.

"You want me to come back up boss, what tonight? ….Alright boss, I'm not arguing, if you want to handle this situation yourself then fine. Yeah I'll try and find out who this geezer is and I'll give you the details."

Barry went off into another long tirade of swearing and instructions. A nurse looked sternly at Mickey and pointed at the no mobile phone sign. Mickey turned his back and ignored her.

"Fine boss, bringing Leon and Bobby is not a bad idea, this is one bad dude boss, he's a pro and if he's a pro then that probably means this Adam fella is connected… the reason I'm saying that boss is that this was no random mate coming to help another, he never shouted out, there was no sound, nothing. If I'm mistaken then fine, but in my experience civilians don't act like that. Now if he was the muscle and he came to the protection of this little Adam fella, then I'd want to know who the fuck is this Adam guy, is he a player?"

There was a silence on the end of the phone; Mickey could hear Barry breathing and could almost hear him thinking, mulling the information over. Barry then began slowly and deliberately asking Mickey questions.

"Boss, I think we've got it wrong...think about it? We just assumed that this guy was a monkey that Melissa had ripped off, a stooge? But we got that info from Gemma. Maybe, just maybe it's what we're supposed to think?"

Mickey got up and began pacing around the waiting area. Jonno had long disappeared into the cubicle treatment areas; Mickey's head wasn't exactly a high priority. Mickey moved close to the automatic doors and slid out as they opened. He leant against the wall and responded to the latest question from Barry.

"Yeah I do think that. Melissa has done a runner to this guy and he's protecting her. What he gets out of it is the £100k she nicked. Makes sense to me, I always doubted she had the gumption and nerve to nick from us. With the backing of some firm she might think she's safe from retribution."

Mickey paused to let the idea sink in.

"Whether this guy Adam is the whole deal or simply part of something bigger, I don't know. Clearly he has some muscle and good muscle at that." Mickey moved his hand over the back of his own head. It fell upon the large wadding of cotton wool and gauze taped over his balding crown. "I think they have to be taken seriously. He played it very straight with us, must have been delaying until help arrived. Adam? Adam played it straight boss... he did a great job of seeming completely useless..."

Mickey had mixed it with a lot of tough people. This wasn't the first and probably wouldn't be the last time he'd been put down, but to put him and Jonno out of action so easily had never happened before. Mickey had run through the how's and why's of it, even allowing for complacency, he knew that his attacker could have killed him on the spot if he'd been so inclined.

"So boss, we've to be careful. Provincial numpties or whatever they are, they need handling with respect..."

Mickey listened carefully to what Barry said next, putting his finger in his free ear to shut out the beeps, noises and shouting children of the casualty ward. "Ok Barry...you're the boss. If you still want me to come home and mind the shop, I will. I'll find out what I can about these two first... it's a small town and I'd be fucking surprised if they had any serious competition down here. I'll let Jonno know what the score is and I'll bring the car back up to town tonight."

Mickey terminated the call and looked ruefully at his phone. He didn't get why Barry wanted to come down and deal with this himself, he certainly had no idea why he wanted him to leave it alone. After all, he had a score to settle with his mystery assailant. It had been a long time since someone had levelled him so easily and the way he went on to deal with Jonno actually inspired a sense of respect in Mickey. It was very good work, he thought.

The doctor walked towards him, his tie was loose and he was unshaven. Mickey quickly shovelled the phone in his pocket, expecting a reprimand.

"Mr Finnigan?" the doctor asked.

"Yes", said Mickey, rising to his full height.

The doctor looked at the chart in his hand and ignored the show of bravado.

"Your friend.." he began, eyes on the chart, "… sorry to say, is not a well guy. We can confirm his nose is broken, but so too are both his cheek bones."

Mickey nodded, unsurprised.

"It means that his face has effectively caved in.. his sinus cavities are also damaged and he'll need extensive surgery to reconstruct his face…so", the doctor finally looked up and realised that where he thought Mickey's face was only contained a massive chest. His eyes continued up the body until they reached the big man's face.

"So.." finished Mickey, "He's unlikely to be driving me home tonight?"

The doctor gulped.

"Yes, er I mean no - he'll be in hospital for some time I'm afraid, he's sedated now. He was in quite a lot of pain."

Mickey nodded. He understood pain, he'd inflicted a lot and received a lot. There was no shame in Jonno hurting now. He'd been well and truly sorted.

"We do need some patient details…." The doctor prodded the chart at Mickey, as the nurse had done an hour before.

"Leave it with me doc." Mickey broke into his unpractised smile and took the chart. "Can I see my friend for a moment… I know he's sedated but I need to leave him a message."

The doctor led the way down the corridor and past the row of drawn green curtains. Various grunts, groans and moans of people in pain abstractly emanated from behind them. The last booth on the right contained the stupefied Jonno.

He tapped his partner on the shoulder as the doctor drew the curtain behind him and left. Mickey rifled through Jonno's coat pocket and found his phone. He flicked through the mobile's menu and quickly typed in a diary action and a note. He set the reminder to go off at 9.00am the next morning. Jonno would be out of sedation and painfully awaiting rounds. He'd get the message.

Mickey didn't look at Jonno again. He left the unfilled form on his trolley and exited casualty. It was the afternoon now, not too long before door men came on duty, if you want to know who runs what in any town, they're a good place to start.

Mickey wasn't ready to head home just yet.

* * *

Jake flipped open his clam-shell phone and held it to his ear, saying nothing. The voice on the other end quickly and

122

succinctly downloaded some information. Jake nodded, and then remembered he needed to speak to confirm receipt of the information. "Fine…stay there; keep an eye on the car and see if the big fella turns up. Call me as soon as you see him". Jake snapped the phone shut and looked immediately at Adam.

Adam caught the look in his eye and knew Melissa hadn't returned before Jake said anything.

"She still hasn't shown up. Why didn't you say the box room had been turned over? As if, and I quote, "someone in a state of panic was hunting for something". He looked at Adam and comically raised his left eyebrow.

Adam had returned to the house an hour or so before, it was in exactly the same state he and Melissa had left it in after their initial sexual acrobatics. An hour on and she hadn't come back. Adam understood immediately.

"It would appear she's done a runner. Now why would someone who'd just handed £100k to her ex…ex whatever, run? Why would you do that?"

Jake looked at Adam hard, as if staring at him might produce a coherent answer. Adam stayed silent.

"Maybe, and I'm going out on a bit of a limb here, maybe she saw or knew that the people she took the money from had turned up and were chatting to you." He emphasised the final point by extravagantly pointing at Adam.

"Mmmm, it would seem odd....I can see why you think that's the most likely conclusion," Adam offered by way of a weak reply.

"How nice of her to stick around and see if you were ok. Must have been oh so concerned for your well being." Jake didn't want to hide the sarcasm. Adam just looked at his scuffed shoes. He fingered his mobile phone.

She hadn't called, but she had texted.

He debated telling Jake.

He had decided though, not to complicate things further.

The message was short and sweet.

"I did what you said. Sorry not as planned. Forget what we talked about it can't happen now. Mel x"

"Doesn't seem she had much faith in my ability to protect her does it?" Adam offered. Jake sighed and turned his gaze to the window and its view of the cathedral.

"Be fair Adam, that's the one thing the dizzy bint has gotten right."

Adam ignored the rebuke, "Maybe she's just hiding and will be back...."

"Shut up! Smell the coffee - She came back, checked for the cash, ransacked the room, it was gone, she didn't even hang around to ask where's my cash gone, git of an ex -thingymebob – no, she's done a runner, but why?"

He held his hand up at Adam as he was about to speak. Adam's mouth opened and then closed silently.

"Rhetorical Adam. She saw what happened to you...get it? She knew no matter what happened the game was up. This changes things..."

"Yeah" agreed Adam. "It certainly does," 'but for very different reasons to yours', thought Adam.

"We don't have her as a bargaining chip any more; in fact she's a bit of nuisance all round. A rogue element in the unfolding drama."

Adam thought hard about the permutations and quickly pieced together a version for Jake. "So, your theory is that the thugs, they wanted Melissa and pretty certainly the money, but they don't know the two have been separated, they certainly don't know we've the cash."

Jake nodded.

"If Melissa is out there she can tell them we've got the cash in an attempt to take the spotlight from her..." concluded Adam.

"Bingo. My gut feeling is, she's shit scared. Panicking and on the run. Therefore we've a bit of time before she gets her head together and does anything involving rational thought."

"Don't underestimate her..." Adam knew he needed to speak to Mel and warn her of what might be coming next, his text message wouldn't have been enough.

"Good point. No, we've to remember that these guys who came for you and her probably work for someone else. That's usually the way of things. She has only got one thing going for her, she knows we've got the money, so the sooner we remove that as a weapon in her armoury the better for us."

Adam mused on the scenario Jake had painted. He had worked on the facts, applied logic and rational deduction. It's what he was trained for, but it was flawed. It relied on truth.

"I don't think you need to worry about Mel, not short term anyway, if she has run then she'll be focused on that…." Adam looked for a reaction in Jake.

Jake rubbed his hand over his short blonde hair and thought carefully. He knew the best method of defence could often be attack. He hated applying clichés, but fuck it, sometimes they worked. He mulled over the potential actions in his head. "Pretending the thugs and the situation will go away is tantamount to burying our heads in the sand. These guys are coming and if unchecked they will come in force and they look like they could do some serious damage."

Adam watched his friend.

"Maybe, just maybe, they would settle for getting the money back and walking into the sunset. That's our best shot, meet them head on, present a united and bold front, offer them the chance to walk away and hope they take it." He nodded to himself pleased with his thoughts. He then opened his ringing phone slowly.

Dave, the sentry at the car, reported back.

"Mr Simons, the big fella is back at the car. Fuck me he's a big bastard as well…one sweep put him down did it sir?" The 'sir', a respectful by-product of the militaristic nature of Jake's business empire.

"Just a matter of force, angle and gravity Dave."

Jake paused, looked at Adam and smiled. "Dave- engage. As discussed."

He shut the phone and tapped it gently on his lip.

* * *

Mickey didn't like hospitals. They contained officials and officials ask questions. Jonno would be taken care of – being on hand with flowers and chocolates wouldn't matter now.

He turned right out of the casualty entrance onto Romsey Road and began the steep walk down towards the town centre and the Peninsular Barracks. The view across the town to towards the cathedral that thrust its way through the low level buildings and trees to dominate the Winchester skyline, was an impressive sight. Mickey took a moment to enjoy it, the sun shone and he thought what a nice quiet place Winchester must be to live in.

Mickey pondered as he walked, it seemed clear that Melissa must be in cahoots with this Adam. Knowing Melissa and her history and the way the attacker had dealt with him and Jonno, Mickey jumped to only one conclusion.

They were villains.

Finding them shouldn't be too hard. He'd ask some direct questions in the local bars and it would only be a matter of time before someone turned up to see who he was. He turned off Romsey Road, passed the Gurkha museum and headed into the estate where they'd left the Lexus..

Dave put his mobile phone in his pocket and emerged from a darkened recess in the corner of the estate and quietly moved along the pavement towards the Lexus and the very, very big man that was opening the driver's door. He strode off the pavement and into the middle of the road, standing directly on the middle of the T-junction facing the parked Lexus. He stood and waited for the big man to notice him.

Mickey pulled the door shut as he slumped into the car, he glanced up and saw the man in the street. Not a big guy, but trim and thick set, he had the look of a man who was confident in his ability.

"Who the fuck is this guy?" muttered Mickey, perturbed that for the second time in a day, someone had sneaked up on him.

Dave made the signal for Mickey to put his driver's side window down, by rolling his clenched hand. Mickey ignored him and opened the door instead. He pulled his massive bulk out of the vehicle and lent on the open door, the car listing to the right as he did so.

"What the fuck do you want?" Mickey said, conscious to appear like he was not going to be fucked with.

"Get a nasty bump on the head today big man?" Dave responded, his Essex drawl Jamie Oliver to Mickey's Mike Read.

"You a funny man, mate? Is that what you are?" He slammed the door shut and began moving towards Dave.

Dave didn't move.

In fact he smiled.

"Easy big man. We don't want you slipping over again."

Mickey stopped. He didn't want to; he'd rather fold the little monkey up and stuff him into the bin on the corner. But he relented. Discretion, he decided, was most definitely the better part of valour, when dealing with these guys.

" My boss wants to talk to you. He told me to tell you... he can help you find what you have mislaid."

Mickey stared at him, suddenly interested by what the irritant had to say.

"Go to Bar J on Market Street on the Market Square." The blank look on Mickey's face prompted him to expand on his directions. "It's right out front of the Cathedral. Follow it round and you can't miss Bar J."

"Who do I ask for?"

"They know you're coming, big man, you're not hard to spot you know. If you want to ask for someone, then you should ask for Mr Simons."

Mickey stiffened at the slight. He didn't like the smirk on this guy's face and he didn't like the idea of going straight to the dragons den. "Are you the fucker who blindsided me this morning?"

Dave laughed a little. "No big man that would have been Mr Simons. Don't you worry about seeing him, he only wants to talk. If he hadn't wanted to do that, he would never have left you able to respond. Count yourself lucky."

With Mickey pondering what he had just heard, Dave waved royally at him and strode off down the road to his right. Mickey watched him go. He realised he was standing in the middle of the road, so he stepped over the white lines as if they were dangerous and folded himself back into the car and shut himself in.

"Who the fuck are these people?" he muttered to himself. People didn't usually tell Mickey what to do and he certainly wasn't used to being intimidated.

He fished in his pocket for his mobile phone and thought about making a call to Barry, but stopped himself. Barry would be down tomorrow, he would call him once he had some more concrete information to go on. Risky or otherwise Mickey knew he had to respond to Mr Simon's invitation. If nothing else he wanted to look into the eyes of the man who had the audacity to take him down, even if only temporarily.

Chapter Fourteen

Irma and Irena Petrov could have been twins, but in fact there was a four year age gap between them. You couldn't describe them as attractive, but neither would you call them ugly, largely because if you did then you may illicit the reaction that they were becoming famous for - their propensity to cut off the testicles of their enemies and leave them to bleed to death. The Petrovs, so far, had never had to assassinate any female rivals, though Irena had pondered what calling card they could leave if the situation arose. Irma had done the same; they were yet to compare notes.

They both stood exactly five foot tall, no one knew precisely how old they were, but you wouldn't have got much change out of mid forties. If they had a style, then they were modelling themselves on Dolly Parton with Slavic highlights. Their high cheek bones, blonde hair, dour demeanour and slightly retro 1960's dress sense made them look like a transvestite tribute act in a working man's club up north.

They hadn't been in London long, a couple of years. Originally they came over from Tallinn, Estonia in 2004 with their husbands, moved on in their homeland by the expansion of corporate organised crime that emanated from the Ukraine and Russia. Unable to compete with the oil and gas oligarchs, they knew their days were numbered if they didn't find a new market for their particular skills.

London was viewed as and happened to be, for the Petrovs at least, the city of opportunity. Unlike Barry Hunt and others who were part of the Mr G network, the Petrovs had no manor, no official turf. They answered to no-one but were therefore at the mercy of everyone. They lived off the criminal scraps of the London underworld table, but they weren't without ambition. London had become the land of opportunity for a new breed of criminal.

Irma, the elder of the two, realised very quickly that her husband Juri wasn't adjusting to working in London. He simply wasn't adjusting to work.

His limited English inhibited his already crippling lack of ambition to take on established territories. As he squandered their money and setup fund on partying and gambling, Irma realised that if she wanted to succeed, to make the life she had been promised, then she needed to do it without him. Her concern was not the removal of Juri, rather of his partner, the more psychopathic Ivo. He had not managed to retain the fearsome troops that were with him in Tallinn, and had failed to make effective use of his time in London. His brand of skills merely competed in an already congested market.

In fact Irena, the younger sister, planted the first seeds of sedition, casually stating that she sometimes wished her husband Ivo would go back to Tallinn or simply die and "do her a favour." From there, the sisters joked that they should run the business and what use did they have for these silly men?

As the idea took hold so did their commitment to the cause. It opened a personal window into a life they had viewed and participated in only from the periphery. The transition into central criminal figures didn't prove too big a leap to make. Within eight months of being in London, Juri and Ivo had disappeared, later found in the Thames estuary tangled around the anchor chain of a domestic Dutch barge houseboat called "Amanda".

Irma looked out of her first floor Fulham office window, surveying the bustling London street below. She smiled as people pushed and shunted one another entering the lair of the tube at Fulham Broadway. She knew it wasn't London proper, but it was close enough for a girl from the back streets of Tallinn. Every time she stood at the window and took in the view, she knew she owned all above and below her. The daughter of a dock worker, who had no one but her sister in the whole world, was now somebody in the greatest city in the world.

The door opened without a knock and in walked the younger and marginally slimmer Petrov. A thin-lipped smile spread across her face. "Sister... it is public."

Irma turned, her mouth mimicked the actions of her sister. "Good...and was it found with its balls in its mouth?"

The sisters smiled at the memory and the thrashing limbs of their victim.

"Yes...this time they stayed in. You were right, we needed to close the mouth more if we put the body into the water."

Irma nodded. Killing Gregor Bartok had been a bold move, a statement of intent. The Petrovs were ready to come out of the shadows and begin mixing it with the big boys.

* * *

Mr G did not like being made to wait. He had developed a hatred for queueing and waiting as a young man, and now it manifested itself into a generic frustration. In fairness a man in his position rarely waited for anything.

He had people for that kind of thing.

Beano ran his immediate circle of runners and helpers, a glorified PA is how the uninitiated looked at Beano's role, but that would be underestimating the man. He had an impressive elephantine memory to match his gargantuan frame and he could recall almost to the word any conversation, instruction or deal made if he cared to. When combined with his network of informers, flunkies and runners, Beano's word on any situation could be considered final. However, being made to wait for Beano's unquestionable facts did not please Mr G.

He lifted himself off the aircraft carrier-sized sofa unit and with his slow West Indian stroll, ambled over to the stereo. Consciously he scanned the empty penthouse room before deftly flicking the stereo off. He hated 50 Cent. He basked for a moment in the silence, and then he ran his manicured hand along the CD rack, but saw only Tupac, P-Diddy and their like. He really fancied some Neil Diamond.

'Pretty amazing grace' would have suited his mood.

Unfulfilled he turned and moved to the floor to ceiling window and gazed out over south London. His manor.

His father used to take the young Winston Gerald Goodman's hand and walk him around their Southfields garden, no more than forty foot by twenty five; little more than a walled in allotment. That patch of garden was his father's pride and joy. Neat, lovingly tended, Mr G's fondest childhood memory was walking in that garden with his father.

"A man is defined by his land, boy. You don't have land, you don't have nut-ting" He could hear his father's words even now. Their evening strolls began the same way, his father taking his hand once dinner had been finished and asking him, "son, shall we walk the estate?"

Mr G smiled at the idea that from Bexley Heath to Twickenham, south of the Thames, was now technically his estate. Sure he had manors and landlords tending them, like Barry, but he ruled the roost.

Beano had been taken aback when, a few days before, he demanded to "walk" his estate. Taken aback he may have been, but Beano hadn't wasted any time in making it happen. Mr G knew his father would disapprove of his lifestyle. Mr G gave thanks that his parents moved back to Jamaica and passed away contented and believing their son had become a market trader.

Why now, thought Mr G, do I have to wait for the answer to a very simple question, Beano should know everything, his question should not have posed too many difficulties, "What the fuck is the story with Barry Hunt?"

Mr G had seen red when he discovered the cheeky fucker hadn't deposited the cash for his monthly retainer. Any delay in the supply chain meant a chance for the cowboy organisations to infiltrate and supply where his organisation was not. Barry had been good for business ever since Mr G's rise to power in the "Reefer Wars" of the early 1990's, he had been loyal and kept his manor in good order. Now though, it seemed that things were slipping, mistakes kept being made and decisions taken that concerned Mr G. The word on the street said that Barry Hunt had lost his bottle, no longer the Barry of old, he didn't have the same fire in his belly.

Mr G threw Barry a bone; sort out Bartok and we're fine.

Now not only has Barry not resolved it, but Mr G has to find out through the grapevine about Bartok's demise. This is not respectful, and now Mr G wants answers and Barry is making him wait... this is getting serious.

Mr G was forced out of his thoughts by a loud rasp on the door, he turned to see Beano heave his bulk through the door. Beano never waited for a response. He wheezed and looked like he was sweating profusely as he moved into the room and leaned, one-armed, on the sofa back.

The sight had become a common one for Mr G. The lift to the penthouse didn't go to the top of the building. You still had to climb a flight of fifteen stairs to get to this upper level, and it knackered Beano every time. Mr G knew Beano would begin as soon as he was able.

"Barry Hunt...couldn't get him by phone, Mr G. He was always busy, always asking me to leave a message."

"Is that my answer Beano?"

"No way dog. Beano wouldn't leave his bro hanging like that. Haven't done it before, aint going to start now," Beano said, genuinely quite hurt by the accusation.

"Your man Barry, Barry mother fucking bullshit Hunt, well he's been hiding from us man. Making out he was Mr fucking busy, lord of the manor. Too damned busy to take my top dogs call" Beano moved into full flow.

"Can't raise the bitch on the phone...what you do? You go down there and make the bitch listen...am I right?" He didn't want a reply and none materialsied.

"You bet your sorry arse that's right. But, I was thinking, sure Leroy and Clem can bust a few heads, make some noise and encourage him to talk to us...but why should Mr G hear his news, the answer to his question, second-hand?" He held out his massive arms in theatrical emphasis. Then he clapped his hands in a dramatic and somewhat regally camp fashion, letting out a burst of giggle as he did so. The door swung open and two heavy-set black men, dressed head to toe in black Armani, escorted a somewhat more diminutive and bedraggled figure into the room, his features obscured by a black silk bag.

Mr G smiled at the entrance. He didn't let it linger for long.

137

The man, clearly bewildered, got plonked into a chair that Beano had pulled up from the dining table. The man's hands, were tied behind his back, so it made it difficult for him to sit comfortably. Beano moved forward and with the flourish of a third rate magician, whipped the silk mask off.

He revealed a slightly scared, dishevelled and annoyed Barry Hunt.

Barry blinked his eyes to get them accustomed to the light change, he wasn't surprised to see Mr G standing in front of him. He looked away and lowered his gaze, embarrassed at his undignified entrance.

Mr G now had a broad grin on his face.

He nodded, sage-like, to Beano, happy at the answer he had provided. Definitely worth the wait.

"Barry...where you been bro? Don't you know it's good to talk?" Mr G kept his voice measured and controlled. He avoided exaggerated gangsta' speak and where practical discouraged his people from doing it.

"Beano has been wanting to talk to you... you know why?" Mr G paused, but got no response from Barry. He nods his head at Beano, who promptly raises a paw-like hand and cuffs Barry across the back of the head.

"Answer Mr G Barry Bullshit, you can't hide behind yo' fucking voicemail now boy."

Barry sighed, his shoulders lifting up and down noticeably. It doesn't take long for bad news to travel around the criminal underbelly, Barry had heard the news from several sources.

Bartok had been found.

He had desperately tried to get Mickey back from Winchester before Mr G's anger could rise too far. If he could have got to Winchester before this forced meeting he would have been able to buy a little more time and have the fringe benefit of being out of the firing line. Barry needed to think on his feet and do it quickly.

"Sorry Mr G – no disrespect intended….I know you wanted to find out what's been going on, but I wanted to be sure of the facts before I spoke to you, you know get my ducks in a row, so to speak."

"Fuck your ducks. The facts are real fucking simple. You set me up with a fucking arsehole of a partner. He fucking stole from me." Mr G glared at him.

"That made you my extra special bitch. I asked you to take care of the fat cunt for me. You said and I quote….."

Beano chimed in effortlessly…"Don't worry Mr G, I am on the case, I am all over the situation. Bartok's head on a silver platter by the end of the week."

"Did you or did you not make that promise Barry?"

"I did." Barry felt ten years old again. This time he wouldn't be getting the cane; maybe a bullet in the head, but not the cane.

139

"Well, we've a discrepancy between your fucking word and subsequent actions. Talk me through why the fat Ukranian is currently lying on a police slab with his bollocks missing, but retaining his head?"

Barry stared up at Mr G, "His bollocks were missing?"

"Yes. His fucking bollocks had been hacked off. Not sliced or cut Barry, but hacked off. My man is telling me that he died from loss of blood, from having no fucking bollocks…"

Mr G's voice had risen to a near shout, it echoed around the penthouse.

"Now Einstein, the fact that you didn't know his bollocks were missing tells me something very important. You had nothing the fuck whatsoever to do with his death did you?" If Barry Hunt was a cartoon, he'd have had a big thought bubble protrude from his head at the moment and it would have said the words, "OH FUCK."

Barry regretted his stupidity immediately. He searched for an answer, but could only come up with…. "No."

A moment of silence followed, Mr G had expected Barry to claim he had carried out the hit and say sorry for not delivering Bartok's head as planned. People usually cried or begged for forgiveness when they failed Mr G.

"I did order the hit on Bartok," he nervously began. "As we discussed. I had my best man on the case…"

"Mickey Finn?" asked Mr G.

Barry paused, contemplated his answer and its implications in a millisecond, "yeah – Mickey."

"Continue," ordered Mr G.

"Well, you see, Mickey, he entertained the possibility of a third party joining in…but I can't lie to you Mr G, Bartok, as far as I know, was not taken out by anyone officially connected with me...sorry."

"Sorry! Barry I don't want to hear sorry. I want to hear … 'Mr G, here is your money back, the man who hit Bartok is…' These are the words I want to hear, Mr Bullshit."

"Yeah…of course you would". Barry grasped for an idea, a thought that would give him a way out. Beads of sweat had formed on his forehead.

"But, you see, I do know who hit Bartok…I mean I found out, er I had it confirmed about an hour or so ago." Barry had the burgeoning of an idea, it could save him some time and maybe get his plan back on track.

"You know who did the hit?" Mr G arched his eyebrows in surprise.

"Yeah, they're an odd bunch, usually sound but prone to doing some stupid things. Real, wannabe hard men. They're based in Winchester would you believe?" Barry was getting into his stride, he could see the lie panning out, a chink of light at the end of the tunnel had just appeared.

"Winchester?"

"Yeah Winchester. Down in Hampshire…."

"We know where fucking Winchester is Barry... the ancient fucking capital of England... largest gothic cathedral in the world...you implying something by that?" Beano barked it out like he could follow it with a bite any moment.

Barry ignored him, "My man Mickey is on the case as we speak. Trying to resolve why they did what they did." Beano and Mr G exchanged looks; they then turned to Barry, then back to each other.

"You said that whoever hit Bartok had nothing to do with you," Beano offered.

"Officially their hit was nothing to do with me...but well they did the hit... and they thought they could blackmail me... yeah they wanted leverage!"

Mr G sat down uneasily on the sofa and patted the seat to encourage Beano to join him. He waved away the two heavies and looked long and hard at Barry.

"Tell me the fucking story, Barry."

Barry swallowed and nervously began, shifting his gaze from Mr G to Beano,

"As you know, we do some work in the provinces, and make a nice margin on some of the gear we get from you. Beano will vouch for that, we've been above board with it. Well this is the mob who we sell to in Winchester. Mickey deals with it, it's his thing really. He sometimes does some freelance heavy work for them. I don't ask any questions, I just let him get on with it. Anyway he convinced me to lend them some money, peanuts really, a bit of finance, they needed to get some shooters…or something, and we would get paid back with a percentage of whatever job they were planning, as I say Mickey was dealing with it."

Beano and Mr G nodded – fair enough, Mickey had his side thing going. Mickey Finn is a capable man, Mr G had backed him and won when Mickey was still a fighter. They settled a little on the sofa, this was like a gangsta' Jackanory.

Barry cleared his throat and began again more confidently, "It seems that they decided to hit Bartok. Somehow they knew about it, maybe Mickey spilled some news, maybe they knew the fat bastard, I don't know. Anyway, to encourage me not to ask for the cash back, they said they would come running to you saying that they hit Bartok and not me, insinuating that I stole from you, which you know, I wouldn't do!"

Mr G leant back on the sofa, exhaled audibly and looked back at Barry. "So what you're saying is these guys hijacked our deal on Bartok, in an attempt to put you in my bad books. They are also reneging on a straight money deal with you?"

"Yeah…Mickey is sorting it out, in fact I am due to go down tonight and have it out with them. Mickey is laying the groundwork…"

"Cool." Mr G sat back and restored the look of gangsta ambivalence to his face. "Can you trust Mickey on this one Barry? I mean it would seem he might be at the centre of this, are these Winchester boys like his pet crew?" he asked.

"Yeah I get that, I understand that, that's why I've ordered Mickey back from Winchester once the meet is set up, I'm going to get my dosh back, find out if he's involved. I mean these guys steal from me they steal from you don't they?"

"You reckon?" said Beano doubting the validity of Barry's story.

"Well yeah. These guys owe me just over £100K, it was supposed to be a sure-fire thing, lend them the cash, a few days later I get a big pay off. Hasn't happened. I mean I don't go round lending £100K everyday of the week, to be fair, it did dent my cash flow."

"Is that why you ain't paid me my monthly retainer?" Mr G lowered his shades so Barry could see his eyes. Not many men that saw them and owed Mr G money stayed alive for long.

"Not holding out on me, are you Barry?"

"NO – me hold out on you? Never. Cash flow - you got it in one Mr G." Barry winked, touched his forefinger to his nose and pointed it at Mr G.

"Don't do that Barry… it annoys the fuck out of me!" The shades popped back into place. "So you're down in Winchester sorting this problem out, back tomorrow?" Barry nodded.

"Well Barry you're usually a fine partner, been in the business a long time. It's a reasonable explanation. I am a reasonable man. You have until Saturday my man, to bring back my fucking £100k."

Barry leapt to his feet. "Yes, no problem, I'll take these monkeys in Winchester to school. I'll have your money back. All sorted by Saturday, deal." Barry started to head to the door, eager to get out and to catch his breath. He had reached the door when he heard Mr G's deep dulcet tones once again,

"Barry…my man, you'll be paying the £200k retainer on Saturday as well… right!"

Barry mouthed shit, his back still facing Mr G. He looked over his left shoulder and said, "Of course Mr G, Mickey will be back to take care of all that." He spun round and left through the now held open door.

Mr G looked at Beano and the pair shared a shrug.

"You believe him Beano?"

Beano frowned, and slowly shook his head.

"His manor is under-performing. Word is it has a lot of leeches, lots of scavengers scrapping for a foothold. Barry ain't cleaning house like he used to…"

"Like he should," said Mr G, "has the old man gone soft?"

"Maybe…" offered Beano.

Mr G nodded. He sprawled a little on the sofa and tried to lounge. It didn't suit him. "Beano… work the manor, find out what you can. Make contact with Mickey when he comes back. You know the man. See how he views things."

"You think Mickey is raising an army with these Winchester boys- kick Barry's arse out of the manor?"

"Do you?"

"No."

"Why not?"

"Mickey Finn is old school. He does loyalty, he's aligned to Barry all the way," Beano said.

"Yeah that's my feeling. He's a good man is Mickey Finn. If the shit goes down, I'd like to know which side he's on…" Mr G left the phrase hanging.

Beano nodded.

He swung his bulk round and waddled toward the doors, as he reached them they opened, as if magically, and he stepped through.

"Oh and Beano," Mr G yelled after him, "Bring back my fucking Neil Diamond CD."

Chapter Fifteen

Olly and Mark stood outside the main door to Bar J. It was 7.00pm on a Thursday, it should be a quiet night, but the bar would still be comparatively busy compared to a lot of places in town. The mix of chic furnishings, good food and live music had turned Bar J into the must-go-to place at the weekend; as a consequence, the week nights had developed into the buzzing venue to be at. The drinks and food were priced to keep the riff raff out and the dress code simply stated, "Be smart enough to get in." Half the poorly dressed punters denied entry completely missed the double meaning.

Bar J didn't strive to be especially snobbish, it didn't care who you were. It only cared that you wanted to have the good time it offered and could afford it.

Olly and Mark had been with Jake and his various security ventures for three years. They were his "trouble shooters" the first on the doors at any new venture, sometimes working the door of the original pub prior to its redevelopment into Jake's vision, to begin the process of weeding out the undesirables, or touring in a car to be on call to assist at any venue.

Both men had seen action as Royal Marines. Jake hired them because they epitomised the calm, controlled and totally trustworthy qualities he required. They earned a lot of money through Jake, so when he called them and told them to do basic door duty, they didn't question him. When he told them to watch out for a special guest, they didn't ask a single question.

Jake had attracted a fair degree of unwanted attention from "have a go likely lads" and he had always dealt with it head on. Locally his reputation for being squeaky clean but never backing down, had gained him grudging respect. The small local gangs knew he wasn't interested in their dive locations. They understood that peddling drugs in his venues or generally trying to influence him met with a severe reaction.

"Did you see her?"

"Who?" said Mark absentmindedly.

"Chloe...you know the little red head. Did you see her?"

Olly was referring to a Bar J regular, Chloe. A tidy little thing Olly had been going on about for some weeks and as yet had failed to pluck up the courage to ask out.

"Yeah Olly I've seen her. She's lovely. I don't know how many times I have to tell you that I think she's lovely. She's lovely, ok?"

"Yeah she's lovely isn't she? Maybe she'll be out tonight...you think?"

"Mate, maybe she will. Who knows for sure. But she's here most nights...but let's be fair, what difference will it make?"

"What d'ya mean?"

"You have droned on about her, her perfect bottom, her lovely hair..yada yada for weeks and have done exactly zero about it. If you're thinking about asking her out, for chrissake do it."

148

Mark hoped he'd finally do it and shut up, he also hoped he'd do it carefully and not get caught chatting up the ladies while on duty. Jake had his rules.

Olly just smiled, he hoped she'd be in. He knew he wouldn't ask her out, he knew he was all talk, but he loved the feeling he got, when his heart skipped a beat as he saw her. He didn't know exactly what was going on behind those captivating eyes of hers. But he loved the effect she had on him.

"You hear the story about Jake today?" Mark had been given the lowdown on the situation from Dave.

"Sort of yeah. He takes out two guys, hired heavies or something?"

"Two fellas, one a monster apparently, they were taking a liberty or something with Adam and well Jake stepped in. Both went to hospital, one still in there, may be eating with a straw for the foreseeable future."

"Hasn't lost it then has he."

"Not a chance." Mark stepped aside as a trio of Winchester's finest ladies closed in on the door. They pushed the door open and the ladies strolled in. "Good evening ladies," welcomed Olly. The ladies smiled, they always did and moved in to the bar. The boys found themselves the centre of a lot of female attention. They were in their late twenties, Olly dark and Latin coloured, Mark blonde, thicker set and slightly taller, his Scandinavian looks the silk to Ollie's hirsute velvet.

149

"I wouldn't fancy anyone, one to one with Jake. I mean yeah he has the special forces background, but it's the fighting instinct that scares me. He doesn't wait, if he thinks it's going to go down he gets in first, worries about the consequences afterwards," Mark said.

"How's Cindy?" Mark had been dating Cindy off and on for a couple of months. He had never divulged too much. Mark coughed slightly, "Yeah its good. Sort of…no, it's good."

Olly noticed the hesitation; he sensed maybe Mark wanted to talk about it. "What's the problem matey?" Mark was glad he'd asked, he wished he had been more subtle in hinting that he wanted to talk about something, but fair play to Olly he had picked it up. "Well, it's hard to explain, we, you know, have been out a few times and she has stayed over…"

"What like a sleepover?" Olly jested.

"Yes just like a sleepover but with the exchange of bodily fluids," Mark jousted back. They both laughed.

"Anyway, you know how Cindy, is well, gorgeous?" Olly certainly knew, she was in his humble opinion, model material.

"Well she's great, unreal body, nice girl, great laugh…"

"But..." offered Olly.

"But…well... she's a bit crap in bed."

Olly muffled a smile and laugh… "You what?"

"She's crap in bed. Don't you tell no one about this…Olly?"

"What?"

"Promise…you'll keep it to yourself?" Mark looked serious.

"Promise," said Olly, "now get on with the details."

Mark sighed and shuffled his feet. " Well we get all steamed up, nice bit of stroking, all of that….then as we move to getting naked….well she just freezes up…just lies there…I mean she joins in, sort of, but lies there moaning and stuff, but just lies there…"

"You mean no…wriggling, no writhing?"

"No nothing… and well she won't let me, you know deliver my special love…and won't go near the old chap."

"Oooh no oral, no taking… blimey, that's a bit a harsh. Have you mentioned it to her?"

"Well I've asked if she enjoys it, the sex like and she says it's great, says it's the best sex she's had…"

"Fucking hell... let me guess, it's the worst you've had?"

"Yeah" said Mark frowning, "Without doubt it's the worst I've had."

The two men stood in silence for a moment.

"I mean how do you tell someone who looks like a fucking angel, she can't shag for shit?" Mark offered.

"Well someone better had hadn't they, poor love is missing out big style."

"Yeah I suppose…harsh though. It's a first for me, telling a girl she's no good in bed. I mean, maybe there is some truth in the adage…you know?"

"What mate…" asked Olly.

"Ugly girls try a bit harder…cos you know, they don't get offered as much…"

The two men fell into another contemplative silence. It was interrupted as the unmistakeable figure of Mickey Finn came round the corner. Olly and Mark immediately and almost imperceptibly went into character, there wouldn't be another matching the description. The special guest had arrived.

Mickey had rounded the corner and seen the two doormen. He watched as they clocked him and looked on, intrigued by their reaction. Neither was a big man, but they were professionals, Mickey could tell that instantly, men of kindred spirit he thought. Like the man at the car, they were solid, trained and fit looking. Confident they could handle themselves.

He stopped five feet from them. More than an arm's length away. The safe distance. "Good evening sir," offered Mark.

"Evening boys," smiled Mickey back.

"You're expected sir. May we have the pleasure of your name, we'd like to introduce you properly," Olly said.

"So polite boys, students of Roadhouse are we?" The 80's Swayze cooler movie reference passed them by. Patrick had said to his new doorman recruits, 'no matter what happens' be nice…'

"My name is Mickey Finn…and I would like to meet the man who put me down today."

Mark and Olly exchanged a brief glance. Mickey was clearly the monster of the story. The suited figure dwarfed them,

152

his giant calloused hands and scarred eyebrows told the story of man that had hit and been hit. Olly and Mark never deferred to size, it was irrelevant in their line of work really. Doormen were traditionally big, simply to deter trouble; mostly it had the opposite effect. In Mickey they recognised a fighter, a capable man, a man to watch.

"Follow me sir, Mr Simons is expecting you". Mark led the way into the bar and round through the security coded door, Olly followed behind, never crowding Mickey, but close enough so he knew he was there.

Olly and Mark's places on the main door were immediately replaced by two more of Jake's team. They had been on standby in the cloakroom.

Adam paced back and forth, his mood one of agitation. Jake looked more composed but still clearly anxious. They had been over their strategy again and again and had agreed to play it cool, sit back and see what they could draw out of the thug and to make sure they didn't play their hand too early.

Jake had briefed a small circle of his best and most trusted employees, they would follow the instructions, only asking questions once it was all over. The security headset ticked twice. The signal from the door that their visitor had arrived.

"Sit down in the corner Adam, try to look important and not like you're going to shit yourself…" Jake gestured to the Eames armchair he had moved to under the window. Adam smiled nervously and sat down.

153

At the top of the stairs Olly politely told Mickey he had to be frisked. Mickey accepted. The inspection over, Mark knocked on the door to their left and entered immediately. Mickey entered the room and had to duck his head under the door frame, Olly and Mark stayed close. Sitting behind an expensive looking desk he saw for the first time the man that took him out, Jake Simons. In the corner on what Mickey thought looked an uncomfortable designer chair, Adam Warriner stared at him intently.

After taking a moment to scan the office and the men he had encountered, Mickey nodded perceptibly, like a man deciding he liked the place so much he might buy it.

"Let's do this properly..." offered Jake. "I think introductions are required." He held out his hand across the desk. Mickey took a casual step forward and grasped it. His hand dwarfed Jake's, they shook convivially. "Jake Simons, owner of Bar J."

"Mickey Finn. Pissed off from Putney."

Jake smiled. Mickey looked across at Adam, expecting an introduction. Jake didn't offer one; instead he sat back down and indicated for Mickey to join him.

"I prefer to stand if that's ok with you..."

"Frankly I don't care one way or the other. Gents, you can wait outside." Olly and Mark moved back and out of the door.

Mickey knew he wasn't in a strong position, he hadn't planned to do anything silly, but as with everything in life, you can only be sure of your part in something. Everyone else provides the unknown element.

"What can I do for you gentlemen?"

"How's your colleague…Jonno I believe…that's his name isn't it Adam?" Adam nodded.

"Jonno's going to be fine. You bust his nose and face up pretty bad though. Police were sniffing about asking questions when I left. Jonno will keep his mouth shut mind."

Jake ignored the police reference, and kept quiet.

"Where's Melissa?" Mickey asked.

"Why do you want this girl so badly?"

"What does it matter to you? We want her, it's private."

"It matters to me, because in the pursuit of this girl you decided to try and break the fingers of my colleague." Jake let the final statement hang in the air.

"Why are you protecting this fucking girl, do you even know her?"

"I'm not protecting her…"

"NO! You're protecting him…" interrupted Mickey, thrusting a thumb angrily towards Adam. The remark and gesture took Jake and Adam by surprise.

"I don't know what the fucking deal is between him and that bird, but I need to speak to her. I'd rather not have to go through you and your little private army to do it. That's a fucking hassle I don't need. So, I want to resolve this amicably, my boss wants to resolve it amicably. But, I want to do it fucking quickly."

155

Mickey's words were strong and hid an undertone of violence that Jake understood.

Jake pondered what Mickey had revealed. They had assumed he reported to someone else, but it was Mickey's views on him and Adam that intrigued him the most.

"So do we. Trust me; a quick resolution is what we all want. Now this Melissa girl, I can assure you that she has no connection with us. We're not protecting this girl. She's someone, frankly, we do not want to trouble ourselves with."

Mickey nodded, pleased they were getting somewhere.

"Now, lets be clear about this, this Melissa is however, a former colleague. An unreliable one. One that we've not had contact with for a number of years, until she turned up on his doorstep."

Mickey decided the time was right to sit down.

"As you are aware Mickey, may I call you Mickey?" Mickey nodded. "We don't like to divulge our part in anything we do, force of habit. So I apologise for the ferocity of my riposte earlier today, but I am sure you understand the situation."

Mickey nodded again.

"I feel it only appropriate to tell you that this Melissa character disappeared from our lives under something of a cloud. She stole from us, now it wasn't a particularly large sum of money, but then, that's not the point is it Mickey?"

Mickey smiled and shook his head, "No it isn't."

"Glad we agree. Anyway, the story that Adam told you prior to your man's rather clumsy attempt to maim him, was in essence true. She really was declaring a wish to head off to foreign climes. Maybe she hoped to help herself again before she went, we can't be sure."

"Where is the girl now?" Mickey was bored with hearing Jake's voice.

"Gone," said Jake almost instantly. "It appears she may have witnessed your attack on Adam and somewhat panicked. We've not found her or any of her things where she stayed last night. It's our assumption that whatever her plan B was, she has decided to implement it."

Mickey sighed. This was not what he wanted to hear, he couldn't be sure if these guys were holding out on him or not. Either way he had to be certain they had nothing to do with the money and if there was any doubt then they would be hit, hard. Mickey decided that laying his cards on the table was the best policy.

"Ok, let's level up here. I don't want to dance round this any fucking longer. The eventual outcome of what I have to say will be in your hands. We're men of the world and I don't need to spell out the consequences of our failure to agree to a mutually beneficial course of action."

Mickey tried to mimic the cadence and patterns of speech Jake had adopted. He'd been told it lulled people into a false sense of security, it was a subtle form of flattery that appealed to people.

157

"Melissa stole from us before she decided to do a runner. She stole a lot of fucking money. Truth is, I'm here to get that back as priority one. Priority two is to persuade the thief to understand the error of her ways."

Jake nodded.

"So? Can you enlighten me as to the missing cash, or has that, like the girl, vanished into thin air?"

"Mickey, I understand your point. We don't want to fight with you. If we can resolve the situation, find the missing elements and maybe deliver them to you...will this expedite the speedy removal of you and your like from the area?"

"You what?"

"If we find and return the money, will you remove yourself and anyone connected with you and your employer from this area and agree that you shall not return, oh, and do it quickly." Jake said slowly.

"If you can get me the money and the girl then yes I'll happily fuck off and not return, old world charm has its limits boy!"

Jake stood up. "Do you have a number I can call you on?"

"What the fuck for?"

"I think we can make this happen for you Mickey. It can't happen right now. It's not that we've been holding out on you, but we had to test the water, understand the issues. You understand?"

Mickey thought he did, so nodded.

158

"Thank you for being honest Mickey. When we've resolved it I'll call you and you can collect your missing money at a, how shall I say, a neutral venue."

"When?"

"Hopefully later tonight Mickey."

"My boss might want to collect it personally. You won't mind?"

"As long as our agreement stays firm, you can send the fucking Pope for all I care."

"Let me hear him say it." Mickey pointed at Adam. "I've heard a lot from the monkey now let's hear the organ grinder."

Adam stood up and took a step forward, he buttoned his suit jacket as he did so. "We will return your missing money, in return, you will remove yourself and your colleagues from the Winchester area permanently."

"The girl?"

"We can't deliver the girl, you must understand this."

Mickey shook his head,

"Fellas, if you have the money you have the girl, if you have the girl you have the money….do you follow me?" He couldn't care less about Melissa really but he needed to be certain of the actions these boys were taking.

"Melissa stole from us originally Mr Finn, we like to take advantage of opportunities that come our way…do you understand me?" Mickey nodded slowly not fully getting Adam's meaning.

"We're able to return the money because we took an opportunity…" Adam leant forward as if he was going to spell out his theft.

"This is why we're happy to return the money to its rightful owner, but we'll deduct £10,000 from the monies recovered, to cover the expenses of retrieving the debt for you and as payback for the money she took from us once before."

Jake's eyes flashed momentarily with astonishment. Only Adam noticed. "That's not unreasonable; I'll await your call." replied Mickey.

The big man spun round and headed for the door and marched out of the bar.

Chapter Sixteen

Melissa sat in the plush surroundings of what could have been any small London ad agency and idly watched the Fulham commuters busy themselves with going home. They looked hot and bothered, frustrated by the actions of the person ahead of them, desperately trying to sneak a metre here or centimetre there, as if it would magically get them home quicker. She was sitting in what was in fact the reception area of a small import business called Taste of Home. Irena Petrov had come up with the idea; importing large amounts of traditional East European foodstuffs and wholesale delivering it to the ever increasing number of shops opening up in London and the south east that catered for homesick Poles, Czechs and former Soviet block country residents that had recently poured into the UK.

It had proved to be a convenient and profitable cover for the Petrovs and much of their cross border activities. It had helped them to develop the human, gun and drug smuggling arm of their business. They had few qualms about how they made their money or who they hurt en route. Irma and Irena believed in legitimacy, but like all vices, only in moderation.

Melissa didn't look her best after her hasty retreat from Adam's. She had done what she could with her hair and make up, but she did not feel or look like a sound business opportunity. She hoped she wasn't getting them involved too early, it wasn't her plan to be here so soon, but she had no other options. Barry had spoken of the Petrovs as newcomers, irritants that trod carefully, avoiding the toes of London's big fish. They had ambition, that much Barry admitted to and when they had based themselves just over the river from him, he really began to take notice.

Melissa had learnt early on that in her position she would be wise to always keep her ears open and her mouth mostly shut; except when working. She found it incredible what would get said around her, confidential information bandied around in front of the stupid whore. After all she didn't matter, what would she do with it? She just hoped that what she knew would be enough for the Petrovs to bite, to take their ambition and turn it into action.

Irena and Irma spoke excellent, if a little broken, English. They had made it a rule that while at work they spoke only in their adopted tongue. It had been a good policy and they had subsequently learnt quickly. They spoke with that almost comedic, heavy eastern-bloc accent, somewhere between Arnold Swarzenegger and every Russian peasant stereotype you have heard on TV or film, but they understood the sarcasm and nuances of British wit, even if they didn't show it often.

"Who is she again?" asked Irma.

Irena was sitting at the computer on the far side of the first floor office. The desk was glass and chrome, the chairs high-backed expensive leather affairs. It matched the reception for ad agency style, bright walls, clean lines and prints of famous artworks on the wall. Design by catalogue.

"Melissa… I don't know her second name. She used to work for Barry Hunt, in his brothels. She's a big earner, his favourite girl I think."

Irena delivered the biography as if they might be reviewing a secretarial application.

"Does she know about our business, about our deal with Mr Hunt?"

"Yes. Is only because of this that I granted her audience. She says she has information that as 'business women,'" she made the quote marks with her fingers, "would want to know."

Irma nodded.

"It seems that Mr Hunt does not have her work with him anymore…."

Irena nodded, her hair-sprayed bouffant didn't move.

"Could she be trouble?" Irma asked.

"Yes she could be."

The sisters had learnt to keep their English conversations short and to the point. They did business much the same way.

"But nothing serious I think." Irena continued. "We hear what she say and then we decide what we do with her…if she knows too much and is of no helpfulness, we say to her, goodbye." She made the throat cutting gesture.

"But maybe she has something to offer," Irma replied.

She chewed the end of her pen. The sisters had taken the aggressive approach to the expansion of their criminal activities. They had found it was quicker to intercept small drug deals rather than mass import their own. They had a ruthless reputation and so far their business had grown quickly and thus under the radar of the big London organisations. When they hit other gangs' mules or traffickers and sometimes even the transaction itself, they took no prisoners, why leave room for retribution. Most of their conquests had been low key, small time and something that the bigger gangs viewed as collateral damage, something to be tolerated, or even as a service if it eliminated other smaller scavengers.

Now, though, the Petrovs had begun to source some of their drugs through more conventional methods, they had taken the biggest step of all, the move into a major league and exposure to greater risks. They knew they were on the cusp of straying onto the more established gangs radar, they wanted and needed to control their exposure.

They were fearful of the wrath of gangs like the G Men, no matter what happened under Mr G he usually protected those that ran his manors from attack by smaller ambitious operations like their own.

Melissa, upon being beckoned by the stern receptionist, followed her behind the reception's glass partition and up the stairs. They moved along the corridor, and the receptionist rapped the door with her knuckles.

"Enter," came the muffled reply.

The receptionist turned and without a word, strode back toward the reception, leaving Melissa facing the door alone. She pushed it open and stepped into the office, taking a deep breath as she did so.

The sisters welcomed her from behind the desk, Irma seated and Irena standing.

Irma indicated that Melissa should sit down. Melissa more meekly than necessary, moved forward to the chair. Embarrassed by her appearance, she sat down, pulling her knees together and folding her arms in.

"Welcome Melissa, I am Irena and this my sister Irma…what can we do for you?"

Melissa swallowed, her throat was dry and for the first time in a long time she felt nervous, little balloons of adrenalin bubbled around her stomach.

"Thank you for seeing me, also I'm sorry for the way I look, it's been a crap couple of days…" she trailed off, the sisters just smiled fixed grins and offered no platitudes. Their hair remained rigid, despite the gentle breeze coming from the open window behind them.

"I used to work for Barry Hunt, I was one of his HD girls from the Palace."

HD was brothel jargon, it stood for Hi-Def, as in top of the range. The sisters knew the term, they may have been women in a man's world, but the oldest trades still made money.

"I have left Mr Hunt's employ, I tried to leave voluntarily, but it isn't easy to resign from such a position. I have had to run …escape."

The sisters stayed silent.

"Barry is a jealous man… he's unhappy about my leaving."

Irena cocked her head to the side and looked at the beautiful but bedraggled Melissa up and down. Melissa noted the action, she was more familiar with men checking her out that way.

"Were you not his favourite girl Melissa?" Irena asked.

"I was… yes. He would do almost anything to get me back I think…."

"Or keep you quiet." Irma's voice was cold, it chilled Melissa momentarily.

"Yes…maybe."

"You think maybe we will protect you?" Irma asked.

"Why we do that?" Irena chimed in. Fake smiles adorned their heavily made up faces.

"Maybe you'd consider it after I have told you what I know… it might be in your interest to help me, so that I can help you." She searched for a reaction.

Irma smirked a little, what could this girl have that is of value. Irena however, smiled, Melissa was a pretty girl and Barry was a very ugly man. That told Irena a lot about Melissa.

"Why don't you tell us what you want, if information is as important as you say, then we talk more. Please be brief…."

Melissa noted the frustration; she could sense she might not be being taken seriously. What her story, her information needed was spin. Melissa knew that any power she might have was in how she presented it. Half truths wrapped in distortion, based on an

166

actual truth. But, given the right timing and said in the right ears it could be an incendiary device that could get her where she wanted to go.

"What I want, is money, a large amount, up to £100,000 and a new passport, not some Pritt-stick job either, but a decent one that I can travel with and create a new identity."

Irena smiled, a small unemotional smile, what she asked for could easily be achieved if what she had was worth it.

"You ask for a lot, this means either you have a lot worth listening to, or you are an idiot time waster. If you are idiot then I assure you, you will never earn money from your face and body again."

Melissa stared at both of them.

"So, if it is worth us helping you, stay. If not leave now, your features intact. You understand?" Irma joined in.

Melissa stayed silent. The sounds of the Fulham Broadway filtered through the open window. A child cried, a car beeped its horn. The sisters didn't move.

Melissa took a slight breath, straightened her shoulders and began…

"I heard a lot when I was close to Mr Hunt…"

Irena admired Melissa's steel.

"He used to talk to me, tell me his problems and his troubles, his secrets as well. I understand his business, his investments, I know who owes him money. I know who he owes money to; I know about his relationship with Mr G. I know the truth."

Irma and Irena's ears pricked with interest.

"You need to know that Barry Hunt is completely broke…he has had a large sum of money stolen from him… which he won't get back. His biggest problem is he owes a lot of money to Mr G and the G men, and about now they are starting to chase him for it."

Irma and Irena stiffened, they kept their faces calm and the smiles fixed, but Melissa definitely noticed them bristle. Strike one she thought.

"Why should we care?" Irma had stopped the gentle side to side swing of her seat. Her attention piqued.

"It concerns you, ladies, because if Barry doesn't have the money for Mr G, don't think he's saving it for you. He won't have anything for your final payment…"

She let the information sink in.

"I know about the drugs deal…and I'm here to tell you he doesn't have your money."

Melissa held up her hands, placating the growing sense of dread she could see in their faces.

"Mr G doesn't know about your deal, at least not yet. It would be very bad for Mr Hunt and for you if the details of this deal were to leak out!"

The sisters exchanged glances. The information was valuable, now they understood how Melissa might earn her money.

"You come here to threaten us with this information?" Irena's aggression was rising. Irma, under cover of the desk gently tapped her sisters thigh, by way of chastisement, for the drop in guard.

"Please, don't misunderstand me ladies. I don't wish to blackmail you. My coming here in person, is evidence that I don't want to do that. If I go to Mr G, sure he'll be happy to get the information, but he won't think twice about getting rid of me, if for nothing else, disloyalty."

She watched for any relaxation in the sister's demeanour. There was none.

" If I know this information then it's possible that others do. I wanted to warn you that Barry has no money. If you have made commitments based on Barry's finance then you need to be made aware of the situation so you can plan for it." Melissa's words resonated through the sisters.

The information had proved to be very important. If Barry Hunt had no money and owed money to Mr G, then not only were they going to be out of pocket on the deal, but there was a very real chance that they would swing markedly into the sights of Mr G. He wouldn't tolerate this level of encroachment lightly.

"The information is valuable, but is not worth what you ask Melissa…"

"Maybe not now… that's just to prove to you that I am serious and worth listening to. I also know you are not stupid people."

The sisters didn't bite at the attempted flattery.

"The problems that Barry has in paying you are an inconvenience, for sure, but they hide a greater opportunity."

There was an uncomfortable pause.

"Melissa... stay with us, be our 'protected' guest, we can talk more once we fix...one or two problems."

Melissa nodded her thanks.

"Talk to your people, get word from the street. There will be rumours to endorse what I say."

The sisters nodded.

"I have a possible solution..."

Irma held up her hand. "Dmitri," she called. A pug-faced little man with cauliflower ears walked in.

"Dmitri, please ensure Melissa is made comfortable in the rooms upstairs, and when you have settled her come down and join us." Dimitri nodded and showed Melissa out, closing the door behind him.

Irena sat on the end of the desk and looked down at her sister in the chair. She began mulling over out loud all the permutations of the news Melissa had given them.

"If what she says is true, then our deal with Mr Hunt is over and we will be left with more drugs than we can sell. At least not without Mr G noticing us."

Irma nodded her agreement.

"Also if Barry is caught by Mr G, he will probably offer us like a sacrifice. Mr G would squash us like little fly, just to make an example of us." Irena added.

Irma nodded again and said, "We keep this girl close little sister, if she speaks the truth then we can find out very quickly, but we need another buyer for these drugs."

Irena added, "We need to speak to Barry, see what his options are, if we take out Barry, we stop the Mr G threat?"

Irma looked up at her little sister. How had she become so ruthless. She was right though, they needed to speak to Barry to get to the bottom of it.

Dmitri appeared at the door. Irena beckoned him in, he and his soldiers had been posted over London listening for the reaction to the Bartok murder.

Now they would have a new job to do.

* * *

Melissa sat on the stylish but uncomfortable sofa in a flat converted from office space on the top floor of the Petrovs' offices. She looked at her phone and saw one message received.

"Meeting going ahead. Not sure we need this charade. Expect to be back on plan soon."

She read it and shrugged her shoulders. She knew he would sort it out eventually. She flicked her thumbs across the buttons, drumming out her reply.

"Seeds have been sewn. Stick to the plan, a new deal can be made."

Chapter Seventeen

Jake had assembled the who's who of ex-military experts from within the ranks of his organisation. The handover had to be planned. They had selected a potential site they knew well. Open, but not easily available to passing public, yet, still highly visible to ensure no silly behaviour. Adam looked on, bewildered at the speed and efficiency of the men around him.

Bar End, the Winchester University sports ground, would be the handover site. It had three exit points, though the unfamiliar would only know about one, a narrow lane off an innocuous suburban road. It seemed perfect. The hidden access points came in the form of connecting gateways to some council-owned football pitches to Bar End's western perimeter and to the east, from the municipal King George VI playing fields. These fields each had their own access to other main roads.

To the south of Bar End sat St. Catherine's Hill, the wooded geological dome that provided the wondrous backdrop to the view of the Cathedral city. Nestled at the foot of the hill was part of the M3 motorway, which cut controversially through the countryside around it. The carriageways stood about half a mile from the handover point, close enough to see activity on the fields but far enough away to ensure detail would be scarce. Jake and his team judged that this mixture of secluded entrance and open vista would deter Mickey and his friends from being silly at the handover.

Another factor in the location's favour was that it took just two minutes to drive through the back streets to Jake's house. The narrow main entrance led to a single lane drive of about fifty metres long. The large trees around the entrance, car park and whole northern edge obscured the grounds from the houses and partially from the motorway traffic. Jake and his team surmised, that with the noise from the motorway and the tree cover, people would hardly hear or see anything. Combine that with conducting the handover in the half light of a late summer's evening and with any luck no one would notice a thing.

Rob Hargreaves, Adam and Jake sat on the sofa in the VIP suite of the Later Lounge, Jake's other plush bar in Winchester. Olly and Mark stood to their left. Rob had been brought up to speed with the situation. He and Jake had stared down a few local villains and rival security firms in the past, the situation wasn't totally alien to him. Rob believed in managing risks, you need to limit your exposure and, where possible, expose yourself to no risk at all. To Rob, this whole situation was extreme exposure to risk.

"Right, you know my feelings on this whole load of bollocks, but that aside… here's the plan. Three cars, one with a team of four at the handover, in situ at Bar End, but parked near to the hidden exit point into King George fields. Car two with a duo, on the council pitches to the west, hidden behind the trees and storage building, they'll ensure the path through that gate is open, if it's needed. The final car, car three, another duo, will watch and tail the incoming traffic down Bar End road; it will then go through into the King George playing fields, shadowing the hidden exit into King George. The gates all open in towards Bar End. We'll leave them ajar, so we can charge vehicles in and out easily or open the gate quickly if required."

Rob stopped and looked at the two faces staring intently at him. He realised they were not going to say anything until he had finished his impromptu briefing. He brought out a roughly drawn plan of the area and added several large Duplo building blocks to represent the buildings and Lego bricks for the cars.

"So car one is in place at Bar End for the handover. At the point of the handover the other two cars can offer support and additional exit routes, or reinforcements should anything silly happen."

He sipped his coffee.

"The basic plan is that we, via car one, hand over and then drive out through the King George exit, with car three moving behind and blocking that exit route."

He moved some red Lego blocks to mimic the actions of the three cars.

"Car two will have come round, in tandem, from the football pitches and be ready to close off the main Bar End exit, effectively blocking the enemy's vehicle in."

The final Lego block moved into place.

"If we do it coordinated and fast, they won't have time to react. It should ensure that car one doesn't have any tails once we leave Bar End."

Jake smiled. Rob had always been a good strategist.

"The cars that remain then simply wait a moment and head for the gate they didn't enter from. It'll confuse the hell out of the enemy. If they had an intention to follow then they'll be clueless as to where to go."

Rob paused again and took another sip of coffee. He cleared his throat with a little cough and began again.

"Now, for the scenario where it gets silly – we're assuming they'll be coming tooled up, we don't have any firepower, and I don't advocate that we do, despite Adam's assertions."

Adam shuffled in his seat.

"We can look like we're armed and act like we are, but if this turns into a fire fight then everything you have built up Jake, goes to cock."

Jake nodded. He knew all of this and he agreed with the strategy Rob was proposing. He understood Rob's hesitation and reservation, but despite it all Jake was having fun, he couldn't wipe the cheeky little grin off his face.

"If there is any silliness at point of handover we head back into the vehicle, both the two support cars will come through and drive at the enemy, drawing attention and perhaps fire away from us."

He looked at Olly and Mark. They both nodded.

"We will then leave by the nearest available safe exit. The point is to create as much confusion and mayhem, ideally we want it so that they can't recognise which car is which once we are on the open road."

Adam nodded again, really not thinking about the details of the handover, he was more concerned about the money.

"When charging the enemy target, use the smoke grenades. Look to knock down or separate people from their vehicle. Whatever it takes to draw their attention and then slow their re-grouping."

Rob sipped his coffee again.

"Jake, you're still happy to use the three Range Rovers?" Jake nodded. He had recently purchased three black Range Rovers as support vehicles for his chauffeur bodyguard service.

"They good enough?" asked Adam.

"Each one has bullet proof tinted glass and is super charged to do 0-60 in 5.5 seconds and a top speed of 135 mph and come with bull bars." Rob said.

"Wow," offered Adam.

"The Oligarchs love them," Jake said, "British stars love being protected by a British car. I prefer the BMW X5, but business is business."

"Number plates?" Olly spoke for the first time.

"Covered on all three cars. Simple tape and paper job. Remove it as soon as is safe and sensible to do so," Rob ordered.

177

"Gents, let's look upon this as a trial; it's probably the most action they'll ever see, but a good trial none the less." Jake often found ways to justify his decisions; Rob knew not to argue but to simply make the best of it.

Olly and Mark nodded.

Rob held his hands open and looked at the others. He had stopped, he had nothing more to add. He got to his feet; Jake rose with him, patted him on the shoulder and guided him out of the door. Olly and Mark followed. They had three cars to prepare.

Adam watched as Jake slowly shut the large glass door, sound proofing the room. Jake turned, but didn't look up.

"When we go to the handover Adam, let me do the talking ok? I want this done and dusted as quickly as possible. We put the money on the floor, he walks up, checks it, we all nod our agreement and we then fuck off out of it."

Adam nodded his agreement. Jake now looked at him earnestly, "forget about keeping the money or conning this guy Adam. That's not our game. I didn't appreciate the little stunt with Mickey."

"What do you mean?"

"The bollocks about a finder's fee and deducting the money… we agreed we would look like we meant business, not that we would do business."

"Yeah I winged it, but you saw his face, he wasn't shocked or upset by it. I think it would have looked strange if we had simply rolled over."

Jake held up his hand to stop Adam talking.

"It's not something I am going to argue about Adam, I didn't like it, ok?" Adam nodded.

"Mickey Finn has gone away thinking we're something we're not, that's fine in the short term, but I don't like the way he thinks that I protect you, it implies I work for you or there is some other authority in all this..."

Jake hadn't said it outright, but he found the notion that he may answer to Adam an odd one, he wasn't sure why, but he didn't find it comfortable.

"Maybe you shouldn't come tonight?"

"No chance Jake, these fuckers hunted me down and tried to break my fingers, fuck knows what would have happened if you hadn't come along... it fucking well shit me up!" Adam was breathing a little heavier, anger bubbling inside him.

"You can do the talking but I am doing the handover, we agreed that... I hand over the bag." Adam pushed his open hand repeatedly into his other palm to emphasise his point.
"You need to understand Jake, I'm no bruiser, no fighter, that was the second time you have come and rescued me, frankly I would quite like these arseholes to get a little personal pay back from me... I can't do it with my fists, that's your game."

The two friends swapped a knowing glance.

"Maybe though, subtracting a ten grand commission from them is more my style, anyway it would be some kind of victory for me!"

Jake sensed the tension, he'd only seen it in Adam a few times, and he knew he could be stubborn in a mood like this. He held up both palms, placating Adam and easing the mood.

"Fine, fine, sorry. I didn't appreciate that's how you felt. Come along enjoy the show, play bag man… but leave the talking to me, ok?" Adam smiled and nodded.

"You have the money ready?"

"Yeah…it's ready" he said

"Anything at all from Melissa?"

The question surprised Adam, "No…still nothing…well it's not even been a day has it…"

"No.. I suppose not."

Adam and Jake just looked at each other, neither knew what to say.

"Right, let's call Goliath and sort this handover out."

The handover time was set for 9.00pm. It would be dusk, that magical time in the summer, when the sun had dipped down over the horizon, but a warm diminishing glow of light remained. It faded so slowly that you can go from bright light to dark without noticing, your eyes adjusting to the slow change in light. It was this change from semi-light to darkness that Jake and his team would rely on. By the end of the handover it would be dark, easier for the three Range Rovers to disappear into the night. Driving without lights was no issue for guys who knew the area like the back of their hands.

* * *

Mickey surveyed the scene ahead of him. Winchester sat in the valley below, he looked across the city toward St. Catherine's Hill from his vantage point outside the County Arms pub, a glass of coke in his hand.

He'd called Barry and updated him on his meeting.

Barry asked why he hadn't headed home yet. Mickey hadn't been able to answer. He thought he had done the right thing, it was his job to protect Barry.

Mickey's phone rang. It vibrated and bounced across the picnic table. He clutched it up and looked at the number on the screen; it took a moment to recognise it as Jake's.

"Mickey?" he enquired.

"It's me," he replied.

"I have a location, easy to find – sign-posted in fact."

"Details?"

"Bar End Sports field. Bar End Road, near to the M3 at the end of Chesil Street…do you know it?"

Mickey raised his eyebrows. Of course he didn't know it.

"I can find it."

"9.00pm tonight. One car only."

"No problem. I'll check the venue out and inform my crew. But i won't be there. The boss is handling this himself." Mickey added. Jake mulled the news over and then said "Fine." They both shut down their phones. No goodbyes.

181

It had been short, concise and almost militaristic he thought.

The drop off point would be quiet but open. Easy-to-find Jake said.

These boys didn't want a fight, that seemed clear to Mickey. Everything they had done had been neat and controlled, no posturing, no histrionics.

Mickey preferred it that way.

Mickey's watch said 7.00pm. Barry would have left London already, they'd make the handover time no problem. He levered himself into the driver's seat of the Lexus and fired the engine into life. He tapped the names Jake had given him into the Sat Nav. He compared the location with that of his standard road atlas, satisfied the machine wouldn't take him via Papua New Guinea and he moved into the traffic and headed for Bar End.

* * *

Irena and Irma had waited patiently for Dmitri to report back. They didn't speak too often, both mulled over the events of the day and reconciled their own ambition with the threats the news offered.

Finally they watched him amble through the reception on the CCTV monitor. A minute later he knocked on their door and entered without waiting for a response.

Irma began the de-brief.

"What have you heard about Barry Hunt and Mr G while you have been on the streets Dmitri?"

"Is bad," he said. Dmitri hated having to speak in English. He found it slow and cumbersome, but the sisters insisted and he accepted he needed the practice.

"Things are bad for Barry, how...?"

"Mr G, Mr Barry owes money to Mr G, all know this."

"Is that all Dmitri?"

"Bartok." Dmitri's face broke into a broad grin at the memory of cutting the fat man's balls off and standing side by side with the sisters as he bled to death.

"What has that fat dead fuck got to do with Barry and Mr G?" Irma asked.

Irena pulled herself off the desk and looked at Dmitri, "Did Mr G work with Bartok Dmitri?"

"Assassination", said Dmitri stoically.

She opened her arms out, pleading for him to say more.

"Mr G tell Barry Hunt to do assassination of Bartok, he pay early. We laugh. Him already dead, Barry in trouble for not doing it, for not cutting head off."

Irma and Irena looked at each other uneasily, what the hell did Barry Hunt and Mr G have to do with Bartok? The Petrovs had invested with Bartok in illegal gambling and dog fighting. He'd fucked up and taken nearly £50,000 of their money. You didn't rip the Petrovs off if you wanted to keep your balls.

"Do you think little sister that Bartok stole from Barry, like he did with us…or maybe stole from Mr G?"

"Maybe… he was stupid enough to try. But if this is so then we completed Mr G's contract, this could be helpful…Barry does not know this?"

The Petrov sisters understood now that they could be partly responsible for the current woes of Barry Hunt and architects in the suspension of their own drug deal.

"Melissa could be useful, if she knows Barry's business well, knows secrets – she could help us to strike first." Irma's eyes were open to a host of opportunities but she couldn't shake off the nagging doubts about the threats that came with those opportunities.

They had to find Barry Hunt.

* * *

Barry's hand tapped up and down on his thigh. A monotonous and rhythmless patter that tested his companion's patience. Neither man said anything.

Bobby drove and Leon sat on the back seat behind Barry, trying to ignore the fidgets and tapping of their boss.

Barry's phone chirped into life. He snatched it to his ear and barked.

"Mickey!"

"It's me."

"I've scoped the location for the handover. It's not ideal but it's ok."

"It won't be a fucking problem…stop worrying."

Barry couldn't see Mickey shut his eyes in irritated concern.

"I'll hand you to Bobby in a minute, give him the details…" Barry coughed and then took in a big sniff.

"Don't you want to know the details for yourself…?" Mickey asked.

"Fuck it. Bunch of monkeys, what they going to do?" Barry sniffed again.

"They have the money, that's for certain. As I said before they're straight talkers Barry. All they want is a quick handover and for us to leave them be…doesn't have to be difficult." Mickey cautioned.

"Mickey, you forget. I do the telling!"

Mickey said nothing.

"Have you left Winchester yet?" Barry sniffed again. Mickey heard the sniff and knew the reason. He's loaded he thought, he won't be thinking straight. He never does, not with a dose of Peruvian marching powder up his hooter.

"In the car and heading up the M3."

"Mind the shop when you get back, Ok?"

"Ok."

Barry coughed a little and let out a laugh.

185

"I haven't been on a road trip for a while – this is going to be fun."

Mickey listened to the strained tones and fast pace of Barry's voice, he was completely off the wall.

"Maybe I should stay boss – act as hidden back up?"

"For fucks sake Mickey – I don't need my hand holding. Who's the man in the situation?"

"Well Jake's the muscle and did the talking…but I reckon the man with the power, the guy pulling the strings is Adam."

"Really?" Barry thought back to Mickey's earlier briefing on how they accosted him in the street.

"Stands to reason. He's no heavy, no soldier. If he isn't the power, the brains, then why is he there and involved."

"Get back to London Mickey… don't do any more thinking. Mind the business… make sure the money gets delivered to the G-Men. They're getting arsey."

"Have they not been paid?" he asked.

"No they have not been paid, open the safe in the office and take the cash over personally."

"Personally. You want me to deliver the money?" Mickey failed to hide the surprise in his voice.

"Yes personally. Is that difficult? Too much to ask?"

Mickey allowed a moment's silence to pass. He took a deep breath.

"No problem boss," he muttered.

"Good, now fucking talk to Bobby."

Barry threw the phone at his driver and let out another laugh and a smile broke out across his face.

Mickey Finn gunned the accelerator of the Lexus hard, his brief passion for the suburban delights of Winchester fading in his rear view mirror; the big car ate up the road ahead. His mood, ostensibly dark anyway had reached pitch black. The odd behaviour of his friend and employer niggled at him, he had never been slighted by Barry like this, 'keeping shop' was something Barry took seriously; Mickey understood and respected this. After all, Barry had become very hands off in recent months and Mickey had assumed more responsibility for the running of it. But ordering Mickey back to base and being tasked with handing over the retainer money from the safe to Mr G's G-Men. That's a bag man's job. Jonno did things like that. Bobby or Leon did things like that. Mickey told them to do things like that.

Mickey Finn is no bag man.

Chapter Eighteen

Adam checked his watch again, it read five minutes to nine. Jake, Adam and Rob along with Olly, sat in car one. Rob had parked on the Bar End playing fields about one hundred metres away from, but facing, the narrow entrance. To their right the perimeter hedge ran south towards the motorway, the gate into the next field partially hidden from view stood ajar and only a matter of yards ahead of them. Even if Barry Hunt and his people charged them all guns blazing they could be through and away in seconds.

Jake checked on the radios, all other cars acknowledged their readiness. Car three, the one destined to come round and protect their rear, sat in a parking bay on Bar End Road, waiting for Barry and his boys to arrive. Adam rubbed his clammy palms on his trousers, he had a slight knot in his stomach.

"Nervous?" asked Jake.

"Yeah…you?"

"A little.." said Jake.

Adam wondered if it would be more akin to first night nativity play nerves than pre battle jitters.

"It's been a while since I've done something like this," he finished.

Adam knew Jake liked this feeling, he'd confessed that to feel fear was to feel alive.

He glanced across at Jake who was gently biting his bottom lip and gripping the overhead handle harder than he needed to, his fingers turning paler as a result. Jake hadn't shared all the details of his conversation with Mickey, but all had agreed it odd that Mickey wouldn't be attending. Jake had immediately added more lookouts to make sure no one tried to sneak in unannounced.

A loud chirping and simultaneous buzzing of a mobile phone broke the silence. Everyone looked at each other and self consciously tapped their pockets. Adam grabbed at his pocket and dug his ringing phone out. Jake was about to tell him to put it down, when Adam flicked it open and spoke,

"Mum…what is it? This really isn't a good time…Yeah I know I answered…yeah that should mean I am prepared to talk to you, but if I don't answer you, you ring continuously until I do answer…no mum I don't mind you ringing me." Jake held his watch face up to Adam and mouthed "put the phone down tosser," Adam nodded and shrugged his shoulders in a 'what can I do' gesture.

"Yes mum I can come on Sunday, I told you that the other day and yes I will fix the light…no I don't mind doing a couple of other jobs…mow the lawn? Right I can mow it. Mum…I love you but I have to go."

The crackle of the radio interrupted the conversation.

"Red leader… Red leader, the chicken is in the basket."

190

Jake smiled, his guys liked messing around, it lightened the mood, took the edge off the fact that Barry Hunt had started down the Bar End Road.

"Mum…see you Sunday, yes about 12.00, yes, right, bye," he slammed the phone shut. He looked at Jake and mouthed "sorry."

"Red leader the car is coming to the end of the road."

The urine yellow Lexus cruised at that indeterminate speed, the speed where the driver knows where he is, and where he's going, but unsure how to get there.

Jake took control.

"Ok fellas, less fucking about."

The car and radios fell silent but for the static hiss.

"Keep your eyes open and let's make sure this goes off without a hitch. Where are they?"

The radio crackled, then a voice broke in, "they're at the end of the road, they've paused, now turning into the entrance, they should be in sight red leader?"

"Affirmative car three, they are in view. Final positions everyone."

Barry Hunt sat in the passenger seat of the Lexus, muttering almost constantly, the type of commentary chatter you would expect from an elderly passenger. Bobby, his afro brushing the ceiling of the car, was at the wheel, as simultaneously they peered forward at the road ahead, as if it would make the view any clearer.

"Down there? That little road between the houses, on the right?" Bobby looked incredulous.

"That's what Mickey said man," Leon piped up in the back seat.

Barry just waved his hand vaguely in the direction of the narrow lane, impatient to get this whole farce over with. The Lexus crept along the little road, between the houses, hedges on either side, it was no more than fifty metres long before it broke out into a wide playing field. Lime trees shadowed a small car park to their left and then further on from that, the recently constructed two storey clubhouse appeared.

"Is that them?" Bobby motioned to the black Range Rover, parked about one hundred metres away, half way down the large field, no more than ten feet from the hedge that ran down its right-hand side, headlights on.

"Must be," said Leon.

They slowed to a halt on the edge of the grass, the Lexus staring down the Range Rover. The Range Rover's lights flashed and it inched forward, encouraging Bobby and the Lexus to do the same.

"Nice fucking car man"

"Not bad," agreed Leon.

They both hated the Lexus, especially its colour. The luxurious Range Rover made both men nod in childlike approval.

192

The cars came to rest some fifty metres apart, the Range Rover had in fact hardly moved at all. Rob had enticed the Lexus to meet him halfway, but he'd ensured he never went beyond his escape route. He could still spin the Range Rover through a sharp right and be out of the field in a matter of seconds.

The exit remained hidden from Barry and the Lexus.

Jake opened his door and stood behind it, his feet and part of his head the only parts visible. Dressed head to toe in black, he would be hard to make out in the fading light and glare of the headlights.

Barry watched as the door opened and a man stepped out.

"Right, listen up," ordered Barry.

"Bobby, stay at the wheel and keep the motor running. Leon, on my shoulder alright? Let's have a bit of a giggle boys." Barry's smile swamped his face, a mixture of maniacal and childish glee. He pulled a small silver vial from his pocket and snorted violently from it. His eyes glazed momentarily, and then he pulled himself together by shaking his head and wiping the excess powder from his nose.

"Any sign of them tossing about, let fucking rip, I want these fuckers to know we mean business."

Leon nodded. He checked and then locked and loaded his small Uzi 9mm sub machine pistol, a big lad, it would hide easily in a rear waist holster on his back, hidden by his John Rocha jacket. Barry and Leon emerged from the car together. They shut

193

both their doors and moved in front of the car, swaggering with over confidence. Their headlights were off. They stood bathed in the lights of the Range Rover. Leon looked around, studying the location for the first time, the natural light fading fast.

"Mr Hunt I presume." Jake raised his voice to be heard, but it carried easily across the empty playing field, no wind to break it up.

"Right first fucking time...you Adam?"

"No, I'm Jake, Mr Hunt...we have your money here. I presume Mr Finn enlightened you as to our arrangement?"

Barry turned and looked at Leon "Mr Finn, Mr Fucking Hunt, who do these fucking jokers think they are? ...YES..." he bellowed, "He has told me about the deal, which I am not discussing with you....bring out the boss man."

Jake stayed quiet, eyeing Barry's demeanour. He didn't like Barry's tone.

"Did you fucking hear me? I don't want to discuss this with the fucking monkey. I want to speak to the organ grinder. So do me a favour sunshine, shut up, go deliver some fucking Milk Tray, whatever, but let me speak to Adam."

Before Jake could answer, the Range Rover back door opened and Adam hopped out. Jake made a gesture to speak, but Adam held up his hand.

They shared a look and Adam did his best to reassure Jake.

Barry, too far away to make out the little exchange squinted at the smaller figure carrying the black bag.

194

"You Adam?"

"Yes Mr Hunt, I'm Adam. Would you like your money?"

"Yes I would…but before we get too nice and cosy let's understand the situation a bit better, I don't want to sound a bit thick, but I don't get how you have my money."

"Well Mr Hunt, we've got it, what more do you want to know?"

"I want to know how it came about and where the fuck Melissa is?"

"I would say that we probably came about the money in much the same way as you lost it. As for the girl, well it seems she didn't want to hang around and explain about the money and is long gone."

Barry stamped his foot and then shrugged his shoulders.

"You nick the money off Melissa did you?"

Adam remained silent.

"Stealing from her is like stealing from me, I take issue with that," Barry shouted across.

Adam swallowed hard; the man seemed to be spoiling for an argument.

"Mr Hunt, we're returning the money to you, that's why we're all here, that's what you wanted. How can we be stealing from you?" He enunciated his words, conscious that Jake should hear them as clearly as Barry. Barry, as if in some pantomime villain role, arched his back and spread his arms wide in response.

"Don't get smart with me sonny, do you know who I am?"

Adam's head dropped a little, unsure he'd actually heard the line Barry had delivered.

"No Mr Hunt not really, do you know who I am?"

"Of course I fucking don't …why…"

Adam cut into Barry's reply. "Then we're in a similar situation to each other Mr Hunt, I for one err on the side of caution in these situations, you never know completely, who you are dealing with."

Barry contemplated the remark for a moment. Rising onto the balls of his feet and then settling back down, teetering for balance in between. He couldn't tell if it had been an insult, in fact it might have been a threat.

"Melissa had that money with my permission, she was going to do a deal with it for me…it wasn't for you to take and it wasn't for you to put the frighteners on her…" Barry faltered, his brain not working as quickly as his mouth.

"So I am concerned for my employee….who was working with my consent … you come along and steal from her, which means you steal from me…so you see…I'm not fucking happy." The final line carried little punch and no threat. The ramble ensured Barry looked and sounded like an uncoordinated fool.

Adam turned his head slightly and whispered to Jake.

"What the fuck is this guy on? He can't believe this bullshit, can he?"

"So you see *Mr Adam*….you see my situation?" Barry's head was dowsed in sweat, his breathing heavy and he was swaying as he spoke.

"Mr Hunt this conversation is at odds with our conversation with Mr Finn…he stated, Melissa had stolen the money, as she had once done so from us sometime ago…"

"MICKEY GOT IT WRONG." Barry lurched forward, the venom of his riposte heaving him on to his toes.

"THAT'S WHAT HAPPENS WHEN YOU SEND A MONKEY TO DO BUSINESS - they make a fucking balls up of it!" Barry took an exaggerated breath, "You have taken some liberties sonny boy," continued Barry, unaware of Leon looking uneasily around, he hadn't seen Barry like this and he for one didn't relish having a fight with these guys without Mickey.

"Mr Hunt, Melissa stole from us long before she began working with you. She stole from you; we know this because she told us. She misjudged our interest as concern and not revenge. As soon as we discovered that she had taken the money we knew someone would want it back. Relieving her of it was a means to an end for us, revenge and a revenue opportunity."

Adam waited, keen for his words to sink in.

"We're happy to return the money to you," Adam breathed hard, he had been impressing himself so far.

"Yeah you got my money, but you want to keep a fee, a fucking finder's fee for taking my money from my people, a liberty that's what that is…" Barry's temper, rising by the second, had made his face turn a blotchy red, he stumbled forward getting further and further from the safety of his car. Leon unused to the situation, shuffled after him, his hand edging behind him toward the hidden Uzi.

Jake and each of his men in the cars watched studiously as the scene unfolded, the communication constant, Jake's radio buzzing with the commentary of his men. They had all noted the shambolic forward movement and the now strange behaviour of what they described as the bodyguard. Jake's nerves fluttered in his belly once more. He whispered commands to the team, his face still partially hidden by the door.

"Mr Hunt, I can only state again," Adam took several small steps forward, "We recouped our money when we took the cash from Melissa. We had no idea who exactly it belonged to; maybe the owners would come looking, maybe not? From the moment we acquired it, it became ours." Adam spread his arms in his best 'open posture'. He'd attended a business seminar that said when dealing with irate and irrational people you needed to placate and cajole. Open your body language and ensure you presented a non threatening posture.

"We agreed with Mr Finn, that we would, out of courtesy, return the cash, minus the fee, we've asked for assurance that you won't interfere in Winchester…" Barry waved his hand at him, dismissing his remarks.

"As for liberties, well it was your men that took a few with me.. and look what happened to them!"

Adam had now covered over ten metres of the gap between them, with Barry's stumbles they now stood no more than twenty five metres apart, close enough, despite the near faded light to make out the detail each other's face.

Barry stopped and stared hard, his patience wearing thin. He held himself upright, infuriated by Adam's last swipe.

"Who do you think you are you little cunt...I'm Barry Hunt, I have run a London Borough, my manor, for over twenty fucking years. I have seen the Yardy gangs come and go, dealt with the Turks and the rise of the Russians. I am in Mr G's pocket, the G Men and Barry Hunt could squash you like a bug." He rammed his fist into his palm.

"So let's not fuck about any more. I have bigger deals to do and you monkeys are holding me up. You will give me back my fucking money, every last penny."

Adam threw the black bag down in front of him and held his palms up in a placating gesture.

"Your money... as agreed... just take it." Adam glared at Barry nodding his head at the bag slightly. He edged backward, never taking his eyes off Barry, willing him to simply take the bag.

"Every last penny... hahahahahhh" bellowed Barry... "fucking weasel..."

Barry moved his right arm quicker than Jake thought possible and whipped out his own automatic pistol, it had been tucked into his belt under his baggy suit jacket. He raised it slowly into the air, a broad Joker-like grin of triumph on his face.

Jake reacted the quickest, shouting the order for containment. The cars didn't need the order. All three motored into action, they had anticipated it, both Range Rovers roared into the field, car three charged, engine growling, from Barry's left, the faded light making it seem like it came straight through the hedge.

Adam sprinted back towards Jake who came to meet him, and within seconds the big black vehicle slid and screeched between them and Barry, blocking the line of fire. Jake bundled Adam bodily back into the car.

Further away to Barry's right the other Range Rover careered across the field straight at Barry. The engine, stuck in a low gear, screamed malevolently as its headlight beams fell on a transfixed Barry.

He stood, frozen, open mouthed at the speed it all happened. He lamely swung the gun from where Adam had been standing to the fast approaching Range Rover to his right, he had bluffed with the gun, why weren't they scared?

Leon, blinded by light, scared of his own boss, finally snapped into action and half ran to try and get ahead of Barry, all the time fumbling to retrieve the Uzi from its holster. He got to a few yards ahead of Barry as the car closed, now travelling at sixty miles an hour. Its driver, Mark, planned to fly past and cover the escape of the other two cars. But Leon had finally pulled the gun clear of its holster and his coat, he spread his legs and braced himself, Uzi raised to his shoulder, and aimed at the speeding Range Rover.

Mark had driven in war zones, with years of experience in hostile situations, he reacted without thinking. He jerked the wheel to the right.

The car hit Leon square on and never slowed. The giant bull bars smashed into Leon's chest blasting him down and, tearing across the grass, the Uzi flew from his hands. The Range Rover stayed on course and accelerated straight over Leon, his head bouncing off the undercarriage. Not that he felt it, he had died instantly from the collision, the life blasted out of him by two tons of steel.

Barry dived for cover as the car destroyed Leon, he stayed down, head in his arms as he heard the ownerless Uzi begin firing. The poorly maintained weapon had flown ten feet in the air before landing on the arid turf, the jolt setting it off. The gun discharged its violent cargo at three rounds per second, the first wave ripped into the defenceless Lexus. Lacking any of the protection of Jake's Range Rovers, Bobby, who had been rooted to his seat, never stood a chance. The bullets scorched through the door panel, imbedding themselves in Bobby's legs. His screams went unheard as the Range Rover roared behind him and out of the main gate. The next few rounds that fired from the errant Uzi sprayed through the window, showering Bobby in glass before striking his neck, cheek and right hand. Having blasted through his flesh and bone they carried on their destructive journey up and out of the roof of the Lexus.

It took a moment, but Bobby went from his upright position to being slumped forward onto the wheel, his lungs wheezing under the pressure, forcing out his last dying breath.

The Uzi's unplanned symphony finally came to an end. Barry, shaking in fear from the gunfire and charging cars, unclasped his hands from his head and looked around. He raised his head just in time to see a black Range Rover screech to a halt in front if him. The door sprang open and Jake Simons leapt out, swung a sweeping back kick and hit Barry square in the face.

He was unconscious before he hit the floor.

Jake took a moment to scan the now eerily quiet field, he scooped up the black bag and jumped back into car three. The other two vehicles had already left the scene, Adam safely bundled into one.

Olly eased the car into gear and it pulled away from the carnage. From the moment Barry had raised the gun to their innocuous departure via the council football pitches, three minutes had elapsed.

Chapter Nineteen

Mickey Finn sat down in Barry's studded leather armchair, the whisky tumbler in his hand filled with a fine sixteen year old Dalmore single malt, on ice. He didn't care if the purists scoffed, it's how he liked it. He rubbed his temples, it had been a shit journey home. The M3 crawled into London and the A316 had been even worse. He checked his watch, 9.45pm. It should be over and Barry on his way home with most of his money retrieved.

He'd resisted the urge to call and check up on things; Barry had managed to do the same. Mickey gulped the whisky, it warmed and spiced his throat as he swallowed. He already knew he'd be having another.

He picked up his mobile phone and hunted for Beano's number. Beano arranged every pickup and every deal. You could go via him and no one else. Monkeys did the leg work, but Beano called the shots.

He answered on the third ring.

"It's Mickey Finn. I have the money for the retainer. We'll deliver it to the usual place at the usual time...ok?"

Mickey listened and his face crinkled, then his brow furrowed, he didn't quite understand.

"Cashflow? Not sure about that Beano, no, money shouldn't be an issue, I'll bring it tomorrow...what?"

He cocked his head to one side, it's not that Beano spoke softly, Mickey just wanted to be sure he heard correctly. Beano rattled on for a few moments.

"I don't know anything about that…my pets in Winchester?"

Beano moved into a higher pitch.

"Yeah, I should get them better trained, you're right Beano, yeah, its shit when the protégé tries to teach the master!"

Mickey endured a few more seconds of Beano's righteous babble before, at last, he could click the phone shut. He stared at it, utterly confused by the conversation. He hoped the phone might speak up and explain how Beano knew about Winchester.

The spouting crap about Mickey's pet crew going off the rails and some bollocks about Barry having to step in was odd, but stranger still, was Beano asking for assurances that cash flow wasn't an issue.

Mickey gulped the last drop of whisky. He rattled the ice around the tumbler. His eyes focused on the wall of the office and particularly on the hideous 1970's framed picture of the Nestle office building in Croydon. Behind it, the wall safe lay hidden. Mickey never really understood why Barry kept the picture. He said he liked the naffness of it, it reminded him of simpler times, he'd said.

"Shit times," Mickey thought.

He stood up and, for the first time in his long service to Barry Hunt, he doubted what he had been told. Barry had been erratic for a while now, in fact as Mickey cast his mind back he found it hard to recall the old Barry, the one more fondly remembered. Barry had been on edge long before the situation with

Bartok had come up. Business, Mickey knew, had not been as good as it could have been, it seemed as if London had given up all its traditional vices for Lent, but forgot to start up again. Mickey looked hard at the crap Nestle picture, could money be that serious an issue? Barry usually confided in him, shared the worries, surely he would know if there was a problem.

Mickey plucked an ice cube from the glass and tossed it into his cavernous mouth. He crunched down, nodded to himself and strode up to the picture.

He pulled it away and dialled the safe's combination.

He pulled the handle and eased open the door.

* * *

"Fuckity, fuck, bollocks" Jake paced quickly, he avoided emotional displays when he could, but he was pissed off. He moved back and forth across the large storage facility in which the Range Rover teams had holed up. The facility formed part of a farm storage unit near his soon to be premier property, the Stockbridge Hotel. He stored, repaired and serviced all his vehicles in it and it had been earmarked as the nerve centre for his new chauffeur and bodyguard business.

"This is fucking serious Adam, serious fucking shit…" at a loss as to what else to say, he booted an old desk chair and it wheeled across the room with a squeal. The last of the Range Rovers had made it back to the farm unit ten minutes before. Each one had come in via the fields and had avoided the local village. They sneaked in, under cover of dark with their lights off.

Parked side by side at the back, they resembled a police line up. Olly and Mark had begun their clean up with Rob attending to the detail. Job one, change the tyres on all cars. Before the night ended they would also remove the bull bars on car two, cleanse it of any lingering bits of Leon, and then hose it down.

All who remained knew that they had Barry Hunt trussed and bound in a small locked room at the end of the facility. No one asked why. The old order of things settled in, some men gave orders and others took them.

"I can't believe the silly bastard reacted like that. I mean Mickey seemed so reasonable, he just wanted to get the cash and move on..." Adam said.

"Jesus, this is fucking serious…" Jake continued pacing. The death of the two men at Bar End didn't upset him. They amounted to casualties in a pocket war. If you want to be safe, stay away. No, the deaths didn't bother Jake. The potential ramifications did.

Adam looked at him quizzically.

"You've said that Jake. We know."

"Forgive me Adam, for being just a little concerned for my life and the lives of the people who work for me."

Adam didn't reply.

Jake blew the air from his lungs in a long sigh. Every action must have an opposite re-action. He needed to think through the options.

"Are we certain that the two bodyguards are dead?" Adam asked to no one in particular.

"How did I get caught up in this bollocks…" Jake muttered

Adam went to say something, but he waved his hand at him.

"It's rhetorical Adam. I am thinking out loud at the moment."

The tension didn't diminish. Rob decided to break it by answering Adam's question.

"Yes," he said looking at him.

"I'm certain. No bastard could have survived that collision with the Rover, not at that speed, surprised the fuckers head didn't come clean off with the impact."

"What about the other guy, the driver?" Adam asked, unmoved.

"Dead," interjected Jake. "He had at least two maybe three gunshot wounds to the head, from what I could see anyway."

Olly and Mark stopped working. The storage unit fell silent as they contemplated the dead.

"How?" asked Adam.

"The bodyguard's Uzi…it discharged when he dropped it," Rob said.

Jake nodded his agreement. Olly and Mark began working again and the unit filled with background noise once more. Rob waved Adam and Jake in.

"Let's go over this one more time," he said.

"None of the cars had correct number plates. All three are identical and so when we came out it may well have been confusing as to exactly how many there were."

Jake nodded. Adam yawned.

"Time frames, we had cleared the field within two minutes of the Uzi firing. It's unlikely that anyone saw all or maybe any of the cars take positions on the field. Or leave. Our weak spot is the motorway traffic…they, in theory, could see it all; but luckily it was fast moving tonight and in that half light, we should be ok, at worst they would think we were joy riders."

"Cameras?" Jake asked.

"None in the local vicinity. Several on the motorway but focused on the road only." Rob searched for anything else of relevance.

Jake nodded again. They knew little actually linked them to the scene. They had all driven out different ways and taken very different routes to Stockbridge. The cars had not been on the open road more than once or twice before tonight. The vehicles had no real connection with the farm and it was unlikely anyone had seen them return.

"Don't worry boss, I think it's covered."

Jake nodded once more.

"Well done Rob." He patted him on the back.

"The most important thing is there's nothing to connect us to the bodies. We never met them before and we left very little evidence at the scene. We'll be cool."

"Except the two bodies," Adam said.

Jake glared at him.

"About the bodies. Mark did what he had to do, we all did. What are we going to do about alibis?" Rob asked.

Jake had decided that all of his team had earned a cash bonus, he knew they wouldn't say anything, they would all be implicated if anyone did.

"I'll rework the rosta, we had a security strategy meeting tonight. We'll be eachother's alibi, the meeting took place at the Later Lounge, and we discussed the new chauffeur business and its development. Adam attended as our financial advisor."

Rob nodded. Keep the lie simple. "I'll spread the word."

Jake took his cue from the clock clicking round to midnight and rose to his feet. Everyone bar he and Adam had now left, they alone would deal with Barry Hunt. Adam trotted after Jake as he strode down to the improvised cell. Barry's cell stood at the end of the single story pre-fabricated office units which had been erected on the right side of the big storage unit. The room had a heavy secure door, its original use had been for the storage of Jake's valuable surveillance, navigational and computer hardware he planned to acquire for the chauffeur business. Now the heavy door and steel windowless walls housed a London gangland boss.

They reached the door; Jake removed the padlock and pulled the lever bar back with a clatter. He strode through without pausing.

Barry Hunt had crawled into the corner, and cowered in the foetal position. The room had no carpet, no furniture and the walls stood bare, the only colour, apart from the metallic blue of the steel, came from the smudges and spots of Barry's blood on the floor. Black gaffer tape secured his hands and feet. Another dark strip of tape, caked in dried blood, covered his mouth.

Barry looked up at them, fear and panic in his eyes. His nose leaked a slow steady trickle of blood. The stain spread from his nose, down his chin and onto his neck and chest.

Adam took a moment to adjust to the harsh strip lighting in the room, as he did so the shock of Barry's appearance sank in.

He lay there, completely naked.

Jake moved forward and as he did so Barry tried to edge away, pressing himself into the steel panels. Jake squatted down in front of Barry, paused and then spoke.

"Now then Barry, I need to tell you that you're in a steel room, which is deep inside a large building, which is a long way from anywhere." Jake paused to allow the information to sink in.

"No one knows you're here." He looked for a reaction. Barry shrank away.

"If you cooperate and do as you're told, you'll be ok. We don't want to hurt you…don't make me hurt you Barry?"

Barry let out a low mournful whimper.

"Do you understand?"

Barry simply looked back at him, his eyes wide and nodded. Jake got up and turned back to the door and took Adam with him. They locked the door, the room shaking and echoing as they did so and moved back down the corridor and back into the main storage area of the building.

Adam felt ready to speak.

"Why the fuck did we pick him up?" he asked.

"Because leaving a pissed off gangster in a field with two dead mates didn't seem like a good idea to me ..." Jake replied.

Adam shook his head. He moved clockwise round the desk as Jake perched on its edge.

"Why didn't he just take the money and go, I mean the big fella, Mickey, was so chilled in comparison to him? He was supposed to just take the money," Adam said, breaking the silence that had descended.

"Yeah well our Barry in there was off his tits on coke, fried. Seen it often before." A rueful expression of disappointment appeared on Jake's face.

"Gangsters hey....not what they used to be." Adam offered.

They both smiled, the tension eased.

Jake conjured back the memory of Barry ranting and stumbling in the field.

"It doesn't add up, I mean fair play, he may have thought he could scare us or whatever, but he simply rode up, no plan, no idea and tried to railroad us...," he trailed off trying to fathom the

211

reasoning, before finally giving up and saying... "yet all he had to do was take the bag."

Adam nodded.

"Simple...how could you fuck up something so simple?"

Jake fiddled with his fingernails but offered no response.

"So what do we do?" Adam asked.

"Well one thing is for certain, that man in there is totally shit scared, I mean he's scared for his life. I don't think it will do us any harm to keep that going."

"I was wondering about that, he came to see us tooled up, that means our little act for Mickey must have been convincing..."

"Yeah maybe too convincing, you and your retainer fee...pratt!"

"That's what convinced him we're serious...I mean he came here expecting trouble, so he came and tried to front his way out of it, despite the fact a deal was done...why would you do that."

"Why did he come down anyway? Why did he not just have Mickey pick up the money and head home, he needn't get involved, he had no need to be here. I mean he bigged himself up in that rant, how he had run his manor and all that. If he was such a big shot you wouldn't waste time with us would you?"

Adam shook his head and then shrugged his shoulders when he realised he didn't actually know the answer.

"One thing is certain" said Jake, "There's more to all this than we know. But our problem is that we now have a London gangland boss naked and tied up in my store room…what happens when his pet gorilla starts to miss him?"

"Mickey?"

"The same. He knows us."

Adam nodded.

"Best we ask the man himself. The fear of what we could do should loosen his tongue enough for us to work out where we go from here."

Jake moved to follow but Adam blocked his path, "I think I should speak to him alone…keep up the pretence he already has of me as boss…do you mind?"

Jake frowned, "Sure…I'll check on what the boys did with the cars."

As Jake moved away Adam called after him.

"Why is he naked?"

Jake smiled.

"Makes him more vulnerable, you don't act the hero with your dick out".

Adam chuckled as he moved to the door, 'nope,' he thought, 'especially not with a dick that size.'

Chapter Twenty

Barry eyed the back of the steel door of his makeshift cell. He hadn't moved. He had no idea of the time or how long he'd been there. A while though, the blood on the floor had dried in patches and he felt cold. The lights had been on permanently since he came round. What bothered him the most, despite everything, was the thought that someone had stripped him. He had no recollection of it all, but then he hardly remembered anything after arriving at the handover.

He knew he shot his mouth off and remembered the sickening thud as that Range Rover mowed down Leon. Leon had been killed, the realisation of that took a while to register. He liked Leon. And Bobby? There had been shots, Barry remembered shots. Had they killed Bobby?

Barry felt scared, more scared than he had ever been in his life. His world was no longer unravelling, it had completely disintegrated. Soon, if not already, Mickey would discover the truth. Mr G would want to know why Barry hadn't sorted out his business in Winchester, Mickey would be squarely in his firing line. 'Sorry old friend,' he mumbled to the empty room.

Mickey could take care of himself.

Barry shut his eyes, why hadn't he just picked up the bag?

The sound of footsteps outside interrupted his thoughts. The door shook as the lock clanged and the door swung open.

He recognised Adam as he stepped in and pulled the door closed.

Barry watched him squat down, placing a bottle of whisky on the floor.

Adam pushed his finger to his pursed lips and let out a long "ssssshhhhhhhh," – then looked at Barry with raised eyebrows. Barry nodded, he wanted to be quiet, he wanted to behave. These men were killers.

Adam ripped the gaffer tape from Barry's mouth in one strong tug. Barry's head bobbed forward as he did it, his lips chapped and stuck together. A layer of skin came away with the tape. Adam swigged from the open whisky bottle then offered it to Barry, who nodded. He cupped the back of his head with his right hand and using his left he poured a large and generous slug into Barry's open mouth.

Barry gagged a little before coughing and settling back against the wall.

Adam eyed Barry's gut and pasty frame. His greying chest hair emphasised his plump unkempt appearance. He'd had Melissa, this thing, had owned her.

Adam bit down on his teeth, braced himself and began.

"Barry, both of your bodyguards are dead…"

"Leon," interrupted Barry.

"What?"

"Their names are Leon and Bobby, they are good guys."

Adam paused to regain his composure.

'Don't let him dominate this – you're in charge now.'

216

"Right...well Leon and Bobby are dead then. You killed them Barry. You're responsible for their deaths." Adam looked hard at him gauging his reactions. Barry nodded at the bottle, Adam gladly gave him another big slug.

"Now listen, please listen very carefully before you speak...You have been a complete pain in the arse. All you had to do was to take the bag. You've created a situation that means I have some difficult choices to make, you complicated the situation, you understand this don't you Barry?"

Barry nodded.

"If you were me Barry, put yourself in my shoes, would simply letting my friend put a bag on your head and drain the life out of you be the simplest and neatest thing I could do?

Barry's face broke out into a little smile.

"Please don't smile Mr Hunt, it isn't an amusing situation. Either you represent a threat or an opportunity. Neither will guarantee you leave this room alive."

The steel in his own voice impressed Adam.

"Barry, I need to understand something. Why would Mr G be interested in squashing us...why would he be interested in little old us? In fact why would Mr G even know about us?"

Barry was taken aback a moment, when had he mentioned Mr G? He wished he could recall all that had gone on before, but his face hurt and the whisky was going to his head.

"Well you stole from me, it's the same as stealing from him, when word gets back... he'll want to resolve the situation."

Adam squatted to the same level as Barry. "So Mr G knows the story about one of your whores stealing £100k of your money… sorry his money, he also knows you're here to ask for it back, does he?"

Barry couldn't hide his reactions. Adam watched as he took on the appearance of a small boy caught in a lie. "Barry, I'm wondering, hypothetically that you may be worth more if we were to sell you back to Mr G…what do you think?"

Adam noticed Barry swallow hard, he could sense the nervous tension in the man, he strained at his bonds, sweat now mingled with the steady flow of blood over his top lip.

"Look, let's be sensible about this…I can see that you are serious. Maybe earlier I misjudged you. I was a bit stressed, things have been difficult recently…"

"Go on", said Adam.

"Well I may have overstretched myself recently, spread my cash too thinly. I have a couple of deals going on that left me needing more money than I had… you know how it is?"

"No I don't."

"Well I don't have the cash to complete a deal, a big deal…"

"With Mr G," Adam rhetorically prompted.

Adam saw Barry pause and think through his answer.

Mr G isn't the only the player.

"Er that's the thing, no not with Mr G, no."

"I am presuming Mr G wouldn't be happy about this extra curricular activity…"

"No, this is something on the side, something I'm doing as a one off…not even Mickey knew about it."

Adam connected the dots, comparing Barry's version to that of Melissa's.

"Barry, you seem to be fucked from every angle…"

Barry said nothing.

"You needed that money back pretty badly didn't you?"

Barry said nothing. Plan B hadn't panned out.

"Why haven't you begged to be let go?"

Barry looked at him, confusion in his eyes.

"You haven't demanded to be let go, made threats, boasted about your importance…nothing. Not a peep from you? Why?"

"Would it help?"

Adam smiled.

"Not a bit…but why would that matter?"

Barry said nothing.

"You don't want to leave… in fact, I'll bet if money is that tight then the safest place for you right now is in here, away from it all isn't it?"

Barry nodded smiling, "You're not wrong…"

Adam thought he saw Barry settle a little.

"So you're dead if we let we go?"

Barry said nothing.

"You may need to try a bit harder Barry…"

"Try harder?"

"To convince me you're a dead man walking."

Barry shrugged.

"Look at it from our point of view Barry. You try and convince us you're dead no matter which way you turn. Maybe we think sod it, let him go, let the old fool take his chances. Why would we let you go that cheaply Barry?" Adam eyed him carefully.

"I'm worth nothing. Why keep me?"

Always the grifter thought Adam.

"I think you're worth something Barry…"

"I had my last throw of the dice…I aint got nothing left boy."

Still trying to play the game. You don't know what I know. Time to deliver the hammer blow.

"Tell me about the Petrovs?"

Barry looked at him, shock at hearing the name of his partners written across his face,

"If you don't tell me about the deal, I can't help you Barry."

Barry visibly sagged. He breathed deeply and his face gave away the fact that he had begun to weigh up his options.

"Think about it Barry. If I know about them, it won't take long for the word to get out to other … bigger fish."

Barry grimaced. His eyes dropped to the floor and he slumped. His chest rose and fell heavily as he laboured to a more upright position. Sweat dripped from his head, the steel cell radiating heat. He looked a beaten man.

"Well, £100 grand has been paid to them," he began, "£100 grand more is required on delivery."

"When?"

"That's technically due this weekend. What day is it?"

Adam looked at his watch. "Saturday…early."

"It's due tomorrow."

"What's the product?"

"Its five kilos of cocaine…worth about six times that once cut and put on the open market."

"You can't pay?"

Barry nodded. Adam watched him, timing would be crucial. The pause became pregnant.

"Can someone else buy in?"

Barry eyed Adam curiously and considered his reply.

"Maybe…what you thinking?"

"We take your place, meet the final payment."

"What's in it for me?"

"Jesus Barry… you don't get killed, not just yet anyway."

"Mmmmm, you pay £100 grand and get £200 grand of coke…I stay breathing."

"For now. The Petrovs, would they buy it?"

"Maybe. If I provide them with a new buyer and you have the money…as long as they are kept away from Mr G's radar, they'll be happy."

"Do you know the Petrovs well?"

Barry tossed his head from side to side mulling the question over.

"I know them a bit…"

"And…"

"Mental, but ambitious. Greed will be the driving force…"

Adam nodded. Money talked, it always would.

"What about Mr G?" he said.

Barry shrugged again, a more resigned look on his face.

"What do you owe Mr G?"

"I was supposed to carry out a contract hit, on some fat loser called Gregor Bartok. He paid up front, £100k, but someone else got the fat bastard before me."

"I suppose Mr G now wants his money back".

"Wouldn't you?" Barry asked.

"That's the only reason?"

Barry shook his head, "No, but it's the main one."

"I owe him a retainer – proceeds from the manor." Barry blushed a touch with embarrassment.

"How much?"

"You going to pay it? What's it to you?"

Adam raised his eyebrows…

"Another £100 grand ok."

"So you owe £200 grand… Mr G would kill you for £200 grand?"

"Mr G would kill me for £2. It's the principle."

"Live by the sword hey…."

"Fuck that – No free lunch boy. You earn, you pay – you can't, you're out. Mr G can't afford to have passengers. No one can."

"That what you are Barry? A passenger?"

"Yes boy – I'm a dead fucking weight."

Adam took renewed stock of the old man. He might be beaten, but he had a little fire left in his belly.

"Forgive me for thinking that £200 grand shouldn't be a problem for a top gangland boss like you… where is all your money Barry?"

Barry shifted uneasily, "It's not as easy to make money in this game as it used to be. Top dogs like Mr G take more and more and people take more and more from the bottom. It's not what it was."

"So if the Petrovs take our deal – you should be safe from them. We'll take the bonus of the deal in lieu of killing you…that's two death threats off your back."

"Mr G will hunt me down."

"You matter that much?"

"Don't matter a jot. As I said, it's the principle."

The two men stared at the walls of the temporary shell.

Barry spoke first.

"If you did the deal with the Petrovs… you know you run the risk of crossing Mr G."

Adam nodded.

"You could eliminate the risk…sell the drugs on to Mr G ."

"Would that not be suicide?"

"You're not London – you're not a real threat. It would be business…"

"Go on." Adam sat down, resting against the door.

"He'll want to know how a deal took place in London without his knowledge and may pay handsomely for the information …offer up the Petrovs."

"Why are you telling me this Barry?"

Barry smiled, as a fox does when it eyes a helpless chicken.

"If the Petrovs fall into Mr G's radar, maybe, just maybe, he'll lose interest in me…"

"Especially if word got out the Petrovs killed you in a drug deal," added Adam. "Got a good pension plan Barry?" A stony silence broke out between the two men. Adam rose slowly, his back to Barry as he began opening the door.

"I'm not sure your not worth more dead than alive."

Barry didn't look up, but he heard the clang and thump of the lock.

Adam walked back into the main area of the barn where Jake stood facing him. Their eyes met, the rage building behind Jake's eyes was palpable. The black holdall sat open in his arms. Adam stopped a few feet away and could see into the bag.

It's time to bring Jake up to speed.

"I can explain…" Adam said.

Chapter Twenty One

Mickey Finn yawned, he had not slept well. The near empty shelves of the safe proved to be a shock. A big shock. Mickey knew that Barry kept pockets of emergency money in various locations around the manor, but it would not be enough to cover the shortfall, not nearly. He bumbled around his Wandsworth flat, his boxer shorts at half mast and recent tea stains on his once white, but now grey vest. Mickey pottered around the flat, casting anxious glances at the phone; he made toast and more tea and tried to piece the jigsaw together. The small flat didn't lend itsself to roaming, after he'd banged his shin for the third time on the coffee table he settled into the tattered armchair. He stroked the greying stubble on his chin, always looking at the phone, willing it to ring.

It didn't. At 9.30 am Mickey Finn realised he had to act alone. With an old biro he wrote out the budget on the back of a piece of junk mail. He did so with careful attention, double checking his calculations.

Mr G headed the list of priorities to resolve. £200 grand was the price that needed paying. Mickey had pulled everything from the safe onto his living room floor. A little under £100 grand stared back at him.

The phone still didn't ring.

A final gulp of now tepid tea saw him lumber into action.

Shit, showered and shaved, twenty minutes later he pulled the flat door closed and moved into the weekend throng of Putney.

Mickey had made several calls through the night to the various establishments the manor ran and all said they had paid up a week or so ago, virtually nothing outstanding, no more to come in. Where had all that money gone? If the manor had paid up and on time as claimed there would be nearly half a million quid in the safe. He knew the businesses had paid up, they always did. None of his lads gave him any reason to worry. It had been business as usual.

Mickey did what he does best. He menaced. He warned every establishment to have as much cash ready for collection that morning, and Saturday morning is not a good time to be dealing with villains, even the ones that worked for you. They were hung over and generally scattered to the winds.

They all showed up. Mickey had that effect on people. They all paid as well. Mickey knew it was bad business, robbing tomorrow to pay for today. With the money haphazardly bundled into a brown satchel, he dialled Beano and waited.

The Mucky Duck, the pub where Beano and Mickey liked to meet, stood on the northern bank of the Thames in Twickenham. It was a favourite with the pre and post rugby international crowd during the winter months, but in the summer months people came for its bankside garden and its views across the river to Eel Pie Island and the Surrey fields beyond. Mickey sat with the leather

228

satchel on his lap, nursing a pint of Guinness. The bar staff knew Mickey, he often came to the bar for a beer, he liked the tranquility, a pleasant hideaway from noisy roads, people and work.

He sipped the Guinness, Mickey had never been a big drinker, but when he did, the black stuff hit the spot. Beano had decided to meet him. Mickey usually sent a minion, Beano likewise. Why would today be different? A breathless and rasping voice interrupted his thoughts.

"You got a black drink for a black brother?" Beano pushed his walrus like bulk through the small wooden gate and padded his way across the grass to the bench table next to Mickey. "You a Guinness drinker are you?"

"Yes brother Finn, I am. My mother swore by it, why you think this nigger is so big?"

"Over eating?" The pregnant pause was only shattered by Beano as he burst into a raucous laugh, he even slapped his thigh.

"You're a funny man, Mr Finn, very fucking funny man…is that for me?" He raised a podgy finger and pointed at the bag on Mickey's lap. Beano raised his arm and waved at his companion. The man, a tall Somali looking fella, nodded in return and went into the bar.

"So, no Barry? Barry is absent…he said he would be here Mr Finn?"

"Barry said he'd be here at a handover… he's not usually at these, Christ you and I don't usually do them."

229

"No, but this time is unusual, funny times, a lot of complications." Beano licked his lips and his gaze flitted from Mickey to the pint of Guinness.

"You spoke to Barry this week then, about this meeting?" Beano nodded. "He didn't mention it to me when he asked me to handle the handover." Said Mickey.

"Well maybe he thought you were too busy sorting out these monkeys in Winchester, this side bar you have going on. Did Barry get it resolved, they pay up?"

"I haven't heard back from him to be honest Beano, he's not back up in town, hence why I'm here alone…" Beano snorted a little. Before he could muster a derogatory response, the tall Somali put a pint of Guinness down in front of him and he took it up without thanks and downed half of it. He pushed his fat paw of a hand across his face, removing the telltale froth from his top lip.

"That does not sound good to me Mickey, if he's not back then the money he went to collect for Mr G is not back, right?"

Mickey nodded slowly, his mind racing, trying to compute all the new information and mix it with his own. Barry must have known there wasn't enough money, and was happy for him to walk into the lion's den and he hadn't been told the lion was unfed! Also, Beano knew about Winchester…why did he know about Winchester?

"No, Beano. Barry has had a few issues this month, he really hasn't been himself. I have the money for the retainer here, as always…"

Beano took the satchel and handed it to the now much closer attending Somali. "That's good Mickey, it's important you understand that missing payments is not an option. Barry needs to be reminded of this issue. Mr G asked me to specifically deliver that message to your Barry bullshit personally. But the man aint here is he Mickey?"

"No, but I'm sure he'll be back today, with the money..." he probed.

"The money is not that important, £100,000 for the Bartok balls up..." Beano chortled at the pun and the fat Ukrainian's missing testicles.

"Can you believe they cut his balls off? Why would you cut the man's balls off? I mean for out of towners that's pretty hard core man."

Mickey looked up at Beano. Bartok was found minus his bollocks, this was new and important information to Mickey, and he also recognised the calling card.

"The trouble with a calling card or signature style is people get to recognise it too quickly", he fished.

"True Mickey, but these out of towners of yours, what were they trying to do, impress you? Put the scares on you and Barry? Dealing with the wrong mother fuckers if they thought that, hey?"

Mickey watched as Beano chugged on the remnants of his pint. He was confused as to why Beano kept going on about out of towners. Then another penny dropped.

231

Barry had lied to Mr G. He went running down to Winchester to get away from Mr G and the debt he couldn't pay.

"I mean what did these boys hope to do, seriously blackmail you to impress Mr G – he ain't going to waste his time with these no hopers is he."

The final penny dropped. Barry had stiffed Mickey. Mickey, his oldest and most loyal friend had been left in the firing line. *Some fucking friend you are*, thought Mickey. Without realising it, Mickey moved into survival mode.

I'm a fighter, it's what I do.

"No, Mr G needs the likes of Barry and me, to filter these little upstarts out of the system." His fist clenched and unclenched under the table.

"So Mr G is pissed with the Winchester boys for the hit?" Mickey asked.

"No man, he couldn't give a shit about them Winchester boys man. They is no one. No, he's seriously pissed with Barry, you understand that Mickey?"

Beano's stare and manner was pointed.

"He's late with the retainer, also not paying up on time for the failed hit, failing to actually do the fucking hit, man…"

Beano threw his blubbery arms up in mock exasperation.

"Mr G is having doubts, I am having doubts about the man's ability." The indictment hung in the air.

"Your part of this Mickey, you and Barry are tweedle fuck and tweedle whatever….you get me guy?"

Mickey nodded. "Yeah Beano I get you... I knew you'd want the Bartok money Beano."

Mickey ran through the numbers in his head once more.

"You'll find the retainer in full – plus there's an extra £45k, a down payment on what is owed back to you..."

Beano didn't react, no thanks, no surprise.

"You need to understand something though... the extra, that's from me."

Now Beano reacted, like a cajoling teacher, a smile moved onto his lips.

"What you saying to me Mr Finn?"

Mickey waited a beat. Timing would be everything.

"I'm saying that I am *personally* making up some of the shortfall and I will make up the rest of Barry's debt to Mr G." Mickey paused, he gathered himself, he had been in the game too long to not be able to read the writing when it became blazoned across the wall.

Last man standing.

Mickey excelled at Rumbles, the fight format where five men entered a cage. No rules. No referee and no limits. The last man standing took the prize.

Mickey had never lost.

Who you chose to engage and when was crucial.

Timing imperative.

"I have not heard from Barry since yesterday," he began.

"He sent me home from Winchester, he hasn't been truthful on a few things."

He watched Beano, whose eyes focused on the river.

"Barry hasn't returned home yet and he hasn't returned a single call, ...I don't want Mr G to think I am not his man, I am..."

"I say what is so...you Mr G's boy Mickey?"

Mickey nodded.

"I'll pay the debt to keep the manor going...if Mr G is amenable?"

Beano looked long and hard at Mickey. His fat face breaking out in a sweat. "This is serious Mickey, very fucking serious, you are telling me that Barry has done a runner, gone to ground with £100,000 of Mr G's money...."

"And the rest....." Timing is key.

"What you mean?"

Mickey sucked in the air. His stature reduced as he hunched at the table.

"Well, I struggled to pull together that pile of cash." He motioned to the bag.

"We should have twice that with a manor our size. Barry has either run the business into the ground or been stealing from the pot, I mean I'm no telltale, but if he's going to leave me with my bollocks dangling, I'm not going take it lying down am I?"

Beano shrugged a half hearted agreement.

"No I reckon he's been skimming from all of us... I don't want Mr G to think I am part of this Beano."

Beano's frame prevented him from getting up and pacing, so he did it in his mind, beady eyes moving back and forth. He let out a low growling wheeze. He made quick and decisive decisions, in contrast to his movements. Mickey's life depended on what Beano did next.

"Mmmmm hmmmmm" Beano said, as if sampling good cooking. "Roll them dice bitch…roll them crazy dice." He smiled at Mickey.

Mickey glanced left to right, then smiled right back.

"I never thought of you as a gambling man Mr Finn."

"Full of surprises me…"

"My man Mickey Finn - consider yourself caretaker of the manor. Caretaker Mickey, you hear me. Caretaker." He extended his arm and forced a finger at Mickey.

"Know this brother Finn, Barry 'fucking' Hunt is a wanted man."

Dead man walking, thought Mickey.

"The word will be out on the street from now... bring this man to us and you'll be rewarded."

Mickey expected nothing less.

"I'm going to send Rodney over to you, show him the money situation, I want independent corroboration Mickey, Rodney's good, and you know that."

Mickey did. Rodney had become famous as the Alvin Hall of gangster money. "Mr G will appreciate your efforts, he'll want a continued demonstration of your loyalty though bro?"

Mickey thought for a moment, he knew Barry had been lying to him, he knew Barry had set the Winchester boys up to take the fall on the Bartok hit.

He had dug himself one almighty hole.

If Mickey wasn't to fall in with him then he needed to make sure Barry Hunt's world got exposed for what it was, a tissue of lies and smokescreens.

"I need to tell you the truth about Barry and the Winchester thing...it may shed some light on the whole situation and then after that, if you want Barry, then you best get to where the trail is hottest man...

"Oh and where is that?"

"You best go to Winchester...see a man called Adam."

Chapter Twenty Two

"Things change…my time is over Irma." Barry's voice crackled over the phone. He sounded drained, the vigour removed from his tone. The Petrovs listened in their shiny and polished office, straining to make out his words over the distorted speaker phone. Each sister leaned in and cocked their heads unnaturally.

"It's a young mans game, I can't do this anymore…. " Irma Petrov looked at her sister. The elder shrugged and repeated her question. Irena moved close to the speaker, keen not to miss a response.

"Why you out Barry? Is a good deal."

"I tried to juggle too much, you only know how much trouble you're in once you're in over your head…" Barry let the statement trail off.

Irma let out an audible sigh.

"Barry, I don't give a shit about your problems. I understand you loose everything. My heart it bleeds, truly it does." Maybe if she could see Barry she might have felt different. The conversation was only possible because Jake held a phone to the still naked and bound former gangland boss.

"I want my money… deal is deal. This is not some mate you borrow £50 from down pub… is it?" Irma's face remained as stoic as her tone.

"No" mumbled Barry.

"You owe £100,000 Barry, I have five kilos of coke I need to sell, I can't take it to other dealer in London, not now, Mr G would find out, if not already."

The Petrovs knew the situation exactly; Beano had wasted no time in spreading the word that Barry Hunt had been declared a wanted man. The London criminal underground could move very quickly when it needed to. Dmitri had been only marginally more animated in spreading the news that, while a hit on Barry Hunt had not yet been ordered, it would soon.

Irma knew Mr G wanted the satisfaction of a public humiliation first.

Irena had simply giggled.

"Irma, …I don't want you to suffer… there is no one who knows about the deal that can hurt you."

"Is very bad when people steal from each other, there is no honour in world anymore. You not get money back Barry…is that what you want to ask?"

"No of course not, fuck the money, you have my first payment, keep it…what I am offering is another buyer for you, someone that wants to take over the deal…are you interested?"

Irma smiled. Melissa had been proved right. One hundred per cent. Irma thought through Barry's possible angles: he wanted to stay away from Mr G, maybe get away from this with his life.

"Yes Barry we interested, what is in it for you?"

"You don't hunt me down and you keep my involvement with you quiet, especially from the G Men."

Irma pursed her lips and tapped a pen against her teeth. This was possible.

"Upsetting Mr G is not something we want to do, maybe we can agree, one moment please…"

Irma muted the speaker phone and looked hard at Irena and Dmitri.

"How does he sound to you?" Irma asked.

"He sounds tired, it sounds like man with no hope," Irena responded.

"I wonder where he found new buyers from so quickly?" Irma had always been a cautious woman, not given to rash decisions. Murdering your husband and stealing his criminal organisation is not something you do on a whim.

"Maybe Melissa knows about new buyers? I have concerns."

"Well we will need to meet with them. That is not unreasonable?" Irena offered. Dmitri looked from one to sister to another and nodded.

"Melissa can sit in and observe maybe." Irena nodded as her sister continued. Dmitri nodded as well, eager to be part of the dialogue.

"Provincial is how Barry described them, what does this mean?"

"Not London, it means they not sell within Mr G's territory!" her sister smiled at the realisation. "Barry is using our deal to get himself out of trouble," Irena added.

"What worries me," Irma said toying with a paper clip, "is that Barry is prepared to walk away from the £100,000 that he has already invested with us, that's not normal behaviour."

Dimitri shrugged and Irma comically mimicked him, she turned the speaker phone off mute with a flick of her fake finger nail.

"Barry... Barry,"

"Yes," came a muffled reply

"Can we speak with these new buyers?"

"Of course, I'll give them your direct number, they'll call you within the hour."

"Do not assume Barry..." Irma said coldly, "that this call means we agree to the new buyers. We will talk to them and maybe meet them, then make our decision...understand?"

"Yeah I do..." Barry said.

The receiver suddenly muffled and then the phone went dead. Irma waved an arm at Dmitri who nodded and padded out of the room. A few seconds later he returned with Melissa, clad in a brand new summer dress. Irena nodded her approval.

"Nice dress."

A nervous smile worked its way across her lips. "Thanks."

"Is new?"

"Yes - I needed some clothes, I had nothing. I picked it up from Mango earlier."

Irma cut the sartorial appreciation dead. She wasted no time in bringing Melissa up to speed on her conversation with Barry and their assumptions. They looked at Melissa, awaiting her opinion.

"The word is out that he has no future," she said. "He has to cut and run, no matter what his situation, Barry it seems is over with. It's time to look at the bigger picture." More comfortable than the first time she entered the room the day before, Melissa perched on the end of the stylishly uncomfortable chair.

"Melissa are you ready to become a rich woman?"

She simply nodded, keeping her excitement under control.

"Mr G will need a crew, a strong crew to run Barry's old manor. Why couldn't that be the Petrovs?" she asked.

"No reason at all," Melissa offered

"We need to plan this carefully, you know Barry's joints, clubs and offices."

"I know all his business activities and the various crews he has working. I don't know who would be running it now, maybe Mickey Finn, if that's so then believe me he's no thinker."

"What's your idea Melissa?"

"Simple, we hit the manor, small at first, testing their strength, demonstrate our strength, maybe take a few guys out. You need to send a message to other London firms that they should stay away. I can get to a few, those that were unhappy before and maybe create a mutiny in the ranks." Melissa breathed a little too deeply, conscious of her mounting adrenalin.

Irma nodded. "Where would you start?"

Melissa beamed and then reined the smile in. She caught Irena's eye, who watched her intently as she moved around the desk to join her sister. A united front.

"I'd begin with Ramon the ponce at the Palace."

"Then?"

"The street hustlers, pushers and pimps – they are market dependent, any slow down in supply and their allegiances will fall away." Melissa waited for reaction, but got nothing. "From there it would be the doormen and clubs, the small ones…"

"Idea is, small to start, then bigger and bigger… right?"

"Yeah – no one wants a war."

The sisters looked at each other, as if communicating telepathically.

"What about Mr G?" Irena asked

"If we create a lot of small problems for whoever is in charge…"

"Mickey Finn is caretaker…Dmitri heard this earlier."

Melissa's turn to nod, surprised Mickey hadn't taken the fall with Barry. "Mickey, Well he's bound to be under suspicion, so we make him look bad. Mr G may remove him himself."

"Is that good for us?" Irma asked.

" No…shit maybe. No! We need to avoid that. Ideally we need to be in a position where Mr G would be grateful for us taking over…"

Irma held her hands up trying to slow Melissa enthusiasm so she could take the information in. Irena flicked a rare stray hair off her sister's shoulder back into place.

"If we get this right, then Mr G might be grateful for another crew to come and sort it out, show strength and pay him his dues. But if we strike early then we're declaring war on an enemy we cannot beat." Melissa continued.

Irena looked at her sister and understood her reluctance. The same thing had happened in Tallinn. Their husbands began to be squeezed out of their familiar territories and they lacked the wit or diplomacy to make allies and redefine their roles in the changing criminal scene. Instead they attacked, they took on the bigger firms and simply lacked the muscle and organisation to win.

The Petrovs knew they would never have the muscle to take on Mr G, and a week or so ago Barry's old manor would have seemed too big as well, but with it in turmoil and suspicion all around, maybe they could muster enough power to force Mr G's hand.

"First – we need to speak to the new buyers. Make a deal. You don't know who they might be Melissa?"

"Sorry no idea," she fingered the hem of her summer dress, "if they are out of towners then I wouldn't know them, would I?"

"Let's get them here, you can watch the meeting and see if you recognise anyone, Barry could try and sell us out to Mr G to save his neck."

Melissa nodded her agreement.

243

"Well let us see how that meeting goes. Melissa begin your enquiries, but do it quietly, Dmitri you help…." Irma held her arm out inviting Melissa to leave. Irena admired the wiggle of the summer dress as she left.

"Stop it sister…"

"Is a nice dress."

"Yes… very."

* * *

Barry's food and drink had been laced with sleeping pills, and should knock him out for a good twelve hours. It had been a long weekend and Adam hadn't had a decent night's sleep for days. Olly and Mark were coming over from the club to guard Barry from now on; he and Jake planned to head back to Jake's place to rest up.

His phone vibrated again in his pocket, his messaging service, 12 messages in all. He sat down at the desk in the office down the hall and took out a pen and piece of paper to make notes. He hadn't been at work for the best part of three days. Hannah had left two messages on Friday, the second slightly more frantic, she had cleared his diary on Thursday as requested, she would email him the new appointments. He had, it would seem, failed to turn up to a meeting with Colin Peterson, the wealthy courier magnet and family friend. He was due to help Colin with several mortgages on behalf of his children. Adam knew it wasn't a disaster, he'd call him now. He had several other business related messages, but nothing that critical.

244

He did however have three more messages from his Mum. The first message wanting to confirm his visit on Sunday, the second to remind him that she expected him at 12.00 and that he had to fix her light and mow the lawn. The third message left only an hour before, expressed concern that he hadn't responded to her first two messages.

Adam let out a deep and weary sigh.

There still hadn't been a reply from Melissa, no new message, not a thing. He called Hannah. She didn't answer. He left her a detailed message, telling her he needed more time off for personal reasons and would be off all week. He'd make relevant calls but she needed to clear his diary, moving appointments to a weekend if need be.

Then he clicked speed dial to ring his mum and she answered almost before it rang.

"Hi mum it's me..."

Adam loved the skip her voice did when she realised he had called. Every time he heard it he wished he called more often.

"Not great Mum, I have had a better few days." He glanced towards the makeshift cell.

Mrs Warriner had that all English mumsie tone, slightly patronising but comforting in a soft blanket kind of way. Adam settled back to be soothed by it.

"No, not unwell, nothing like that, just tired, had a couple of long days with work. It's thrown up quite a few surprises, that's all." Adam put his feet up onto the desk and settled back into the big comfy office chair. His mum went into transmit mode, she downloaded all the information from the last few days, using up all the moderately interesting things she would have to tell him tomorrow. He feigned fascination about her trip to the post office and her out-sized mail. "It's very confusing now isn't it?" she asked. And yes he did know the new price of postage.

He sat unmoved by her recounting, word for word her trip to the butchers and bumping into Mrs Rees; whom she long suspected of having an affair with Mr Rodgers, the divorcee from down the road. Adam had tried in the past to explain that Mr Rodgers was in fact gay.

As he listened, he witnessed Jake's return, Olly and Mark, his troubleshooting door men turned gaolers, in tow. Adam watched as he gave them the short tour of the temporary prison and then turned hand on hips and faced the office. His mood looked as black as it had done when he discovered the bag. He headed into the office alone.

"Ok mum, don't tell me everything now, we'll chat tomorrow… yes I will come round and mow the lawn…tonight?...no I am meeting up with Jake, we need to discuss some business…you know, I'm buying the house next door, an investment."

Jake waved to get Adam's attention; he mouthed at Adam,

"I'm coming with you tomorrow." Adam looked back perplexed, so Jake repeated the action.

"Sorry mum, yeah I was distracted, Jake will be coming over with me tomorrow…why? Er yeah good question…" Adam looked at Jake and shrugged his shoulders.

Whispering Jake said, "Because I want to keep an eye on you, you can't be trusted."

Adam rolled his eyes, but Jake shrugged his shoulders theatrically, daring him to argue. Then he whispered, "plus you haven't got a clue how to fix a light, have you?"

Adam made a face back at him.

"Jake is good with his hands mum, better than me, he's offered to help do some of the odd jobs…yeah that is nice…well he also wants some of your roast pork…I'm sure you'll have enough, you normally make enough to feed five or six people."

Adam took another few minutes to end the conversation with his mother. Once he had finally clicked the phone shut, he flopped his head into his arms on the desk. It seemed odd, planning a Sunday with his mother, while two men guarded a naked gangster in a store room in a country barn.

Not your normal week.

"Right, let's call the Petrovs." Jake pulled up the chair and sat opposite his friend.

"You ready for this" he asked.

Jake nodded, he'd had time to think it over, work through the permutations of Adam's plan. He wasn't happy about it, but it did seem to cover all the bases. "Dial them."

Adam picked up Barry's mobile and looked up the number, he keyed it into his own phone and pressed 'call'. The phone took a moment to connect, and they heard the familiar ringing tone. Mid ring the call was answered, but only silence emitted from the other end.

"…is that Ms Petrov," Adam ventured.

"Are we talking privately?" came the clipped reply.

"Yes quite privately…my partner is with me but no one else. Barry Hunt said we should talk."

"Let us not waste time. We have product to sell and you a wish to buy."

"Correct, are you happy for us to move forward?"

"Maybe… what should I call you?" Irma asked.

Adam shrugged and looked at Jake for inspiration, who simply stared back devoid of ideas.

"My name is Jake…Jake Simons," said Adam. Jake leant across and slapped his chest.

"Well Jake…you realise that Mr Hunt is a wanted man…dealing with him is very dangerous." The voice, had a cold indifference to it, it could have been cold calling for new windows.

"Yes."

"We have ambitions Jake, so we would prefer that Mr Hunt is kept off the scene. We would not welcome his return to London once our deal is concluded."

Jake and Adam exchanged heavy glances.

Adam raised his eyebrows in a 'whatever' gesture and ploughed on.

"We can assure you that Mr Hunt will not be a problem for you or us moving forward," Adam said as smoothly as he could, avoiding Jake's gaze.

Silence for a moment.

"£100k…is what remains of the deal; you can pay this?"

"Yes, that is not a problem," said Adam, perhaps too quickly.

"Monday –can you come to us?" Irma smiled, delighted neither party wanted to drag the process out.

"That is fine. We'll come to London, we'll discuss the handover of the merchandise."

"Agreed" Irma passed on the address and they agreed a 10.00am meeting.

The phones hit their respective receivers almost simultaneously. Adam flopped his head back and slouched down.

"Why are you going up there?" asked Jake

"We've to appear serious and we need to get a sample don't we… anyway I'm not going," said Adam.

"Dangerous trip?"

"Yeah, but we talked about this – speculate to accumulate," said Adam."Anyway, didn't you hear, they are expecting a 'Jake'. I need to be somewhere else."

Chapter Twenty Three

Adam and Jake arrived at his mother's shortly before 11.00am. Jake insisted they get there early. He felt it only polite and it would be a nice surprise for Kathleen. If he had hoped to perhaps catch her unprepared or off guard then he had seriously underestimated Mrs Warriner.

The weekend visits of her darling boy proved grand affairs in the limited scope of Kathleen Warriner's life. While she actively celebrated the fact that their family consisted of just the two of them, Adam pushed that fact to the back of his mind and tried to forget it. He had known only two of his grandparents, his maternal and paternal grandmothers. Each Grandfather had succumbed to the rigours of a hearty full English cholesterol-induced heart attack before he made four years old. They had the chance to adore their grandson, but he in return never truly remembered them. He had glimpses, whispers of a memory of each man, but Adam could never be sure if they were actual memories or applied anecdotes he had turned into a collective reality.

Kathleen cleaned. Each and every nook of the house gleamed, she spent most of Saturday completing the task; she had, as usual put fresh linen on the spare bed, knowing full well that Adam would not be staying. No one would be staying, but accepted habits die hard. She had then risen early that morning and again run the hoover and duster around the whole house before beginning the preparations for Adam's favourite dish.

Kathleen's roast pork had a deserved, superb reputation, the crispiest of crackling and beautiful long roasted potatoes with a crunchy outside and fluffy interior. A taste of heaven is how Adam thought of it, every time he journeyed away from his mother's roast pork lunch.

Kathleen could not be described as a shy woman, nor vivacious. She had adopted that uniquely English trait of superior indifference. Tolerant of mild irritations and inconveniences, rarely uttering a word of complaint, she ensured that when truly unhappy, those who needed to, knew it.

She had a close knit circle of friends from the bridge club and the various village committees she sat on. She also volunteered to paint and create scenery for the local amateur dramatics group. Her husband's death had in many ways released her, unshackled by the guilt of the life she thought she had put him through, she started to enjoy her own life again. The cul-de-sac where she lived was located east of Winchester in the village of Easton, a peaceful cluster of old and new houses that nestled in the lee of the Itchen river, an unspoilt English village off the main road to Alresford. Its claim to fame, if you could call it that, was that it contained arguably the finest country pub in Hampshire, the Chestnut Horse. Ken Warriner had determined on a move to Easton largely based on his love for the pub.

Kathleen had flapped at first, at the notion of an interloper on her special day, but when she had a moment to reflect and think about it, she realised that Adam wasn't shunning her or the family moment, he was simply trying to move on. She hadn't got along with Jake when she first met him. He'd done nothing wrong, in fact he had been very polite, no, Kathleen resented how close this man had become to her son. A few years older than Adam, successful, handsome, she wondered why he had developed such a close relationship with her Adam, who talked about him a great deal and rarely did in the same way about anyone or anything else.

She greeted them at the door, already dressed for lunch and ushered them in with a flourish. Jake produced a bunch of flowers and a fine bottle of Chablis on the doorstep. Genuinely surprised and delighted, Kathleen greeted him with a peck on the cheek and effusive thanks. Adam quickly produced the flowers Jake had supplied him with and mumbled "great minds think alike." Unfooled, his mother merely beamed at him and gave him a mother-son hug.

They didn't have time to settle and his mother refused Adam's request for a cup of tea before they began. She knew if he settled, it would be like trying to move a disobedient dog.

"We've only got a couple of hours before lunch is ready and I know you'll be good for nothing after you have eaten." She looked Adam up and down and prodded his rounded belly, "maybe you should be off the pork anyway."

Adam shifted backwards embarrassed.

253

"Well I mean, hardly fighting fit are you, look at Jake, I'll bet you could break rocks across that stomach." Jake laughed silently and raised his eyebrows at Adam. "Don't say a word you, or we'll be seeing if you can actually break rocks on it."

Mrs Warriner walked them through the house, where she had conveniently left post-it notes for on any job that needed doing. It resembled a paper chase, the jobs ranging from changing bulbs, peeling wallpaper to squeaky floorboards and poorly draining plug holes.

"You, young man," she pointed at Jake, "will start in here. I saw that mighty fine tool box you left at the front door, evidently you are good with your hands." Mrs Warriner admired Jake's robust good looks, a mother and older woman she might be, but she recognised a man who took care of himself.

"I suggest you start at the back and work your way to the front of the house, follow the scent of the roasted pig." She chuckled to herself enjoying another young man in the house and pushed Adam out through the rear patio doors.

"As for you, the lawn needs doing and I want that big flowerbed at the back completely weeding out." Adam looked back at Jake in the hope of rescue.

"Don't look at him, he'll be out to help as soon as he's finished in there…right, come on crack to it". She clapped her hands by way of emphasis.

As Adam tried to move off, his mother held up her hand, "hand them over," he sighed and made a sulky face before handing over his mobile phone. Kathleen turned to Jake and held out her hand to him, "you too Mr Simons, ghastly things, encourage everyone to have five times more conversations than are required."

She gathered the phones and put them into the apron that covered her red cotton dress. "They will not be going off and being used while we work and lunch, understand?" Jake tossed his head a little from side to side, conceding he had no comeback.

The bungalow stood in a cul-de-sac, eight houses on generous plots facing a large unmarked wide road and turning circle. Each bungalow came with about half an acre of garden in total, built in the 70's and mostly still owned by the original buyers, they had become an unplanned and uncontrolled retirement community. Many of the front lawns had lost their dividing fences and the space had become a cooperative gardening utopia. The Warriners moved in after Adam left home, they downsized considerably into the two bedroom property and pocketed a healthy amount which subsidised their retirement plans. Adam, surprised his mother had not sold up and moved out after his father had died, liked the fact that the interior of his parent's house looked nothing like the others. No net curtains or chintz and lace. Overt floral tributes whether on the walls or carpets, had been stripped out and discarded within days of their moving in. The house had become a tribute to clean lines and white walls. Photos and art adorned the walls, chosen to draw colours from the carpet and soft furnishings. A bungalow had never looked more chic. Adam never thought of it as home. It didn't have the memories that impart a sense of place. At least not for him.

He had wondered why she hadn't sold up and for a long time he misunderstood the connection his mother had to his father via the building. Now, he no longer fought it, his mother could be a force of nature and as long as she kept smiling he'd be happy.

Adam had been going for no more than thirty minutes; he'd gone past the hot and bothered phase of manual work, and had moved with many grunts and groans, to the tired and sweaty stage. Then he spied Mrs Rollason from next door. It had taken her a lot longer than usual to start her curtain twitching behaviour. He could see the funny dumpy little women scuttling behind the fence panels as he emptied the lawnmower bag. He didn't dislike her, she could be good company for his mum, but he hated the way she hovered, spied and peeked all the time. He also knew that if he got talking to her he would have to suffer the endless updates about her darling son Rupert.

Rupert, like him, was an only child, and naturally the apple of his mother's eye. Rupert it seemed was superb at everything…

"You know he went to Oxford."

"We're so very proud that he's completed medical school."

"He's in Zimbabwe, helping the kiddies. He's doing some wonderful things and in such a dangerous place."

He could hear the anecdotes grating in his head all over again. …

"Rupert has married Lady Isabella what not hooray-snooty fuck knows."

That had been the last Rupert bulletin he could recall, a wedding in a castle somewhere in the middle of the father of the bride's estate.

Adam had never met Rupert and had only seen Mrs Rollason's husband twice. On both occasions he had been pretending to be asleep in a deck chair at the bottom of his garden, a hefty looking gin and tonic at his socked and sandled feet.

Adam glimpsed the plump floral printed pudding flit down along the fence, heading towards him, but looking back up at the house. Adam followed her gaze which focused on Jake, who had already commenced job three, the patio doors. He had removed his fleece top and stood in his shorts and skin tight grey t-shirt.

Pre-emptive strike, thought Adam.

"Hello Mrs Rollason...enjoying the lovely weather?" He said it louder than really necessary; the words forced Mrs Rollason into an involuntary jump. She froze and Adam could see her head swivel towards him, unable to see over the fence. He watched as she stooped to peer through a crack in one of the dilapidated fence panels. Adam waved as he saw her podgy face appear in the gap. She snapped her head back, guilt etched on her face.

"Oh Adam it's you...I was rather worried who it might be, in your mother's garden I mean, I didn't recognise the other young man...you see...."

"That's a friend of mine, he's helping me with some odd jobs around the place."

"Ah yes well what a good boy you are…well done…My Rupert was supposed to be down…"

Adam fired the mower back into life drowning out the final part of the sentence. He put his hand to his ear and looked at the fence…he mouthed "what," and then "sorry," while pointing at the mower.

On the dot at 1.00pm Kathleen came out and called the boys in to clean themselves up; she had busied herself preparing the table outside on the patio. Once clean and presentable they all sat at the table and lunch was served. Jake devoured his pork commenting enthusiastically about it living up to the hype. They quaffed a light New Zealand white wine and chatted aimlessly, Adam had given his usual five minute download on his job, his mother had tried to ask leading questions but found that her interest and knowledge, as usual, was lacking. Instead, Jake became the focus. She expressed surprise at just how successful he had become. She knew he had a bar, but had no idea he owned three and was impressed by all of his other business interests; quite remarkable she had said.

What enthralled her the most was the news that he was to own the Stag Hotel in Stockbridge. It had an excellent reputation and Mrs Rollason's Rupert often took his mother there for dinner. She delighted in the prospect of telling Mrs Rollason that her son and now she, were really very good friends with the owner.

"Friends of the owner get special dispensation," Jake said.

"You'll never pay for a meal at my hotel again...on one proviso."

"What might that be?"

He raised his wine glass and leant in towards her. "That you come and teach my chef how to do a proper roast dinner!"

She slapped his arm in false modesty and blushed a little.

As the conversation lulled, Kathleen fingered her wine glass, her face went a little blank as if lost in some distant memory. Adam recognised the signs,

"Mum... Mum!"

Kathleen broke into a broad smile as she looked at her darling boy.

"Thinking about dad?"

"Yes sweetheart, you know how he loved days like today...it's hard not to miss him." She tilted her glass away from her and Jake took the chance to top up her glass with wine, not wanting to get caught in the nostalgic cross-fire.

"So Adam, when are you going to bring a lovely young girl home for me to meet?" The question surprised Adam and amused Jake, who quickly joined in,

"Yes Adam, when are you going to meet a nice girl and settle down?"

"HA! I hardly want him to settle down, just knowing he has met a girl would be a start. Do you know Jake, I don't think he has had a girlfriend for....ooh I don't know, what, five years Adam?"

Adam smiled, tight lipped.

"I have had the odd girlfriend, but none that would stand the test of meeting the *mother*," he mocked in return.

"Really?" allied Jake, "I remember the odd casual fling but nothing you would call a girlfriend."

"No, Jake, sorry to say, Adam doesn't give his heart too easily, especially not since it has been broken."

The comment invoked a momentary silence.

"Let's not talk about it, hey mum?"

"Got yourself in quite a tizz with that Melissa girl didn't you…pretty girl, man eater though, you can tell the type, …"

Adam stayed quiet.

"…you really loved that girl, didn't you?"

Jake studied Adam from across the table, intrigued, he hadn't heard anyone talk this candidly about Melissa, at least not someone that had met her.

"Yes I did mum. I did very much, she hurt me more than I thought another person could. I'm not keen to repeat the process...if you remember it was a bad summer."

They all fell silent, the spectre of Adam's deceased father casting a gloom over the dinner once more. Jake noted that Melissa's recent return had not been discussed with Kathleen.

Mrs Rollason seized her opportunity to make a dramatic interjection,

"Oooh Kathleen," her voice floated over the fence, an almost startled tone to it, "I say Kathleen, I don't want to worry you but there seems to be three very large coloured gentlemen coming up your front path."

Jake's shocked face met Adam's, he shot out from behind the table and moved to the side of the house by the shed, and stayed low and close to the wall. Instinct told him that from there he could see down the narrow alley and to the back gate, which it was closed and bolted from the inside. As he moved back across the garden, Adam joined him, looking nervous and startled; together they moved into the side garden and watched to see if anyone appeared. An eerily silent pause followed.

Then they heard the voices.

Spilling out from inside the house growing louder as they neared the patio doors, came the unmistakable sound of Kathleen Warriner in conversation with a deep, slow and deliberate West Indian patois, the voices drifted into the garden.

"Well yes, please do come through to the back, luckily we've just finished lunch so, please don't worry you're not really interrupting."

"That's good, I'd hate to be an inconvenience, Sunday is such a family day."

Kathleen stepped out first, her short rounded frame the opposite of what followed. Mr G, 6ft 7 inch, complete with dreadlocks and attired in his signature white Fila track suit with white socks and black sandals. They emerged from the house out onto the patio, from shadow into light. Adam and Jake stood off to the side and watched as a diminutive Kathleen led Mr G towards the table. Beano, the colossus seal-like right hand man trailed obediently behind. Mr G, his eyes covered by huge white sunglasses, sported a chunky gold chain around his neck, his only element of bling. Beano's attire was identical to Mr G's with the exception that he had added considerably more bling around his neck and wrists. Like an out of shape Mr T.

"So how did you say you knew my Adam?"

"We're business associates of your boy and his friend Jake."

"Ooo well it must be an important bit of business if you are prepared to meet up on a Sunday, though Adam didn't mention he might be getting a visitor." She showed them to the table and offered them a seat with hand gestures, she then quickly busied herself tidying the last of the plates and dishes together.

"Well to be fair…" Mr G paused unsure what to call her, he had only found out Jake and Adam's first names. Kathleen made sure he didn't remain uncomfortable for long.

"Mrs Warriner…but seeing as you're a friend of Adam's then Kathleen is fine."

Mr G and Beano sat down, facing out into the garden. Kathleen turned around and saw Adam and Jake creeping in from the side garden and making their way back to the table.

"Oh there you are...I wondered what had happened to you two. Come on your business colleagues are here, come on, come and sit down and I'll get …oh I am sorry," she said turning back to her guests, "I don't know your names."

"This is Beano, the man out front with the car is Devon and I am Mr G."

"Mr G?"

"Correct."

"Is that all? I mean doesn't it stand for anything, I mean surely you can't have been christened that way?"

"No…I wasn't, but I am simply known as Mr G."

"Oh well very mysterious, are you in the music business, a rapper like that chap Dizzy Ice?"

Beano smiled as he interjected, "No, Mr G isn't in the music business Mrs Warriner, he's mostly into property and security services."

"I see, rather like Jake then?"

The four men exchanged glances.

"Just like Jake." Mr G said.

"Well boys?" she indicated to Jake and Adam who had now reached the table, "join Beano and …Mr G….at the table so you can talk business. I'll pop inside and make some lemonade. That would be refreshing for you on this hot day."

"That would be wicked," Beano enthusiastically responded, clicking his fingers as Kathleen moved into the house carrying the tray of used plates. Jake and Adam sat down at the table opposite the two black gangsters.

"Gentleman, I apologise for rudely interrupting your down time, I know it's a Sunday and we shouldn't discuss business on a Sunday, but needs must. Rest assured that I have instructed my man," he pointed at Beano, "to watch his fucking language around your mother," he gestured at Adam.

Adam nodded his appreciation.

"Before we get started I need to understand one thing for certain, Mickey Finn was not too clear in his definitions, who am I talking to?" he moved his hands from Jake to Adam.

Jake and Adam looked at each other for a moment, Adam looked Mr G squarely in the eye. "You'd be talking to me."

"Mickey said that was how things were. Fine. You know who I am?"

"You're Mr G - I believe the correct term would be, the main man?"

"Fucking A right he's the main mother fucker" Beano snorted the comment, it sounded like he had said it before, Mr G's fanfare.

"Beano...easy with the language...be nice, we're in a nice part of the world, I am not too sure where in the world we are but it's nice."

Beano's head dropped, chastised.

"These people aint seen too many brothers in their manor. No need to be hostile. Upsetting the natives is not part of the agenda." He lowered his sunglasses and looked hard at Beano over the top of them, who nodded compliance.

"I'll bet, Adam, you are wondering why I am here?" Adam indeed wondered how the hell they had found his mother's address!

"I am here because of Barry Hunt, I believe you have had some dealings with him?"

Jake sat very still, his hands in his lap under the table. He had managed to pull one of the steak knives they had used at dinner off the table and hid it in his lap. He assumed that both men would be carrying. He sussed out Beano, just because of his gargantuan size, he shouldn't be underestimated, but the bulk would be a disadvantage. The man out front was not an issue initially, he would have to get through the house before he could play any part in the proceedings, the risk would be that Kathleen would become his first target if anything went down. Don't make a move thought Jake, not until you can secure Kathleen. He had already formulated his strategy, if needed, he could be across the table and have the knife into Mr G's throat before anyone could pull a gun. He banked on the assumption that Beano's first reaction would be to protect Mr G and not go for Adam or Kathleen. Beano would be within range once Mr G had been taken out. Jake felt confident he could disarm and immobilise him before he could fire. Satisfied that he could handle the scenario should it come to it, Jake settled into watching the conversation.

"Not dealings…just one dealing," said Adam.

"I see, one dealing, the money dealing, the money his whore girlfriend stole from him, so he claimed."

"Yes…that's correct"

"This is the situation that Mickey came to resolve with you, the time you.." he pointed at Jake, "took mighty Mickey Finn to the ground and had over Jonno, leaving the punk in hospital."

Jake nodded but didn't smile, unsure how to react.

"The man who runs a lot of Winchester, the man with the muscle," Mr G cocked his head and nodded his respect to Jake.

"I have a few issues with recent occurrences, Barry's version of events is on one side, Mickey's version on the other, both delivered while in serious survival mode. For the most part I think Mickey is pretty clean in all this."

He paused, waiting for anyone to contradict him.

"He aint got the ambition to set all this up. No, I think the only way I can get some answers is from you, the Winchester boys!"

Adam swallowed hard. He tried to stay cool, to look and sound the part. When making business deals, dealing with other people's money it was crucial to watch their faces, see their eyes. Adam had always been good at reading people and thinking on his feet.

"We'll try to help, do all we can in fact. What would you like to know?"

"Where is Barry Hunt?"

Jake tensed, his jaw clenched and relaxed. Adam seemed unruffled.

"We'd like to find the man as well, Mr G," Adam said.

Mr G nodded, too deliberately for it to be convincing.

266

"You saw him last…right? Mickey set up a meet a couple of days ago, Friday, what happened at that meeting?"

Adam couldn't be sure what Mr G knew about the goings on of Friday night, the papers and news had reported the finding of two bodies in Bar End, but had not released any information about who had died. To lie about it, to deny it would be silly and tantamount to suicide; he needed to draw Mr G away from anything that implicated them beyond innocent parties. He had to assume that Mickey had given them the whole set up…Adam needed to go on the offensive.

"Barry Hunt, where do we start with him? It seems he has played everyone off against each other," Adam felt his heart rate quicken and voice waiver as he spoke.

"Tell me more."

"Well he spread this rumour amongst his people that a whore of his employ, Melissa Henderson, stole from him…it appears that was a ruse to keep Mickey and his men on side."

"She didn't steal his money?" Mr G asked.

"No… she did bring the cash to us, but on Barry's instructions, as a courier." Adam paused, needing to gather his thoughts and keen to let the news sink in. Lies work best in short bursts.

"She came down here to give us the down payment on a drugs deal…" Adam paused again, interested to see what effect this information had on Mr G. He noticed nothing he could use and had to continue.

267

"…we had a deal going with some continental colleagues. A bit too rich for our purse strings and well Barry's name got mentioned….he sort of came recommended."

"He came in on the deal?"

"Correct - Melissa came down and delivered the deposit money."

Mr G and Beano exchanged glances. Neither spoke and when their gaze returned to Adam, he felt obliged to continue with his story.

"The trouble was she came £100 grand light, she only had half of what was agreed…" Adam opened his arms in a 'what can you do gesture'.

"Now we immediately try to get hold of Barry… you know, to let him know we aren't happy about this."

"As you would…"

"Exactly, as you would! Next thing we know Mickey turns up looking for the girl and a missing £100 grand and gets all heavy with me…"

Adam caught a glimpse of Jake repositioning. Straitening his back, settling into the role of the heavy.

"Big Mickey, well he insinuates we've stolen from Barry… it's crazy talk." Jake joins in.

"Clearly Mickey is not tuned into the reality of the situation. We play along with him. In fact Barry tells us to humour him, and he'll pull him back and come down and deal with the situation himself."

Adam pauses, letting his brain move ahead of the conversation and work it all through. 'Keep it as close to the truth as you can' he repeated to himself.

Too late for that.

"What next?"

Mr G and Beano are slowly beginning to lean in to hear the rest of the tale. "Well…we're expecting Barry to turn up and explain why he's light and to also bring the rest of the money…We think the deal is still on. But instead, at the meeting, he goes a bit fruit loop…"

"Fruit loop?" A confused look on Mr G's face.

"Crazy, nuts," replies Jake.

Mr G nods his understanding as Beano chuckles.

"We're asking for the rest of the finance for a deal he stands to make a lot of money on and he starts blowing his top, shouting the odds, saying we had stolen the £100 grand and had killed off his girlfriend."

Adam paused again, tying up the loose ends in his head. Melissa is still implicated in the theft and he can now justify the shooting. "So we naturally deny all of this, the thing is the girl has done a runner, she did it the morning Mickey arrived in Winchester and got heavy with me…we can't produce the girl, Barry still thinks we nicked the cash and as we're now demanding that he stumps up more, he gets irate."

"Did you take the money?"

"No…we'd be insane to do that…why create a problem with a financier on a deal that could net us all five times the investment? That's no way to do business."

"Mmm, did Barry consider that maybe this Melissa had really pinched £100 grand from the deposit ?"

"Who knows? We should have gotten £200 grand but we only got a hundred from her, maybe she nicked it, maybe he never gave it to her and kept it for himself, we'll never know for certain."

Mr G pushed a paw of a hand around his chin in contemplation of what Adam had told him.

"…So what was my end in this deal of yours, Barry would have mentioned me?" Mr G asked.

"Your end…? This deal was a solo project, whatever Barry's allegiances are, or what he owes you, we didn't know about them. As far as we're concerned it was just Barry, sorry, we only know about you because Barry threatened us with your wrath if we didn't deliver the money and the girl back." Adam rested, he could see in Beano's eyes that the story had begun to fly, he had to continue exposing Barry. The duplicity in what Barry had been telling his own people, the inside information from Melissa combined to give Adam the upper hand. He had to be careful he didn't over do it.

Beano looked from Mr G to Adam, then to Jake and back again, his fat head glistening, he had started sweating profusely.

"Mr G," he began, "Barry was seriously fucked for money, the manor is bankrupt, Rodney says the place is a mess. The facts

270

support our man here. I don't think he ever gave her the money, he was stiffing them like he was stiffing us."

Beano paused to pant.

"He's told everyone this girl robbed him, but where is the girl? I spoke to some of Mickey's monkey employees, apparently he was shouting about her all the time. It's a distraction to buy time from us, from Mickey, from these boys. He's trying to buy enough time to get himself sorted….it kind of all adds up man!"

Mr G sat back and reviewed the situation. He hadn't known what to expect from these provincial villains, and so far he was impressed. They had arrived at Bar J and made themselves known. The place looked well run and the heavies came across as very professional. They hadn't been able to get hold of Jake or Adam, but knew where they were. It seemed fishy but they gave directions and let them drive off to Adam's mother's house, they had explained the situation and asked them to be respectful of it.

Mr G had agreed.

He had also agreed to them being followed. Now, sitting out at the front of the house, four of Jake's men watched the proceedings.

Mr G had liked the fact that they had come to protect their bosses, had acted without direction and looked like they meant business. He liked the manner of these two men, away from work, spending time with Adam's mother, it felt right.

Mr G liked their attitude.

Men you can do business with.

271

He did something unusual; he took his sunglasses off. Adam felt a twinge of victory, it meant Mr G had bought the story, he believed in Adam. Normally by now he'd get the paperwork out and sell a policy.

"Tell me what happened at the end of the meeting, how did two men die and where's Barry now?"

Jake sat forward and answered, "I'm in charge of security, you understand that we never take any situation lightly, we prepared for several eventualities..."

"This I can believe, my man," nodded Mr G.

"Well, at the meeting, things got heated, Barry was irrational and unhappy with our assertions. To cut a long story short, Barry pulled out a machine pistol and began waving it around, he had one of his guys with him, the other was in the car at the wheel, he shot into the air a few times trying to scare us."

Jake paused and looked at Adam, who nodded, as if confirming he should continue. It looked like plausible interplay.

"We simply said, fuck this and decided to head out of there. Barry went to shoot at us, his own man grabbed his arm, we think he was trying to stop him. We had chosen somewhere pretty public, to avoid this kind of thing. We're professional."

Beano nodded.

"The gun goes off as they wrestle, it shoots through the window of that silly Lexus they drove, killing the driver. I'm not exactly sure what happened next but from what we can gather the car was in gear, it lurched forward and knocked down Barry and the other guy. It killed the other guy, his body was found at the scene."

"Barry?"

Adam took over, "we think Barry made it away, he wasn't at the scene when the police arrived, we assume he's alive and very much on the run."

"If you wait a few days you'll see the police reports will corroborate what we've said," Jake chimed in as if perfectly on cue.

The clink of glasses on a tray broke them from their conversation. Kathleen reappeared from the house with a tray and a huge jug of lemonade. Mr G got to his feet and helped her with the tray.

"It's not as chilled as it should be, but lots of ice to make up for it. Beano, why don't you play mum, you look like you could do with a cool drink."

Beano didn't hesitate; he clambered to his feet and began pouring the lemonade out for all of them.

"So Mr G… oh dear I am sorry, a woman of my age really can't call someone Mr G, it sounds simply ridiculous. Please tell me your real name…?"

Mr G smiled, a broad genial and warm grin, lots of teeth and gums, and his dark eyes danced.

"It's Winston Goodmans…Kathleen."

"How lovely, well now that does feel a lot more comfortable. I suppose Beano, that comes from the children's comic does it...?" Beano nodded.

"Beryl the Peril and the Bash Street Kids...Adam loved that comic."

Beano his mouth full with cooling ice shrugged a smile.

"Beautiful garden you have here Kathleen," Mr G remarked.

"It's not your usual country cottage style is it?"

"Good lord no, can't stand all those pansies and forget-me-knots. Far too twee."

"No Kathleen I don't see you as twee..."

Mr G rose from the table and held out his arm,

"Kathleen would you do me the pleasure of strolling with me, around your wonderful estate?" Kathleen threw her head back and laughed, "delighted to," she took his arm and headed for the far side.

"I have zoned the garden," she said, "up near the house are my Mediterranean plants, they need that extra warmth and protection from the cold you see. I have a lovely olive tree in a big planter, it should give some olives this year, over to the right is my savannah, pampas grasses and New Zealand silver ferns. I adore the tree fern, a mighty beast isn't he?"

Mr G inspected the six foot high brown ridged mast with its crown of green feathery fern fronds, genuinely impressed.

"What's that wonderful looking tree over there?" he pointed at a willowy tree about ten feet high, with graceful reddish brown leaves. It had a slender sway of branches and a rounded, layered foliage canopy that looked soft and inviting.

"That's an Acer Palmatum, or Japanese Maple, stunning isn't it? I have three, look at the big fellow at the back." She pointed to another Acer, redder with white tipped fronds that stood on the left of the garden in the shade of a maturing eucalyptus tree.

"They seem to be growing well." Mr G ran his hand up through the foliage, caressing the feathery leaves.

"Slowly but surely Winston. They are quite delicate, it mustn't be too hot or too cold, they need protection from the frost. As with anything though, the more you put in the more you get out. Very slow growing, but in twenty to thirty years they will be magnificent".

Mr G looked at it and tried to imagine this fragile looking tree at over fifty feet tall with cascading branches and billowing leaves. "It's always the way with wonderful gardens, someone has to have the vision to start them, lay the foundations, and ultimately it's others that reap the rewards." He said it thinking back to his father.

Beano, Jake and Adam trailed behind them as she took Mr G through the full array of plants, the tranquil but odd village scene, only broken by the shrill shriek of Mrs Rollason.

"I say Kathleen, is everything ok?"

Kathleen rolled her eyes. "Yes, everything is fine, why shouldn't it be?"

"Oh well no reason dear, but one gets alarmed when, er, um strangers come to call, and there are some other gentleman in a big car just sitting outside on the verge…"

Mr G patted Kathleen's arm, "they are friends of Mr Simons."

Kathleen nodded and Jake looked at the rest of them.

"You have a good team Mr Simons." Mr G said.

"Professional," agreed Beano.

Jake nodded his excuses and made a hasty exit to the front of the house, appeased that any immediate danger had passed.

"They are not strangers Mrs Rollason, at least not to me…They are colleagues of my son, he's conducting some serious business today, aren't you Adam."

"I am," called back Adam, trying to sound authoritative.

"Well I am here if you need me, I'll keep an eye out…"

Kathleen took Mr G's arm and walked away from the fence and Mrs Rollason. "I am sorry about that," she said embarrassed.

"Don't be, we're very aware that looking like we do, Beano and I make the average white middle class neighbourhood a little jumpy." Kathleen nodded,

"Well that's good of you, you see I'm not 100% sure but I think you're the first black person Mrs Rollason has ever seen in real life..."

"Sad, but probably true," Adam added.

276

The group gathered around a large oddly placed Pampas grass so that Beano could touch the soft cotton-like flower, it had been a life long wish apparently.

Mr G took the chance to get Adam alone.

"I need to talk to you about the deal you had with Barry."

"Ok."

"What exactly is he financing?" Mr G had broken away from the group and had his arm around Adam's shoulders, guiding him slowly towards the back fence and some privacy. Adam knew this could be a pivotal moment.

"10 kilos of cocaine, Barry's finance was £200 grand, we were in charge of bringing the stuff in and the provincial distribution. Barry was responsible for the London distribution, 5 kilos for that purpose."

Adam tried to sound matter of fact and knowledgeable.

"But he wasn't going to use my connections and he couldn't push that much coke through his London dealers without me knowing, he must have had another crew involved …who are they?"

"I don't know, what he did with it, I didn't care, not my concern you see."

"Just a supply chain…right."

"Yeah" said Adam, "trouble is I don't have all the money to complete the deal…my suppliers will not be happy bunnies."

"Barry is a foolish man, stretched himself thin, he got greedy. He needn't have been greedy. If I invite people to the trough, there is always enough to go around."

Mr G turned and faced Adam, they stood chest to chest, but he didn't stoop, just looked down on the smaller man.

"I can't have my people making deals of this size, and this is sizeable, without my approval."

Adam nodded he understood.

"He must have another London firm involved. That undermines the status quo, causes a big surge of product and drives the prices down." Mr G flicked his long dreadlocks off his shoulders and looked out across the fields over the fence.

"I don't blame you Adam, you're a business man, you do business, this is a good deal…my irritation is with Barry, not you…"

Adam breathed a silent sigh of relief, and enjoyed the view with Mr G.

"There is no issue with you and your crew… but you don't have expansion ambitions do you?" A smile etched on his face.

"Strictly south of Basingstoke…we don't want to mess with the big boys."

"Hahahh why not man, look how well you're doing…" Mr G put his arm on Adam's shoulder and looked hard at him, the smile gone, the eyes focused.

"I want you to find out who this other London firm is. If Barry is using a rival then I can't afford for that to happen. I need

278

to find out who they are…it's time the G-Men sent a message to London, time to clean house and make people understand I'm still top dog."

"What do you want from us?"

"I'll give you £200 grand, so you can complete the deal…but you find me Barry Hunt, do whatever you have to. Make a new deal with his London contact. We'll hatch a little plan; I want all the rats in a trap."

"I understand, I think we can set the deal up, give you the names…"

"No, I want to catch them in the act Adam, I want them to think they have done it, got away with it. They can have their five minutes of feeling like the big man, I'll enjoy taking it away."

Adam licked his lips and looked back out across the fields, and wondered if Mr G saw them the same way he did, he doubted he could. Adam had just committed himself to the eradication, the assassination of goodness knows how many people, all he had to be sure of was that Jake and his mum would not be next in line.

Adam looked up at the giant man, now smiling the biggest smile he had seen. He turned around and looked back up the garden and waved at his mum, she had Beano kneeling over her flowerbeds helping to pull vine-weed away from her beloved Acer Palmatum.

Chapter Twenty Four

"I don't believe you… I really don't."

Jake's anger had risen slowly but surely on the drive to his house, his temper under control, but his face a redder hue than usual.

"We're now in bloody cahoots with London's biggest gangland boss…how for fucks sake did you manage that one?"

Adam sat at Jake's breakfast bar sipping a cup of coffee. He'd had time to reflect on the day's events during the silent journey from his mother's house. Mr G and Beano had finally left around 4.30pm, with a Japanese Maple cutting and some leftover pork in a doggy bag. His mum hadn't asked about the business that had been done and Adam still wasn't sure what she may have heard, but she seemed glad when Adam had said it went well. She had cast her eye over the jobs they had done and commended Jake on his workmanship. Jake fidgeted noticeably, itching to leave. His mother saw the signs and bade them a fond farewell, Adam promising to stop by during the week for 'tea'.

"I didn't plan for Mr G to turn up. I was just trying to tie up those loose ends, not knowing who knows what made it somewhat tricky…I got us out of one hole…"

"Only to land us in another…" Jake's voice was on the rise.

"I know it isn't ideal…" soothed Adam.

"Ideal…this is so far from ideal," Jake balled his hands into fists in frustration, "it isn't even in the same country Adam. Can I remind you that we're implicated in the murder of two thugs at Bar End last week, have a naked, disgraced gangland boss in my storage shed, who by the way we have to move…he's begun needing the toilet…and now you have agreed to set up a meeting with a rival London gang, to sell them out to another gang….oh no, it's top notch this, sodding spot on."

Adam understood Jake's feelings but he seemed to be missing the bigger picture. Their plans had to be flexible, to change with the unfolding scenarios around them.

"I have it all worked out, we will walk away from this in a few days each of us with a serious amount of cash, virtually no one will know of our involvement and we'll be able to return to our normal lives."

Jake looked across at his grinning friend, confused by how calm and relaxed he appeared. Adam had mutated from the scared and vulnerable friend being beaten up by Mickey Finn a few days ago, into a scheming, totally at home player in a very dangerous game.

"Adam, you understand Mr G is going to kill them. He's going to take them out… Barry too, when you hand him over…you must realise that."

"What else could I do?"

"Barry and Melissa know that all you have said is a lie…" Jake's voice had dropped to a near whisper.

"They do, but they are completely discredited, no one will believe anything they have to say. Mr G will put anything they say down to them simply trying to save their skins."

"You sure of that?"

"As far as he's concerned we're straight shooters." Adam said.

Jake thought for a moment, weighing up Adam's story.

"And what about Mickey? Mr G seems happy to believe he's not involved.

"Mickey has made his play to ensure Barry gets all the blame... our lies help him in his play.."

"And Melissa?"

"We don't need to worry about her..."

"She can still spoil this..." Jake raised his eyebrows as he said it, searching his friend's face for any clues.

"About Melissa...is there something you want to tell me?"

"Tell you what?"

"I don't know, today was the first time I had heard you use the 'love' word in describing how you felt about her."

"Emphasis on felt, past tense! I don't love her anymore." Adam avoided Jake's gaze and focused on his coffee. Jake studied him harder.

"That's a lie Adam. This girl pitched up out of the blue, she gets you involved in all this...you appear to meekly follow, but then start acting like a midget Godfather...I don't buy that."

Adam's head reared a little at the slight on his stature.

"I don't care what you do or don't 'buy' to be honest, my feelings for Melissa are complicated, that much I'll admit. You don't just stop loving someone, no matter how much of a shit they are, no matter what they put you through."

"My neck is on the line in all of this Adam. I can't help feeling she's at the heart of it all. She can't help what she does, it's just her."

"I may not like her anymore, but there is a part of me, a tiny bit tucked down deep that will always love her...you can't understand that unless you have truly been in love."

Jake missed the jibe back at him, he didn't understand, he had major concerns for the whole volatile situation already, without Adam's deep rooted feelings of love coming to the surface. Jake decided to change tack.

"You didn't mention the deaths...being responsible for the deaths..."

"I'm not responsible for anyone or anything that happens to them. They live by the sword then they might die by it."

Adam threw the words down attempting to be as flippant as he could muster. "The Petrovs were doing a deal with Barry long before we got involved, we're just another cog in the works. These people all knew what they were getting involved with..."

"Its not that simple. Promise me something..." asked Jake. "What?"

"Your objective is to get us, you and me, out of this safely..."

Adam shuffled off his seat and stood flexing his back.

"I want to be out of this safely, but richer than when I started…"

Jake gritted his teeth and paused.

"There's more at stake here than just…money," he spat the words out, the disgust written on his face.

Adam sneered back at his friend.

"Don't pretend to me for one minute you didn't want the money too…or are you simply in it for the fight?"

Jake stared coldly at his friend.

"I am in it because you are my friend, no more, no less."

An icy chill of realisation descended over the room.

"Adam, we had a chance today, we could have told Mr G a version of the truth, handed over Barry and said we don't any part of this…"

Adam said nothing.

"We've no obligation to the Petrovs. You could have handed them on a plate to Mr G as well… We could be out and free of hassle."

Adam said nothing.

"Instead we're still playing gangster, but on two fronts. The Petrovs and Mr G. We're about to be drug dealers and party to murder…"

Adam ignored his friend and focused on an abstract print on the wall.

"I have seen death, been around it, and been responsible for it...personally and as a commander. You haven't."

Adam lowered his head but faced away from Jake.

"If you think you can dismiss it and wash your hands of it, let me assure you, you are very wrong."

Adam looked at his friend; he rarely spoke about his past, even refused to make reference to it. Like a dirty family secret Jake kept it hidden as if it had no place being a part of his new life. Adam could see the fear in his eyes and that worried him.

He coughed a little.

"We were party to murder the moment Barry refused to take the bag, that was the moment we were no longer unlucky innocents caught up in this madness, I'm just playing the options..." Adam said.

He had come from around the breakfast bar and he and Jake were now in the centre of his large kitchen either side of the island unit.

"Yeah but why did Barry flip out...he just had to walk away?" asked Jake.

"You said yourself that Barry was on flip out mode that night, look at what we heard today, Barry was beyond desperate, he wanted to pick on us, he was on the wrong end of a shit storm and he thought, 'fuck this, let's have over some little prick.' You can always find someone to pick on. Well I'm not up for being picked on, I don't want to be bullied anymore, not by that cocksucker or any other like him."

285

Adam pounded the island unit top with his clenched fist.

"Life has kicked me enough fucking times without fresh monkeys coming in to have a go…" Adam was shouting, as loud as he could, unconcerned about being heard, careless of the impression it gave. His face red and fists clenched, Adam looked like he was about to explode.

Jake sensing the inevitable eruption, backed away from the kitchen island and turned to the sink under the window… he could still feel Adam's violent eyes boring into his back. Absentmindedly he turned on the taps and washed his hands. Ten, twenty seconds passed, then he turned back to face the room. Adam had returned to the breakfast bar and was finishing his now cold coffee.

"Adam, have you heard the fable, the one about the frog and the scorpion?"

Adam shook his head.

"It's an Aesop one I think – a morality tale… I was told it once…while being held prisoner…" his voice tailed off and into a whisper. Adam turned and looked at his friend.

"Maybe it was where and when I heard it that makes it seem significant, but it's just something I have always remembered…"

"What's it about?"

"Whatever you want to take from it I suppose…it made me look at people and see something else. Something they weren't projecting – the real them. It goes like this…One day, a scorpion

286

set out on a journey through the forests and hills. He climbed over rocks and under bushes and kept going until he reached a river. The river ran wide and fast, and the scorpion stopped to consider a way to cross. He ran upriver and then checked downriver, all the while thinking that he might have to turn back.

On the river bank he saw a frog perched amongst some reeds. He decided to ask the frog for help getting across the river. 'Hello Mr. Frog!' called the scorpion, 'Would you be so kind as to give me a ride on your back across the river?'

'Well now, Mr. Scorpion! How do I know that if I help you, you won't try to *kill* me?' asked the frog.

'Because,' the scorpion replied, 'If I try to kill you, then I would die too, because I cannot swim!'

Now this seemed to make sense to the frog. But he asked. 'What about when I get close to the far bank? You could still try to kill me and get back to the shore.'

'This is true,' said the scorpion, 'but then I wouldn't be able to get to the other side of the river!'

'Alright then...how do I know you won't just wait till we get to the other side and THEN kill me?' said the frog.

'Ahh...' said the scorpion, 'because you see, once you've taken me to the other side of this river, I will be so grateful for your help, that it would hardly be fair to reward you with death, now would it?'" Adam smirked at the simplistic tale and the enthusiasm of its telling. Jake, unaware of the real reaction he was getting, persevered.

"So the frog agreed to take the scorpion across the river. He swam over to the bank and settled himself near the mud to pick up his passenger. The scorpion crawled onto the frog's back and the frog slid into the river. The muddy water swirled around them, but the frog stayed near the surface so the scorpion would not drown. He kicked strongly through the first half of the stream, his flippers paddling wildly against the current.

Halfway across the river, the frog suddenly felt a sharp sting in his back and, out of the corner of his eye, saw the scorpion remove his stinger from his back. A deadening numbness began to creep into his limbs.

'You fool!' croaked the frog, 'Now we shall both die! Why on earth did you do that?'

The scorpion shrugged, and did a little dance on the drowning frog's back. 'I could not help myself. It's my nature…'

Adam blinked self consciously several times and stared into the bottom of his coffee mug. When he looked up, keen to end the silence, his friend was staring out of the window, transfixed by the memory of when he first heard the fable.

"Where were you when you heard that?

"A big hole in the ground…waiting to die."

Adam fumbled with his watch, unsure what to say and how to react.

"What does it mean to you Jake?" Adam asked.

"Oh nothing specific I suppose…just that someone's true nature can't be changed…"

"Do you see yourself as the frog or the scorpion?"

"It's not that literal…not for me anyway. It's a metaphor for life and the nature of the people you meet."

Jake mulled over the fable and Adam's reaction. He thought about what Adam had said earlier, and better understood Adam's behaviour now, but he still didn't care for it.

"It makes me think of the day I found my father…"

A long time ago, when they had first met, both men had shared their sorrow at losing their fathers.

"How?" asked Adam.

Jake shrugged, "Oh I suppose I just wonder what it was about my father that made him commit suicide... stress, pressures of life or maybe he would always just self destruct. I don't know."

Adam thought about how Jake had described discovering his father in the cellar, no one else was home when his father fastened a rope to the cross-beam and stepped off the wooden crate. Only the ten year old Jake could have discovered the body. It seemed to Jake as if his father had planned it that way.

"Life is what you make it Jake. No fate, no luck. It's what it is. People are the same," said Adam.

"Maybe. That would be sad if it was true."

The two men stood in silence, looking at different corners of the room as if they might offer some answers. Eventually Jake broke the spell that held them.

"What are we going to do with the drugs?"

"What drugs?"

"When we make the deal…oh I suppose the drugs will simply go to Mr G." Jake said.

"Yeah, in Barry's original deal he was buying drugs from the Petrovs, in our version, Mr G thinks we're supplying the drugs to the Petrovs for them to distribute. So Mr G thinks he's paid for us to complete the deal and thus set up the Petrovs…"

"You still haven't heard from Mel either?"

"Nothing…"

"How much money is involved now?"

"£300 grand."

"Jesus…"

"Mr G has given us £200 hundred grand for the drugs and information.."

"And we've the £100 grand from Barry…" said Jake.

"Correct."

"I've got it all planned, all you need to do is go and see the Petrovs and make the deal…" said Adam.

"Easy Peasey…." Jake said under his breath.

Chapter Twenty Five

Jake sat motionless in the little waiting room. His palms had begun that gentle journey from clammy to sweaty. He'd overloaded on antiperspirant, hoping to combat the unusually searing heat of the day and his nervousness. His heart thumped and the adrenalin spread through him. While it wasn't the same as the covert and battle operations he had seen before, it was having the same effect on him.

It didn't look like the headquarters of a London gang, but then Jake didn't really know what that should look like. He'd been sitting in the little room on the uncomfortably chic chair for the last twenty minutes, and could sense them watching him, the little CCTV camera didn't scan the room, it just sat motionless in the corner, like a predatory mechanical spider, never shifting its suspicious gaze from him.

Twice, a squat diminutive man of undoubtedly East European extraction had shuffled in, had a bit of a stare and shuffled out again. The man must have boxed at some point, his ears were cauliflowered and the nose so misshapen it looked like it had been moulded by a child from Play-dough. Jake weighed up his chances, if he had to he knew he could take the man out.

Jake had studied what he could of the building before he had entered. The façade was of a genuine place of work and meant the exit to the street would generally be clear and that this waiting room should remain open. The large glass windows meant a clear view in and out of this reception area. Every good soldier likes to know his exit points.

He hadn't seen beyond the door, to his right, the exit and entry point for his squat friend. It presented itself as a standard heavy security door, the sort that required a code punched into it to open, like the ones you see at banks and gyms. Jake surmised that there couldn't be too much space behind the door as the actual building was not of any significant size. However the shop front only occupied a small proportion of the frontage, which it shared with other outlets. How much of the subsequent space the Petrovs owned could only be guessed at.

The security door swung open and the squat man emerged yet again, this time followed by a sharp faced, petite blonde, the peroxide yellow hair and features indicating a nordic origin. She reminded Jake of a mixture of Dolly Parton and a gonk.

"Mr Simons, hello. Welcome. Sorry for the delay. I am Irena Petrov. Before I can take you through, I must insist that Dmitri search you."

She made no offer to shake hands.

Jake stood up and stepped away from the low slung reception chair. He put his arms out wide and Dmitri began his rough and inexpert search. Jake had been counting on this; in the small of his back under his jeans he carried a small flat handled four inch hunting knife.

Dmitri nodded, satisfied with his efforts. Jake followed Irena through the security door, Dmitri close behind him. Jake calculated risk and escape opportunity. As the former rose so the latter became harder. He kept repeating the same mantra over and over "*it's just business*".

He focused on trying to act cool and remain calm, but inside his chest his heart pounded and his palms had completed the journey to sweaty. They walked no more than ten paces before climbing a set of steel-lined stairs to the next floor. A few steps along the upper corridor Irena turned right into an open door which she shut after Jake had entered. Dmitri was left outside guarding the door.

Behind the desk sat a slightly older but similar looking woman to Irena, they weren't twins, this one looked older thought Jake, but because they wore identical pink blouses and blue chalk stripe trouser suits they could almost pass for twins.

"Come in Jake, come in. Please do sit down, these chairs are more comfortable than the ones in reception." Her accent, though clipped East European, had lost some of that traditional hardness.

"Thank you for coming to see my sister and me today, I am Irma, the eldest and prettiest, I am sure you would agree…?"

Jake smiled, "I can assure you that I learned long ago not to judge one lady and certainly not sisters against each other."

"What a nice polite young man, hey Irma. My sister said she thought you were very handsome, I'm afraid we have to confess to a little spying on our CCTV."

"I assumed as much...not to worry; security is an important part of life."

"It is isn't it, I'm glad you said that."

The segue lacked subtlety, Jake concluded that small talk and flirtation were character traits that the Petrov sisters rarely practised.

"This is why we demand that we meet, you see, we know Barry, we are secure in our relationship with him, well, as secure as you can be..." Irma faltered.

Secure? thought Jake.

"So you understand, we're careful of new people?" Irena smiled picking up where her sister left off. As she smiled she revealed polished and capped white teeth. Irena joined her sister sitting on the window ledge behind the desk. She's the prettier one thought Jake, but that amounted to the same as choosing between a rock and a hard place.

"We appreciate that this situation is not ideal."

The sisters didn't protest.

"We understand the predicament that Barry has put you in," he offered.

"You do?" asked Irena.

"Sure... but to be fair to Barry, he needs to find a way to make the deal go through, not to leave anyone out of pocket."

"Why so concerned?" Irma asked, her peroxide mane glistened in the morning sun which shafted through the window. Jake shifted his chair to avoid the glare.

"I think, I know - he believes that this will ensure we all remain friends... and not his enemies." The sisters chimed in together.

Jakes words felt false and he knew they sounded contrived, he lacked Adam's style in these sort of situations. He preferred his enemy to come armed with weapons not words.

He cleared his throat, "I'm glad we understand each other."

Irma stood, she straightened her suit jacket and flicked a stray hair from her shoulder. She missed several others, the hair gave the appearance she had started moulting.

"We worry," she began. " that we never done business with you before."

"We presume our money is as good as Barry's?"

Irma looked hard at him, her eyes piercing.

"There are other issues?"

Jake nodded; keen to move the process along and cover off the points he and Adam had rehearsed.

"Agreeing and understanding the distribution boundaries!" He and Adam had decided that they should go on the offensive, strong conversation would be more effective than passive.

"Yes...that is main one." Irma suppressed her surprise and delight at the straight talking Jake had introduced.

"We will stay south of Basingstoke." Jake pushed on.

"To the east and west?" Irena asked on behalf of her sister.

"We'd like to spread as far as the east coast and round up to the Thames Estuary. West? Well we would be interested in going as far as Bournemouth and up to Swindon." Irena nodded, her appreciation of English Geography had improved in recent months.

"West – that would cover Reading and Slough." Irma said.

"No, we'd not entertain either. We assumed they were off limits."

"They are..you are wise to ignore them."

Jake knew it was all just a game, but he wanted to stress he had no interest in Slough.

"A half circle around London… You will have locals to deal with."

Jake nodded. "Undoubtedly…we'll cope."

Irma smiled her shiny capped smile. "I'm sure you will."

Jake liked having the upper hand, he wanted to press on and wrap it up.

"My concern is over quality…,"

Jake thought of what Adam had kept repeating to him, '*We're saving the day, they need us more than we need them…*'

"Our concern is money."

"We're good for it…when can you deliver?"

Irma and Irena swapped a look. Jake noticed and shifted in his chair. "The merchandise is ready, is waiting." Irma said.

"I presume you are still able to provide a sample?"

Irma moved behind her sister, plucked at a stray hair of hers, her sharp eyes now scanning every movement Jake made.

"You would like a sample? Barry had a sample already."

Jake didn't break her gaze, "Good for Barry."

He held firm, despite two sets of eyes boring into him.

"We need a sample…it's not negotiable."

Irena leaned back and whispered into her sister's ear, they nodded almost together, without further words Irena skipped lightly round the desk, flashed a bright smile at Jake and left the room.

The room fell silent and Irma and Jake held their respective poses.

"It's good you have no ambitions inside the M25."

"Yes," replied Jake, "it appears crowded."

Irma tilted her head in recognition.

"Is best you stay away from Reading, Staines and Slough, the small local gangs have made these nasty places, impossible to run a business like ours."

Jake simply nodded his compliance.

"With regards to receiving the full merchandise and given this is our first occasion doing business together we had hoped we could use a handover venue away from London and perhaps agree some handover rules?"

"Why would you not collect from here?"

Barry's warning echoed in his mind, *'bunch of press gangers really – as likely to hi-jack someone else's deal and nick the loot as to do any real work themselves.'*

"Going here or there adds extra security risk." she finished. Jake had prepared for the question, Adam and he had worked through all of the options and scenarios when they had come up on the train earlier that day. They had to control the meeting and the logistics.

"Yes it does add a little extra security risk, but that is a security risk we will share once we've collected ..." he cleared his throat, desperate for a glass of water.

"The reason is it simply gives us a means of protecting ourselves, we're cautious people, like you, we wouldn't want anyone to think that perhaps keeping the money and the merchandise would be a good idea."

It bordered on an accusation, it certainly felt like an insinuation to Jake.

Irma showed no emotion. "We would have the same concern."

"Yes...but as the seller, it's polite to go to the buyer, especially those that don't want to upset the London, er, status quo. You agree?"

He hoped it would be the killer blow.

The door clicked open and Irena entered, in her hand a small plastic bag tied with a twistex. She immediately joined her sister on the other side of the desk and handed the bag to her. Jake eyed it and licked his lips the once, he had never taken cocaine in his life, sure he'd seen it done, in his business you couldn't get away from the stuff.

"Here is your sample." Irena put it on the desk half way between them, forcing Jake to lean forward, almost rising from the chair to pick it up. As he did so, Irma whispered over her shoulder to her sister again. They engaged in a short rapid conversation in their native tongue. Jake took the bag and simply slipped it into his jacket pocket. He figured they would be discussing the handover request.

The sisters looked up at him a little bewildered.

"You said you wanted a sample…please feel free."

Jake tapped the packet in his pocket, cocked his head a little to one side and flashed a brief smile.

"I don't," he said.

"Never have…we've people that will check it."

"People? What People?" Irena asked.

"We simply call him the Alchemist, he'll let us know the purity and value, I'm sure there will be no problem."

Irena and Irma were still for a moment.

"There will be no issues Jake" Irena said, sounding but not looking offended. "We don't sell bad shit…you told my sister you want handover point outside of London…"

"Yes.We need to agree the rules.."

"You want to agree the rules?" Irma asked smirking.

"Why do we need rules?" Irena followed quickly on from her bemused sister.

Jake took his turn to raise his hands in a gesture of placatory good will.

"Forgive my total Englishness, but I want to be comfortable with the arrangements and I want you to be happy as well, but as the buyer…you understand?"

Irena raised her eyebrows, she could sense that Irma wasn't comfortable with the added complications, her own interest lay in the fact that this man held the key to their futures…the location of Barry Hunt.

"Where had you in mind?" she said keen now to end the meeting.

"Well we're from the south of England, as you know. There is a disused old airfield near the village of Micheldever, it's about ten minutes from the M3, quite open and yet quiet and secluded." He reached into his brown leather man-bag and brought out a piece of A4 paper in a plastic sleeve.
"Here's a map to it." He handed them the Multimap printout.

"Shall we say Wednesday? And one vehicle each, from either side…" Jake added.

Silence as they stared at the map.

"I am not happy with this plan, this adds costs to the deal…" Irma said.

Jake let out an exaggerated sigh.

"Are we to haggle on the price?"

"Complications add risk, risk adds cost…the price just went up…add £25,000 to our deal." The words felt forced and angry to Jake.

"That is a little steep…"

"Fine, pay nothing more and we do the handover here in office?" Irma grinned a sadistic smile. Jake waited a moment, never play your hand early.

"Is something else you can use as payment?" Irena asked, seizing on the opportunity.

"Like?" said Jake.

"Barry Hunt."

Jake held his expression, not letting on the fact that he was happy they had reached this topic without the need for him to raise it.

"You want Barry?"

"We want to be certain Barry is not an issue."

"Barry Hunt is a dangerous for us, we would very much like to control that danger," stated Irma.

"What is he worth?"

Irma smiled, Jake liked the look of success on Irma's face. Winning small battles doesn't mean you win wars he thought. Barry was the ace in the hole.

"If we had Barry, well we'd re-think the extra costs." Irma felt the shot of adrenalin pump through her heart. It made her feel hungry. Getting hold of Barry Hunt would mean they had the key to unlock their ambitions in south London.

Jake couldn't hide his satisfaction that he hadn't had to force them to the handover with the lure of Barry. Irma picked up on it immediately.

"You seem confident you can get us Barry," she said.

"I am," he said without hesitation.

The sisters greeted the confident reply with silence, their brains processing Jake's confidence and assessing what it meant.

Irma wanted to ask more, she liked to deal in certainties. Jake cut the debate short.

"We'll deliver Barry or come armed with another £25,000."

Irma let out a slow blink.

"Fine," she said.

He knew he'd started to fidget, keen to leave.

"One vehicle is fine, how many people?" Irma said, putting aside her worries now the prospect of a deal had become a greater reality.

"I suggest no more than five, we don't want to be crowded now."

"What time?" Irena asked quickly.

"How about noon, high noon." Jake smiled as genuinely as he could manage.

"You think there may be a big gun fight?" Irma smirked back at him. Jake sat up in his chair; her eyes were beginning to get to him.

"I really hope not, we want a quick trade off."

"I was joking about gun fight Jake."

"Yes. I must insist you both attend. No proxies. I will be there and so will my partner, I have always felt there is less likelihood of silliness if we conduct the process personally."

"Agreed." Irena didn't let her sister answer, she was so excited at the prospect of getting her hands on Barry. As she made the statement she rose from her seated position behind her sister. Jake stood up as well and made ready to leave.

Irena joined him and was about to show him to the door, when Irma waved her hand a little and her sister relented.

"Where is Barry now, Jake."

Jake turned to face her and thought back to his preparation with Adam. "Safe, Ms Petrov."

"Irma please, we are friends. You say "We", who is this We?"

Irena questioned from Jake's side.

"I am in a partnership, no man is an island…I head up the logistics side of our business, my partner is finance."

"I like this saying, no man is an island, and can you use women instead of man."

"Yes Irena, woman or man, the meaning is the same, we can't stand alone, we need others."

"My sister and I are not islands Jake…you understand?" Irma raised her eyebrows.

Jake simply nodded, now standing, he'd made the decision to leave, risen from his seat and wanted to move to the door.

"You know that Barry is not in control of his manor?"

Jake said nothing.

"That Mr G has declared him a wanted man…?"

Jake tried to look unsurprised.

"Makes sense…." he said.

"Barry's problems have created opportunity for us and for you…"

Irma tried a coy look, but managed only to look odd.

303

"If Barry is finished for sure, it offers bigger opportunities for ambitious people?" Irma let the statement hang in the air for a moment, Jake felt the urge to reiterate his position more clearly.

"We've no ambitions in London." He looked them both in the eye, "This is definitely a one-off deal for us."

"Sure, sure…, but Barry's old manor holds potential. You would agree."

"Yes it does, but Mr G controls that. Right?"

Irma and Irena nodded together.

"He's dangerous Jake, making an enemy of him is silly game to play," Irena said in support of her sister. They moved towards him together, small steps, appearing to look delicate and petite beside the vast desk; but trying to impose their will on the large man in front of them.

Jake sought to hold them off. "I would have thought that the person that delivered Barry Hunt to Mr G, dead or alive, would have a much greater chance of impressing their credentials to take over in Barry's absence."

The sisters stopped, and smiled.

"We know this."

Jake understood what they had been getting at.

"We wish to stay out of Mr G's radar…" he ventured, looking for a reaction.

"We've no desire or ambition to be connected with him.." he continued.

The sisters nodded their appreciation of Jake's commitment.

"Barry is a loose cannon." Jake continued, "it will help both of our organisations if you had control of him moving forward." Jake felt like a cheap politician. Mendacity abounds.

"Great minds Jake.." Irma tapped her head with a bony finger and winked at him.

Jake moved to the door, but stayed facing the sisters. "Thank you for your time today, it has been most interesting. I am glad your ambitions are local and not national Mr Simons!" Irena offered it as a passing shot. Irma then shook his hand and Irena escorted Jake to the door.

He moved back into the waiting room, his every step tracked by the little mechanical spider in the corner. Jake hadn't understood the comments about Barry's manor at first, but seeing the sisters reaction had been interesting; they too had a vested interest in making sure the handover went smoothly. Security is everything. Objective achieved he thought.

Melissa Henderson watched the grainy image of Jake as he stood in the small waiting room making small talk with Irena. She studied him, as if he were an endangered species. She had seen the face before but could not place him. She wished the system had audio so she could hear what they had discussed.

She wasn't fully trusted yet, she had delivered ideas but not opportunity. She had to rely on others for that. She had her fingers crossed they would.

The intercom crackled and the voice of Irma Petrov came through,

"Do you know this man?"

Melissa leant closer to the screen, "No, he looks familiar but I really can't place him at all."

"Is he Barry's man?"

"No, definitely not, nothing to do with Barry." Melissa knew it for certain.

"Is he with Mr G then?"

Melissa had considered it already and dismissed it.

"No, I doubt it, most of his inner circle are black and dress distinctly, he wouldn't fit in at all."

Way too clean cut and handsome, she thought.

"I am confident he's nothing to do with Mr G or Barry," she delivered her verdict like an antiques dealer valuing something priceless.

"So you are sure he's part of this Winchester gang Barry supplied?"

"As I said...if Barry was going to find someone to take this deal over, he had only one place to go, Winchester...everything else is London tied."

"Yet you still know the face, maybe he's just some guy you fucked... he's a nice looking boy who wouldn't remember."

306

Melissa ignored the cheap jibe. She had only one question running around in her head, *'Why hadn't Adam come himself?'*

"Come on down, walk through the waiting room and see him in the flesh."

Melissa didn't reply, she rose to her feet and strode to the reception area.

Jake thanked Irena for her time and assured her once again that they had no plans for any overlapping business and that if he did find out anything about Mr G's plans he would of course let them know. He tried to turn away again but Irena clutched at his arm. Initially he thought this might be some form of playful flirting; then he realised that the camera would still be on him, Irena grabbing him simply ensured he faced it.

He more forcibly turned his back to the camera and moved towards the reception area. At that moment from a door on the right, a young blonde women walked into the reception, and she peered through the glass and straight at him.

She was striking, her face soft and rounded in stark contrast to the Petrov sisters, she looked perfect. Their eyes stayed locked together until she entered the room. She strode in, smiled at Irena, breaking the lock their eyes held and swayed through to the coded door. Jake's eyes followed and dropped to watch her bottom as she moved to the door.

Irena caught him as his gaze returned to normal height.

"She's lovely isn't she?"

"Er....yes she's, very striking."

"Oh Melissa.." Irena called after the girl, "Could you please make sure you tell Yuri and Dmitri to join us in the office please?" Melissa nodded and headed through the door, she looked back at Jake but he didn't return the look, he kept his eyes fixed on Irena. *She doesn't know me.. but I know her.*

"I must be off," he said turning to ensure no argument, "I'll see you and your sister on Wednesday then, at noon". He shook her hand and then briskly walked out of the waiting room, past the reception and into the street.

Jake kept his pace steady and even for more than four hundred yards, then he turned sharply right into an alley between two market stalls, and waited, his heart thumping. If someone followed he should be able to spot them from here.

Ten seconds passed then twenty.

No one came. Mission completed.

His heart rate slowed and he focused on what he had learnt. The moment he saw her, that beautiful face, he knew he recognised her. Jake had only seen pictures and heard stories, god how Adam had talked about Melissa, he had indeed been captivated, no doubt about that.

Questions flooded his head, they jostled for attention, each one seeking an answer. The most prominent -*What was she doing working with the Petrovs?* Jake thought it through. He had no doubt she was the one manning the CCTV. Irena's little arm grab was the final act to ensure a clear picture. They wondered if she could identify him, but why? She hadn't; that much seemed certain.

Jake swung his head back and forth and scouted the alley. He moved off throwing furtive glances now and then, each time confirming he had no tail. At the end of alley he emerged into the sunshine of a busy street, checked his watch and hailed a passing taxi.

Chapter Twenty Six

"So it's done then?" Jake sat on the Mucky Ducks garden wall and looked across the river to Eel Pie Island.

"Yeah it's done." Adam sat on the grass, leaning against the same wall, his focus only a few feet in front of his feet, ignoring the vista across the Thames. Both men had pints of lager, their second. The first had been consumed too quickly, the pumping adrenalin ensured neither had ever wanted a beer more in their life. They drank the first beer as if their very lives depended on the rapid ingestion of alcohol.

Now halfway through their second, the speed of the first had caught up with them, they felt a little numbed, a little more distant from everything. Jake hopped off the wall and joined Adam on the floor. Two boys hiding.

He rested his hand lightly on Adam's shoulder and gently tapped it, Adam didn't break his stare. A motor cruiser powered down the river, as it passed its bow wave scattered ducks and lapped up against the shore in a series of repetitive swipes, each one slightly smaller than the first until, eventually, the river became calm and still again.

"Mr G understands what he needs to do?" Jake broke the silence.

"Yes, we had a productive chat, everything is in place, assurances made." Adam's voice lacked animation, he sounded flat, like a performer coming down from the high of the crowd.

"He was happy with the sample?" Jake pushed for details.

"Yeah…one of his boys took a toot and gave it the thumbs up."

"Don't suppose it really matters does it?" Jake looked at the boat yard that occupied the end of the Eel Pie island. It looked deserted, no movement, no sounds of boats being repaired or of men working.

Jake picked at some pebbles and threw them into the water, the gentle plop made Adam look up; he watched the ripples dissipate, his focus shifting back to the grass fronds in front of his feet.

"I must have been to this pub a hundred times…" Jake said, "and I have never seen anyone at that boatyard."

Adam said nothing.

"To be honest I think that boat on the right, the one with the red hull, has been in the same spot every time.."

Jake turned to see Adam's reaction. Adam appeared to have missed everything he had said.

"You OK mate?"

Adam looked up, squinted at the sun and nodded.

"Mr G is happy to have financed the whole deal, says we can keep five kilos of the coke for ourselves, it's his gift to us for finding out who the other London gang is."

"We keep all the money?" Jake asked sitting back down alongside Adam.

"Yep. He said the money isn't important, said it was about putting down a marker." Adam played with the parched dirt at his feet.

Jake sniffed.

"What are we going to do with five kilos of coke?" his voice was flat, emotionless.

"Don't worry about the drugs, they're worthless to us." Adam pointed at the black bag on the table. " Have a look in the bag…"

Jake leaned forward and grabbed the long strap that hung down. He gave it a tug and the bag flopped off the table into his safe hands. It took more effort than Jake expected. He yanked the zip back and looked inside, and as soon as he registered what he had seen he quickly shut it pushing it between them.

"Shit" he said.

Adam nodded.

"There's £200k, all in used 20's and 50's 'Mr G's finance." Adam said it as if it were a matter of fact, his eyes never leaving the attention grabbing spot a few feet away.

"I don't think I have ever seen that much cash in real life, Jesus…it was heavy," Jake said.

"Gets the blood pumping looking at that doesn't it…I spent ten minutes just touching the stuff, caressing it. Makes the last few days almost seem worth it."

A silence descended between the two friends. They understood they had moved beyond the pivot point, they knew they had to continue on the path or they would be consumed by the journey.

"What about Barry?" Jake fiddled with two small pebbles as he spoke.

"Mr G wants him, we'll hand him over at the same time. I told him we'd get him alive.."

"Mmmm, what if Barry tells the real story?"

"Doesn't matter," Adam shrugged, "he's so discredited in Mr G's eyes, our version is the accepted truth."

"Fair enough."

Adam pawed at the dirt once more. Jake looked again at the deserted boat yard.

"How did it go with the Petrovs?" Adam asked his first question.

"As planned."

"Cool."

"Odd pair though. Glam themselves up, bit Dolly Partonesque."

Adam tilted his head to examine how serious Jake was.

Jake returned the gaze and nodded he was serious.

"Seriously… had trouser suits, pink busty blouses – the big fucking hair.."

Adam chuckled.

"No laughing matter…mad as bicycles the pair of them."

Adam chuckled some more.

"They'll let anyone be a gangster these days," he said.

"Don't I know it." Jake took a big slug of his pint. He'd already decided to keep some of the day's events to himself.

"They were happy with the handover venue?"

Jake nodded, "yeah mostly."

"Explain?"

"They wanted to do the handover in London – planned to charge an extra fee for doing it the way we wanted…" Jake explained.

"No biggie, did you agree to it?"

Jake shook his head and breathed deeply. "No, it would have looked weird. I teased the Barry situation into it."

"How? – they don't know we've got him do they?"

"No. They want him though. Seemed mighty keen to get their hands on Barry Boy. Seems he's right popular at the moment."

Adam smiled a small lifeless smile. "Or unpopular."

"Indeed… anyway they assume we can deliver him as part of the deal," Jake said.

Adam nodded, "that we can… poor old Barry. What will they do to him?" he said.

"Mmmm, I don't want to think about that," said Jake.

"Damn I'm tired, it's been a stressful day…" said Adam, as he rubbed his hands over his face and stretched out..

"You're telling me, a day full of surprises."

315

"Like what?"

Jake cursed himself. "Nothing, just a figure of speech."

Adam mouthed 'Oh' and did a half-nod.

"What's left to do boss?" Jake asked a fixed grin on his lips.

Adam turned and let a proper smile break out on his face for the first time that day. He got to his feet and dusted down his trousers.

"Well, it's time to go and see Mickey Finn...I presume you called him?"

"Yeah… he was somewhat intrigued, but he said we should head to his pub in Putney, The Duke of something…"

The two men stood side by side. Adam had grown in stature in recent days. The head was held higher and the shoulders more pushed back. They drained their pints and moved out of the pub garden and onto the road.

Walking back towards the centre of Twickenham Adam asked, "How did you know about that pub?"

"It's a famous rugby pub." informed Jake, "we would always come here pre-international rugby matches, its rammed on those days and quite dead otherwise."

"It's really nice, good to see a traditional boozer once in a while."

"Yeah, it is."

* * *

"The meeting was a success?" Melissa fished for details. She and Irma nursed a large glass of white wine while sitting on a sofa. The Petrovs had added a sofa, easy chairs and Ikea prints to one of their upstairs office rooms, in an attempt to have a less formal office space. It hadn't really worked. Melissa felt self conscious and ill at ease sitting on the bright red seat, pretending to be relaxed.

She couldn't be sure if the unease was down to the décor or the company.

"Yes…I think we can do business with these people…" Irena didn't look at her, her attention was focused on the bulbous wine glass in her hand.

"Is the price as expected?" Melissa probed.

"Yes…. there has been a slight change of plan, they have a little bonus, something we can really use…"

"I don't understand.." Melissa, genuinely baffled, leant forward. "Do you still need me to act as courier…?"

Irena leant back in the chair. Melissa had pushed them to meet the new buyers and had offered to be the go between.

"Yes, I think you will enjoy it."

"A solo handover here in town?" Melissa asked.

"No, you won't be making the collection on your own…. Irma and I will accompany you, Dmitri too!"

Melissa forced a smile across her face, and worked hard to keep the alarm from her eyes. Irena didn't notice, her eyes fixed on Melissa's exposed thigh.

"It will be a grand day out," said Melissa. She had recommended that a one-to-one meeting in London would be best, she thought it would be what the others would ask for.

"Yes…after we make the deal the future should be much clearer," Irma smirked. Melissa's right leg wobbled, an involuntary condition that showed up when she felt nervous.

"I don't understand," she said.

"Don't look so worried Melissa, we know what we're doing." She placed her hand on Melissa's thigh just above the knee and stroked back and forth. It should have been a comforting gesture.

"On Wednesday we will have the missing piece of a jigsaw. I do not want to spoil surprise…you'll like it, I promise." She winked and her tongue flicked the rim of her glass a split second before she took a healthy gulp.

Melissa didn't like surprises. There had been too many already.

Chapter Twenty Seven

Adam lay flat on his belly in the wood at the northern end of the disused Micheldever airfield; from his spot in the bracken he had a clear view down the runway to the other end of the airfield plot. Several farmers over the years had used the airfield to graze cows and sheep on, technically still MOD land it had been left virtually untouched and unused since it was decommissioned in 1985. The runway wasn't big enough to service the big Hercules or jet fighters of the modern era, but the MOD had used it and the large hangar to Adam's right, about halfway down the runway, for storage and the site generally for driver training.

The runway, now pothole ridden and covered in patches of mossy grass, couldn't be used for anything. The main entrance to the site had been blocked with large concrete slabs to prevent gypsies settling, but the initiated knew of several farm tracks from the various country lanes that led into the old airfield. Adam trained his binoculars on the hangar, the large grey building about half the size of a football pitch perched uneasily next to the runway. Part of the corrugated iron roof was missing, having fallen in some years before. The whole structure sloped to the right, as if it permanently leaning into a heavy wind. The structure was little more than one large room, now containing nothing but nesting pigeons and a colony of rats.

It had one door, located at its northern end facing Adam. The maps they had provided had shown only one route in and out of the airfield which was at the southern end, in the far corner to Adam's left. Any visitors to the site would have to come through the trees on the left and round the bottom of the runway then either up the service road or the runway itself to get to the partially open door of the dilapidated hangar.

Adam had parked Jake's 4x4 behind him, one hundred metres away, on a dried mud track. All Adam had to do was turn immediately around and walk straight through the thick bracken and wood, he'd need to scoot down a slight incline in order to reach the track and the car which was invisible from the airfield. The woods continued along the track for another hundred metres or so, so it was almost completely invisible.

The track led to a very occasionally used clay pigeon shoot and ended at a fallen down barn, some five hundred metres further down the track. Jake had shot here several times; it was how he had known about the airfield site and its suitability for the day's events. The exit route meant taking the track west, where it wound its way through the large wood on one side of the airfield, across several fields and then down through another spinney before emerging some three miles from any other entrance to the airfield, on a completely different road to which the airfield entrance stood. *Perfect.*

Adam squirmed uncomfortably, the piles of leaves he'd gathered didn't offer much padding against the arid ground and

Jake's insistence that he wear all black meant that as the day got hotter, so he began to boil. His watch said 11.58am, two minutes to D-Day. He refocused the binoculars and trained them on the hangar door. Jake appeared, dressed in cream combat trousers and a black t-shirt, over which he wore a black utility waistcoat. Adam had seen similar garments worn by clay pigeon shooters in the past. Jake looked right in the direction of Adam, his gaze seemingly boring right down the binoculars. Adam knew Jake couldn't see him, but it still made him uneasy and he looked around him to see if he could camouflage himself anymore.

"I'll do the heavy stuff at the handover... you watch and report," Jake had told him. He'd protested, but Jake hadn't been in the mood for a debate.

"On this one you'll do as I fucking say." Jake had been firm to the point of violent. Adam had admired his bravery; he stood out there alone. None of his team were now involved, Jake refused to involve them any further. Only Adam would be on hand to help.

A movement to Adam's left caused him to pan with the binoculars, he wasn't familiar with using them and overshot the entrance. When he panned back more slowly he caught sight of the black people carrier driving cautiously into the airfield, the cars tinted windows offering no clues as to the occupants. Adam plucked the walkie-talkie from his belt.

"Jake...the eagle has landed, the eagle has landed".

Quickly he panned the binoculars back to the hangar door and caught Jake nipping back into the hangar and then re-emerging a second or so later with an aluminium case. He watched him move into what he supposed had been Jake's pre-rugby match routine, punching himself on the shoulders and chest as he tried to psyche himself up. Adam hadn't asked him if he was scared, he just assumed that with his past he would be immune to fear.

The people carrier continued its steady progress around the runway and veered off onto the service road that ran alongside, going not more than ten miles per hour. It came up upon the hangar, slowing to a near halt.

"Still all clear. No other bandits, repeat no other bandits."

The people carrier ended its languid journey about fifty feet from the hangar door and parked so that its side sliding door opened out to the hangar, so that it blocked Adam's view of the goings on. He again turned the binoculars on the rest of the airfield, searching to see if there were any unwanted guests.

So far so good.

Jake stood by the case and watched the car door slide open. First out was a lean, teak tough-looking man Jake didn't recognise, then came the more familiar Dmitri. The squat man held out his hand and Irma and Irena stepped out of the vehicle. Jake could see the driver, still in the car and a final front seat passenger, possibly a woman. He computed the details and flicked his eyes around the airfield.

"Welcome to Hampshire" Jake greeted them with unnecessary bonhomie, "Lovely to see you both again, Irena…Irma," he greeted both with little double air kisses on the cheeks.

Irma, a little taken aback, cowered from the attention. Irena lingered longer at the clinch than she needed to. Jake appraised the group, nothing out of the ordinary, he concluded.

"May I see the merchandise?" he asked.

Irena led Jake round to the rear of the vehicle, the hatchback boot was raised and there, stacked in brick sized packages, Jake set eyes on the cocaine. He reached out and handled one of the white cargo taped packages and as he did so he looked through the car to see if he could spot who was on the front seat.

As he played with the package he sensed Dmitri get a little closer, his left arm cocked at the ready, a stance used in order to pull out a weapon, most likely a gun. He stood upright and tossed the package to Dmitri, who, surprised by the action, juggled with it for a moment before bringing it under control.

"Come on then, let's show you our merchandise and have that brick tested, my alchemist is inside." Jake strode off towards the hangar door and as he reached the case Irma piped up.

"Wait please, before we go further can we see the money please?"

"Irma? Of course." He bent down and theatrically flipped open the case, a bright burst of reflective light dazzling the little group as the lid flipped up. Jake stepped back, leaving the case open on the floor. Irma tentatively moved towards the case almost scared of what it contained; she peered in and then signalled to the lean man.

"Yuri –check it."

The wiry man nodded bent down and inspected the money, then he fingered a wad, before finally holding a single note from the middle to the light.

"Do you really think I would use fake notes?" asked Jake. "You test our product, we test yours." An impertinent, almost condescending edge crept into Irma Petrovs voice. Jake could feel her irritation at being dragged to a field in the middle of nowhere.

"It will be fine" her sister soothed.

Jake extended his arm once more. "Join me inside, it's safer, and we'll get this test over and done with in a matter of moments and you can be re-introduced to your old friend Mr Hunt."

The car rocked - side to side like a weight had shifted suddenly. A distinct and definite movement from the front seat. Irma and Irena turned to follow Jake's gaze.

"Is someone a little jumpy in there?" he narrowed his eyes.

"Do not worry about Melissa, she used to work for Barry. She'll be a little shocked, but delighted to see him." Irma's words flat and emotionless.

"She can decide what to cut off first, " Irena added, her tone not betraying her masochistic pleasure at the thought.

"Is her...how you say... her bonus, Jake.."

Jake swallowed hard, he found it hard not to grimace.

"Nice, let's leave them there for the moment, come this way then people..." Jake ushered them to the door and as they passed he scooped up the case of money and handed it to Yuri. Dmitri led the way into the hangar, still holding the cocaine package, closely followed by the two sisters and the lean Yuri.

As soon as Yuri entered the doorway Jake stamped his foot hard down on the back of the unsuspecting man's right knee. He yelped in pain as he crashed to the floor spilling the case across the floor. As the others turned to identify the source of the rasping metallic disturbance, a mighty West Indian voice boomed through the half light of the hangar,

"BE STILL MOTHER FUCKERS, MAKE A MOVE AND YOU'LL BE SHOT ON THE MOTHER FUCKING SPOT."

Jake caught sight of the fuming faces of Irma and Irena.

"I suggest you do what Mr G requests, he does not like insubordination." He stayed close to the door, watching over the writhing Yuri.

Out of the dim haze, six armed men appeared from behind the roof debris and the now recognisable two black Porsche Cayennes. They were parked to the side of the hangar some thirty metres away but partly obscured by a collection of wooden crates and the dim light.

Mr G ambled towards them, the slow easy walk of an unhurried man. He held a silver coloured Heckler Koch USP in his hand and the two heavies that flanked him carried Berretta Px4

325

Storm machine pistols. To his far right Beano, carrying the same make of pistol, was also flanked by two more similarly armed men.

"Hello everybody...remember me?" The question met with silence. Yuri clutched his ruptured knee and tried to sit up despite the pain. Dmitri stood stoically ahead of his employers, a mumbling sneer of curses playing across his ugly face.

"So this is the Petrovs, forgive me for having not known about you before, your reputation does not precede you...you, bitch number one," he pointed at Irma, "wipe that disgusted fucking look off your face...do it now bitch, or my man is going to put some lead in your head..."

Irma made no movement and her face remained like stone.

"Call the pit-bull off." Mr G gestured towards the now agitated Dmitri who had begun taking small shuffling steps, fists clenched, towards Mr G, cursing him repeatedly under his breath. "I am serious, call the fucking dog off or I will put the fucker down..." Dmitri ignored the raised gun of Mr G and continued his defiant little march.

"Dmitri, niet...stop Dmitri" Irena's words sounded heartfelt, the squat Russian had been with them since their rise in Estonia. Her words didn't halt his progress.

"NIET," she bellowed.

Irena looked at her sister and then cried out to her favourite aide, "Dmitri please, be sensible..."

"CRANG."

Before she could say another word, a loud echoing metallic noise resonated round the building, the bullet passed straight through Dmitri's head and ricocheted violently off the wall of the hangar. Dmitri fell face forward, dead before he collided with the ground. What remained of his face was now pooled in blood.

The others slowly rose from their cowered positions and uncovered their ears as the din receded. Irena and Irma stood motionless, the speed of Dmitri's demise dulling their reactions, then the group heard the unmistakeable **"BANG, BANG"** of two shots and shattering glass, which was swiftly followed by a more muffled third.

The source of the shots sounded like the people carrier, only Mr G and his G Men seemed to have expected them. Jake turned to look at the doorway, unsure what to expect. Without warning a petite blonde woman, splattered in blood, burst through the hangar door, behind her, pushing and guiding her into the vast room, her captor, a freakishly tall and thin Somali-looking man held a smoking hand gun to the back of her head. Tears and blood dribbled down her face as she landed on her knees at the feet of Irma Petrov.

Melissa pushed the hair from her eyes, only to be greeted with the grisly sight of Dmitri's remains. She tried to scream but no sound came out. She thrust her hand into her mouth, staring wild-eyed at the corpse.

"Keep it like that…no fucking screaming, do you understand me." Mr G addressed the whole room, Irma nodded her

327

head quickly. Beano and his little posse moved in amongst the group of hostages, disarming Yuri and searching Irma and then Irena, each one in turn having their hands tied behind their back using black cable ties.

Adam heard the shot from the hangar and it jolted him so much he dropped his binoculars, he ferreted for them in the couch grass, retrieving them just in time to see the lanky black man crawl from the side of the hangar. He stayed low, defying gravity almost and belying his height. The people in the car didn't see him or hear him. He moved around the people carrier and then popped up alongside the driver's window. Adam focused the binoculars, mesmerised. The tall man thrust a handgun to the window and shot once, no hesitation. The bullet ripped through the glass with a deafening 'Bang', hitting the driver in the chest. The victim convulsed with the impact and then settled as the shower of broken glass rained down on him.

Adam's mouth went dry, and his heartbeat rose.

The tall man had leaned back from the shattering glass, and now he calmly reached in and put the gun to the driver's temple and pulled the trigger again. The head exploded and showered the screaming passenger in bone and brain.

'Jesus fucking Christ,' Adam said out loud.

The heartbeat rose again.

His mouth dropped open and he mouthed the words again, the breath taken from him. No longer a game, the reality of what he'd created spanked Adam hard across the face. He stared, even shuffling forward a few inches to try and get a clearer view of the car...the girl, the blood splattered terrified girl that the lanky black man had dragged from the van and marched to the hangar, he knew her.

The woman he loved, the woman who had started it all.

* * *

"Who is this bitch?" Mr G asked the room.

Irma Petrov held her head high, unruffled, refusing to show fear.

"This is Melissa, she works for us…"

The sound of her name settled over the group like a sheet of misunderstanding.

"Melissa? Beano, Jake … aint that the name of the bitch that was Barry's courier?" Mr G asked to no one in particular.

Jake said nothing, he edged toward the door. He counted the guns and memorised the locations, alert to the shifting mood of the room.

Mr G carried on, "The one Barry told everyone had stolen his money. Is this her?" Jake didn't need to answer, Beano piped up.

"That's right Mr G, that's the name of the girl," he boomed.

He stepped forward to join his boss.

"You that girl?" he pointed at her using his gun as an extension of his hand.

"You the ex-hooker that worked for Barry, supposedly played courier to the Winchester boys…that you girl?"

329

Beano shouted and spat the words at Melissa, his heart pounding from his recent exertions, his chest rising and falling dramatically as he wheezed heavily. Without thinking, her senses numbed by shock, lips quivering, Melissa just nodded.

Confused. A confession, an admission of guilt.

Jake side-stepped closer to the door, the plan called for him to deliver the Petrovs to the lunatic West Indian, nothing more. He didn't need to witness mass murder. Not again.

Beano strutted, he had the girl's confession. He looked at the people in front of him and jumped to a host of conclusions.

"So you ran out on dear old Barry… once a ho always a ho? Aint no doubt you stole his money, but you end up with these halfwits." He waved at the cluster of bound people, the disdain written across his bulbous face.

"… a bitch with ambition, ideas above her station. Well baby you are going to pay.. along with every other fucker here." Beano delivered it as statement, a promise.

Mr G placed a large restraining hand on his man's shoulder and patted. Jake watched as Beano calmed. Mr G wanted all the rotten apples in one place, ready to be dealt with in one go, is how he put it. Jake and Adam had looked at each other and exchanged concerned glances when he announced it earlier that morning, "I'm going to make a statement that all London villains will sit up and take notice of."

Mr G began his rehearsed speech, Jake knew it, he'd heard Beano coaching his boss in the car before this mayhem had begun.

330

"Well it seems we're all here…oh no wait, there is someone missing, who the fuck could that be?" No one answered. Jake took advantage of the fact that the focus was on the captives, he stepped sideways and now he had his back to the partially open sliding door.

"Anyone want to hazard a guess who is missing from this happy little reunion of cheating double crossing bastards?" No one answered, Mr G's voice echoing round the cavernous building.

Beano took his two men and moved all the bound hostages into a line and with the back of his foot he pressed on the back of their knees. In turn each one was forced to kneel down, facing Mr G.

Jake swallowed hard. They had been readied for execution.

"Let's bring out the guest of honour, Devon!" Mr G bellowed, the veins in his neck throbbing. "BRING OUT THE PET." The door of the furthest Porsche Cayenne opened and out stepped a short powerfully built coloured guy with a football-sized afro. It scraped the rim of the door frame as he climbed out of the car. He tugged on what looked like a dog lead but the second tug, more aggressive than the first, revealed the head of a man, then a set of naked shoulders, followed by a bruised torso and two bloodied legs.

Barry Hunt fell out of the car, the choke chain around his neck had scarred him. He had been beaten, the welts and bruises across his body fresh, the gash and cuts on his face still oozing blood.

Devon strode forward, Afro bobbing, and dragged Barry behind him, pulling him onto his knees, still naked with his legs tied together via a foot of nylon rope, enough slack so he could crawl. His hands had been bound tightly together at the wrist, forcing him to crawl on his elbows.

Jake blinked hard, his expression being one of a man trying to rid himself of a foul taste in his mouth. Devon strolled towards the line up tugging the blindfolded and gagged Barry behind him. Several times he fell forward, his arms collapsing under him. Devon just marched on hauling the human dog back to the crawling position.

The room was silent but for the sound of flesh scraping on old worn concrete.

Melissa's face was a picture of contorted horror, Irena Petrov sported an inquisitive smile as Barry was deposited at Mr G's side. Mr G nonchalantly patted him on the head. Beano strolled over and removed the blindfold and gag with a violent jerk.

Barry scrunched his eyes shut from the sharp invasion of light. As he winced and his eyes slowly adjusted, Mr G began his speech.

"Well now we've everyone, and I can be certain of your attention, let's begin." All the heads turned from the grotesque Barry to the immaculate white-clad Mr G.

"Barry is a dumb fucker... how long Barry, did you think you could get away with ripping me off before I would notice?" No one moved.

"REMEMBER, Mr G and his crew sees all."

With that he brought his big hand down in an arc and slapped Barry, back-handed across the face. It was a languid rather than violent attack, but the weight and force were enough to start Barry's nose bleeding once more.

Barry spluttered, resigned to an acknowledged fate. He recognised his fellow prisoners, not surprised they were here. Then he found Melissa. She briefly looked up and her eyes met his, they held their gaze for a moment before she turned away.

Barry said, "Oh shut up ya big rasta twat," the words more defiant than his posture.

Beano strode across to Barry and thrust his foot into Barry's ribs with a grizzly crunch, causing him to collapse and wheeze in pain.

Melissa screamed and fell forward, as if lunging for Barry.

Mr G poked out a long Fila covered leg, nudging her back into place. Gagging and trying to catch his breath Barry managed to splutter, "Leave her be Mr G, she's nothing in all this, I'm who you want."

"I fucking have you...and let me see I also have her and her and him...all these fuckers are mine. I decide who lives and who dies"...his arm waved back and forth to show all he owned.

"Mr G sees all," chuckled Barry. "You have no idea what really happens right under your nose - you are in fantasy land fella, I stole from you for years."

Mr G joined in the chuckle.

"Did you get away with it Barry? Did you?" he bellowed, bending to face the naked captive. "I'd hardly call this current situation getting away with it...would you?"

"Fuck you..." Barry said.

"Choose your fucking words carefully my brother, they are definitely going to be amongst your last."

Mr G raised his foot and placed it upon Barry's shoulder forcing him to the floor. He moved his giant shoe up and pressed on Barry's head, squashing his face between his boot and the bare concrete floor.

"You have to understand people, I'm a man with a great many responsibilities, you don't expect people that are well rewarded to steal from you..."

Mr G dropped to one knee so he could get closer to Barry's crumpled face.

"Tell me Barry, what made you do a deal with these Polish halfwits?"

Irma bristled, "Estonian...we're Estonian not Polish" she said with chest beating indignation.

"You're deadski, that is what you are," Beano called out, "so shut yo freaky haired bitch mouth!"

"Barry came to us," Irena joined in. Beano's gaze snapped from one sister to the other. "He told us of the deal, what business person wouldn't miss this opportunity."

"A sensible person would have told him to walk," Mr G replied.

"We are good, a better organisation than you know, we're ready to take over his business in London…" Irma held herself as upright as she could, keen to stand by her sister and show some metal.

Mr G nodded, impressed.

"Touché Atilla. Maybe you are ready, but you know the rules. Everyone knows the rules."

Beano took over, barking out the retort, "you had no right to work in Mr G's manors. He makes the decisions about new teams, not no one else."

Mr G nodded again. "My fucking London. If you aint asked, if you aint been invited then it's an act of aggression…a declaration of war."

"Times change.." Barry spluttered from his prone position, "How did you take power?"

Beano laughed, and Mr G smiled at the reminder of his own ascent to the top.

"Barry Hunt – My man. Old school," he said.

"You been in the business a long time Barry. You know the game. Why steal from me? There was enough for all…"

Barry said nothing, they exchanged a knowing look, sharing a moment as if no one else was there. Two old friends.

"Once you're in Barry – you're in for life…"

"I know."

"It's the life we chose, the rollercoaster that you can't ever get off."

"I couldn't hold on no longer Mr G…"

Barry closed his eyes, as if trying to shut out the reality of how his life had turned out.

"I know…I know my man."

Mr G rose to his giant feet and switched his gaze back to the room.

"You," he pointed at the sisters, "had no business doing business with Barry. You had no business with these Winchester boys."

Mr G hitched his trousers, and twirled the gun on his finger, wild west style.

"It's only because the Winchester boys understand respect that I'm able to deal with this situation, they.."

He stopped as Melissa lurched to her feet, self preservation fuelling her understanding of the betrayals that had taken place. "You don't know the real story Mr G…" she began. Beano stepped forward in case she did anything silly.

Mr G pointed his gun at Melissa's chest, "You going to defend this piece of shit?"

"You don't know the whole story.." she flicked her eyes from Mr G to Barry. Jake watched carefully, he couldn't be sure, but he thought he saw Barry shake his head at Melissa.

Mr G carried on, "this man told everyone you stole from him – to save his own arse he made you the excuse for all his fuck ups and deception…it's a good job you had the presence of mind to disappear or he would have had you up like a lamb to slaughter."

"I did not steal from him.." Melissa ignored Barry. "Maybe you did maybe you didn't – Barry stripped his manor of cash, place is near bankrupt."

Melissa said nothing.

"Silence is a confession," said Beano.

"You stole half the drug deal money, you knew Barry was dying on his arse, you didn't fancy a moonlight flit with the old man. So you decided to take a chunk for yourself," he continued.

Irma spoke in Melissa's defence, "She came to us with nothing, she told us Barry had no money, she wanted to use her knowledge, to help us take over his manor."

"She got greedy. Figured she could make more cash from you once Barry was out of the way," Beano added, "You guys were already tied into the deal with Barry, she just played the angles."

"Just as suppliers…Barry was just another buyer to us."

"Fuck you funny woman – you can't lie your way out of this. We know Barry lined you up as London distribution. Trying to flood the market with cheap shit, undermine our business. You're going to pay with your lives." Mr G's patience had begun to wear thin.

"This is bullshit," Irma barked, "bullshit…we went to Barry for finance."

"What he did with the drugs we didn't care, you know shit," Irena said, emphasising her point by spitting on the floor in front of Mr G.

"What's with the spitting, stop it man," Mr G barked.

"Everyone stop talking, you're confusing the shit out of me…I don't care who stole what or who did what. What I do know is that Barry and the fucking Andrews sisters here entered into a drug deal, a big deal without my say so and without me getting a cut." The veins in his neck pulsed and his voice cracked. Jake stepped back once more, almost out of the door.

"That's taking liberties boys and girls, serious liberties…you need to be made an example of…and that's what is going to happen." He pulled back hard on the automatics slide, the familiar sound of a bullet moving into the chamber rang out.

"You don't need me, I am an innocent in all this, just trying to stay alive…" Melissa sank from her knees onto her feet.

"Girl you aint been innocent since you was twelve."

"I shouldn't be here… this isn't how it's supposed to be."

"It's over. All of it's done." Barry said to her.

"I don't know how or why but something tells me that your sorry arse is involved in this shit from day one…Barry here aint a

dumb arsehole, 'cept when it comes to pussy…and looking at you, I know this dumb fucker has to have been led by his cock."

Jake watched Mr G look down at the little group and shake his head in amazement. *Pull the fucking trigger and get this over with,* he muttered.

Barry dragged himself to a sitting position, his nose no longer bleeding.

"You talk about this Winchester crew as if they have done you some big favour, … they have nothing to do with any of it."

Mr G raised the gun, his arm extended straight, the barrel resting on Barry's forehead. It didn't stop him talking.

"They played Mickey like a fool, convinced him they were serious players and now they're doing the same to you. Adam and Jake are a couple of civilians playing at being villains, I used them to…" mid sentence Mr G leant down and smashed his fist into Barry's face.

He shot a glance at Beano, his face a mask of confused rage, his eyes searching the room for an answer, trying in vain in the dim half light to pick out the face of Jake Simons.

* * *

The sight of Melissa spurred Adam into action, he scrambled to his feet and pushed through the brush and branches, bursting out of the forested apron like a sprinter blasting from his blocks. He surged towards the hangar, his short legs over striding

339

as he ploughed through the ankle-deep grass. Adam's left arm pumped as he fiddled on his belt to grab his mobile phone with his right, tripping and then over compensating, he finally lost balance as his foot hit a hidden rabbit hole. The ankle turned and he tumbled face forward into the ground and with only one arm free to break his fall, he landed face first, with a grunt, onto the ground. He hit the exact point that the grass met the eroded concrete of the runway, his face sliding into the hard ground, tearing at his flesh. He didn't drop his phone.

He pushed himself upright, focused on the phone for a second, pushing the recall button, despite the gravel and stones embedded in his palms and cheek. The call was answered without a ring, Adam didn't exchange greetings he simply bellowed, "NOW, HIT the fucking hangar, change of plan, hit the hangar now...."

Without further explanation he leapt back into his run towards the big building.

* * *

Mr G couldn't see Jake anywhere in the room. "Beano, take Rufus and get outside, find me that fella Jake... I should have smelled a rat when they had no powder here ready."

"They had no powder because we brought it fool." Irma spat the words with disgust.

"Where's Adam – isn't he the main man?" Barry said.

"The main man Adam didn't show up today…" Mr G replied.

Beano moved as fast as he could, his chest heaving with the effort. Rufus, the tall Somali-looking man that had seen off the Petrovs driver, followed.

"Adam," Melissa blurted out his name in anguish.

"What's it to you thief?" Mr G's irritation was beginning to reach boiling point. "He's the brains behind the Winchester mob, the Aryan fucker, Jake, is the muscle."

"They aren't gangland…" Melissa said, sensing a way out.

"No? they made mincemeat of Barry's once mighty Mickey Finn…"

Melissa needed to work it through. Adam *hadn't followed the plan, he'd sold out Barry. Sold out the Petrovs, sold out all of us,* she thought.

"Adam…Adam isn't a gangland boss, he's as straight as they come, Jesus he used be a catering manager before he became a financial advisor." Melissa's voice hovered between desperate and reasoned as she tried to piece together what had happened, knowing that convincing Mr G could save her life.

"Can't be talking about the same dude lady, these boys aint no civilians."

"About 5'11, paunch, normal looking guy, nice mum called Kathleen…" Melissa stopped as she saw the recognition and understanding spread across Mr G's face. She watched as the cogs of Mr G's mind dropped into place.

"He loves me…he'd do anything for me…he was helping me launder money."

"Barry's money, the money you stole."

"No – our money. Our escape money," she slapped her hands to her chest.

Jake exited the hangar and made straight for the people carrier, the plan hadn't worked. Too many variables, too many elements to fall into place. Jake hadn't expected the Petrovs to give in so easily. It should have been a sodding fire fight, they walked in there like lambs, *fucking amateurs,* thought Jake.
He reached the back of the people carrier, just in time to see a figure charging across the field and tumbling to the floor. He watched Adam pick himself up, a big graze across his face, yell something that Jake couldn't hear and then take off towards him again. It took a moment, but then he came into vocal range, "What the fuck is he doing," he mouthed.

Adam, legs pumping, was making good ground now he had firmer footing on the runway, he raced towards the hangar. As he recognised Jake he yelled, "WHAT THE FUCK IS SHE DOING HERE?"

"WHAT?" Jake yelled back, unable to make out the breathless cry.

"MELISSA IS IN THE HANGAR, MELISSA IS WITH THE PETROVS…" he realised his voice wasn't carrying and he put his head down and charged even harder. Within seconds he got to within a few metres of Jake and began slowing down.

"Hold up…Adam…what are you doing…."

"Melissa…" he panted. "She's in the hangar. She was in the car…."

"I know, I know she is… she's working with the Petrovs."

"You know? how do you know…you don't know Melissa."

"I recognised her when I went to the meeting, she didn't know me…"

Adam shoved both his arms into his friend's chest, venom in his eyes,

"You fucking knew she was coming today… you knew she could be here and you said nothing."

"I didn't have a clue she would be here and what difference does it make anyway…" Jake stood his ground, absorbing the shoves with his bigger body.

"It makes all the fucking difference…bastard." Adam pushed past him to run to the hangar, Jake turned and grabbed his friend round the waist.

"You can't go in there, the shit's about to go down."

"LET ME GO, we've to get her out of there."

"No chance, Mr G is about to be wised up to us Adam, it's over."

Adam struggled and wrestled in Jake's powerful grasp, willing himself to have the strength to break free.

"HEY TWEEDLE FUCKING DEE AND TWEEDLE FUCKING DUMBER." Beano and Rufus stood thirty feet from them. Rufus held his pistol out in front aiming at Jake's head. They stopped wrestling and moved side by side, their hands raised up to shoulder height.

"Ok let's not do anything silly now," Jake was talking to Beano but addressing Rufus. "We still have the coke here, there are no issues..."

"Don't talk about issues mother fucker, there is a game of fucking truth or dare going down in there." Beano's bingo-winged arm wafted at the hangar, " and you two aint coming out of it too well." His words were laboured, sweat pouring down his face.

"You don't look too good, you OK Beano," Adam's brow furrowed as he watched Beano struggle to speak.

"I'm fine bitch, just fine..." Suddenly Beano arched his back, his mouth gaped open as he gulped air, pain ripped through his left arm, he grabbed at his chest, and without warning his mammoth legs gave way and he crashed to his knees, panting horrifically, his face a contorted mask of pain.

Jake took his chance. Rufus had strayed into the killing zone with his attention drawn to the fallen man. Jake stepped forward and his lightning fast highly trained reflexes shot into action. He grabbed the gun hand and pushed up, his left hand chopped down on the elbow of the gun arm, twisting the wrist as he moved forward. The pressure forced Rufus to collapse to the floor in pain. The handgun now pointed directly at his own face,

344

his finger locked in place on the trigger. Rufus desperately tried to free himself but Jake's grip was too firm, and now the pain became intense.

"Don't squeeze it man, leave it, let it go…" Jake looked into Rufus's eyes, pleading with him to loosen his grip.

"Let go or you'll die…" Rufus grimaced with anger and defiance and renewed his efforts;

"CRACK"

The gun exploded to life, Rufus, his finger still on the trigger under pressure from Jake, had shot himself in the throat. Jake recoiled from the gunshot, the bullet passing just under Rufus's chin into his throat and out of his body under the right ear. Air bubbles and the hissing sound of escaping gas accompanied the gurgling moans coming from the now quickly dying man.

Jake fell to his knees, the gun still in his hand, his head bowed. Adam stood and glared at his friend, sitting between the bodies of the large black gangsters, Beano no longer writhing or moving, his heart surrendered at last to his great weight.

* * *

"I don't care who the fuck these guys are, the fact is you still all stole from me and a man in my position can't be stolen from, if word gets out that I let you get away with it then we've anarchy … can't let that happen."

345

"Get on with it, Just shoot us…but promise me you'll fucking shoot the Winchester boys as well."

"Shut up Barry," Melissa shouted, "what the hell did you do to create this unholy fucking mess."

"Yeah right blame me…as usual it's my fucking fault."

"What you two talking about?" Mr G asked.

"Nothing."

"This makes me sick. Barry you deluded old fool, never fall in love with a whore. It's their job to make you love them, you are pathetic man."

Irma still holding her head high forced herself to her feet.

"I'll not die on my knees Mr G," her words cut short by the sound of a gunshot from outside. Mr G looked at the two men nearest the door, and nodded his head, they nodded back and turned towards the exit. His eyes never left the doorway, his ears focused on the slightest sound and that's when he heard the unmistakable sound of a vehicle, the low rumble of a big heavy van or truck. As it got closer its engine came into sharper focus, screaming in distress. He swivelled round to face the source of the sound.

At that moment the side of the hangar erupted in a cacophony of noise and shattering iron panels. A Land Rover Defender with caged windscreen, bulldozed its way into the building. Mr G dived for cover as the vehicle careered through the room pulverising a Mr G goon with a sickening crunch and bounce. The vehicle skidded to a halt pinning Irma Petrov between it and the far hangar wall, her head lolling on her shoulders as she tried, in vain, to push away the vehicle which had crushed her to death.

Outside, Adam reached down and picked up Beano's Heckler Koch pistol. The gun felt heavy in his inexperienced hand, he flashed a glance at the distraught figure of Jake, kneeling between the two bodies. He flipped the gun over and noticed the safety catch was off. He flexed the trigger with his finger, it fought his pressure more than he expected. He weighed the gun and then grasped it before walking towards the hangar.

He had travelled no further than a few feet when he saw the Land Rover Defender, some fifty metres away, but travelling at tremendous speed and heading straight for the hangar. His attention was dragged away from the car as two machine pistol-wielding G-men came charging out of the hangar door. There followed a pause, a moment of perfect stillness, as the two thugs recognised the bodies of their two dead comrades. Adam stared back, facing them alone.

On seeing that he held Beano's gun they made their decision without thinking, reflex. Each man raised his weapon. The fear gripped first in Adam's belly and then rose like a shot of pure 'thrill' through his lungs and into his arms.
Time became distorted, his movements became molasses slow. He pulled up his gun and fired. No aiming, no practice, no skill. Three quick shots, unplanned, as if the gun had a will of its own. Then, as

any true brave amateur, he charged, legs pumping as he fired. He roared as well. A guttural caveman roar of fury.

"PHFEESH, PHFEESH." Bullets whistled past him, he fired again.

His first volley struck the first G-man in the right shoulder, sending him spiralling backwards, his body hitting his companion and knocking him down and through the open hangar door.

At that exact moment the Defender hit the side of the hangar.

Adam, threw himself to the floor and tucked his head into his hands. He glanced back quickly at Jake and saw his friend no longer kneeling but lying awkwardly on his side. Adam dragged himself up onto one knee to get a better view.

"PHFEESH," a bullet whistled past his head. Adam couldn't fight the reflex to duck even though the bullet had long passed. His shoulders hunched, he looked back to the hangar and the prostrate figure clasping a hand to the open wound on his shoulder, no gun in his hand.

"PHFEESH," another bullet winged by, closer than the last. The other G-man had got up and kneeling he aimed for Adam's head. Adam lifted the gun to a firing position, Jake's words ringing in his head.

"Hit the target first and foremost. Aim for the biggest unmoving area."

Adam took a more careful aim and fired. The first bullet missed the man and twanged into the metal behind his head, the

348

second ripped into his belly, lifting him off the floor and back through the hangar door. His arms flailed and he screamed in agony.

He's down. Two down and out, thought Adam. He rose to his feet and ran to check on his friend.

You could never have called Mickey Finn subtle and certainly not an intellectual, but what he had in abundance was a total disregard for his own safety. The man personified bravery. The Land Rover Defender reached 70mph and was screaming its dissent by the time it hit the side of the hangar. He had seen Adam and Jake off to the right of the hangar fighting with two men. The plan had been for him to hi-jack the convoy as they left the airfield, to hit, he thought, the Petrovs as hard as he could, taking no prisoners. The removal of the Petrovs, the gang that was doing business with Barry behind Mr G's back, could almost certainly guarantee he kept Barry's manor in the future.

The Winchester boys were in trouble, the Petrovs had double-crossed them. That much seemed obvious. If Mickey wanted to impress Mr G with the scalps of the Petrovs and their illicit drugs then he had to act now. Adam's call had been desperate and implicit, hit the hangar and hit it hard.

He followed the instruction literally.

The Defender came to a halt, a blonde dwarf-looking woman pinned by the bonnet to the crumpled far wall. Terry, the driver, slumped forward over the wheel, his neck broken.

Mickey didn't notice.

He kicked open the rear doors and leapt into the hangar, a Mossburg 500 pump action shotgun in his hands, a big powerful weapon, capable of cutting a man in two at close range. The recoil was as powerful as a horse's kick. The weapon suited Mickey, it looked at home in his hands.

Terry's brother Phil followed Mickey out of the Defender.

Yuri the lame Russian had grabbed hold of the dying G-Man, shot by Adam. The two injured men grappled for the gun in a winner takes all death roll.

Mickey leapt over a pile of rubble from the collapsed roof, not noticing that it hid the trapped body of Barry Hunt. Mr G had gathered himself together and as he witnessed the Land Rover regurgitate its passengers ready to fight, he raised his pistol and fired. Mickey felt and heard the shots wing round him, he dropped to one knee and brought the shotgun up to his shoulder and fired in the vague direction of the shots. As he fired he dropped face down in the dirt, keen to avoid being in one position for too long.

The shotgun erupted pellets at great speed and across a wide area, the shots hitting the debris filled hangar and ricocheting round the building. Irena Petrov clambered to her feet when she saw the body of her beloved sister trapped by the Land Rover. She let out a cry as the volley of bullets hit her squarely in the chest, the blast lifting the diminutive woman clean off her feet and throwing her across the dust filled hangar. She hit the crouched Melissa with extreme force, knocking her down and out.

Phil didn't have a clue who was who and what the score was, Mickey simply said take them down. He hurdled the debris caused by the violent interruption of the Land Rover looking for someone to shoot. Yuri, the lame Russian had begun to win his battle with the G Man, Phil saw white versus black. White had to equal Petrov, so he fired. Phil had never been the sharpest tool in the box, his blast hitting Yuri full in the back, but shielding the G-Man from the blast.   Relieved to be away from the giant's paws, the G-Man turned to locate his saviour. Phil saluted and turned around to look for another foe. The G-Man calculated he wasn't one of his own, so he took careful aim, one hand still on his bleeding gut and fired, hitting Phil squarely in the back, the bullet ripping through his heart and punching a football sized hole in his chest.

Mickey scrambled back up to his feet and took refuge behind the Defender, he tried to locate Phil and did so just in time to see his chest explode and his body slump to the floor. He put the shotgun to his shoulder and waited.

"Come on you little fucker show yourself," he whispered. That's when he saw the head. A smallish man with a big afro poked his head from around some fallen rubble. He had a pistol in his hand, and Mickey offered no warning and wasted no time. Emptying his shotgun the shot struck with deadly force, taking the man's head clean off, and spraying the remnants of it across the hangar wall.

The headless corpse stumbled forward and fell over the remains of Irena Petrov.

As the last shot echoed round the building and slowly died away, an eerie silence settled over the hangar. Mickey crouched alone behind the Defender, listening intently for any sound that may indicate an enemy's location. Mr G scrambled and crawled back to the Cayennes. Who the fuck had hit the hangar and why?

He made a steering wheel gesture to his remaining man, who nodded his understanding, The G-Man clicked open the door of the nearest Cayenne and slipped into the driver's seat. He looked across at Mr G who gave him the thumbs up, as he turned the key and gunned the engine.

Mickey heard the engine roar and the squeal of the tyres on the concrete. He took a moment to plot the car's trajectory then turned and leapt up onto the bonnet of the Defender in one stride.

The Cayenne charged forward turning away from Mickey as it did so and away from the debris and headed towards the less damaged end of the hangar, Mickey levelled the shotgun at the turning 4x4 and fired, once, twice and on the third shot he hit the driver's door, the impact immediate. The driver, showered with shotgun pellets and shattering glass, lost control of the vehicle and it rammed through the increasingly flimsy wall of the hangar, across the small curtain of grass and into the tree covered slope of the airfield boundary.

Mr G seized his moment, advancing from his hiding position he had a clear view of the shotgun-wielding interloper.

His arm outstretched, he took careful aim, but the first shot missed. The second shot ripped through Mickey's left thigh, shattering his femur. He screamed, dropping the shotgun and falling backwards.

His great weight crashed down on the bonnet of the Land Rover, and he slid forward off the vehicle, clutching his wounded leg, coming to rest against the front tyre. Mr G moved forward, gun outstretched, his head moving from side to side trying to recognise any new threat.

He heard nothing and saw nothing.

* * *

Adam reached Jake in a matter of moments; his friend lay in an unconscious tangled heap, the right side of his head bleeding. Adam grabbed at his friend and pulled his head up to his own face, frantically checking for wounds.

No visible injuries to his body or legs.

Adam cradled Jake's head and looked at the bleeding. He sank to the floor with his friend's head in his lap, his eyes filling with tears of relief and joy that Jake wasn't dead and hadn't been shot. A stray bullet had just grazed his head, knocking him out. He hugged his friend hard, whispered into Jake's ear, "Oh thank god, thank god, thank god."

A low murmur from his friend made Adam focus once again. Jake's eyes opened slightly and then closed again, he tried to raise his hand and speak, but only mumbles came out.

"You're ok. You're going to be alright, I'll get you out of here, I'll get you safe." Adam rested his friend tenderly on the floor. He fussed to make him more comfortable, but achieved little.

"I have to go and see what's happened in there Jake," he gestured towards the hangar. The sound of shotgun blasts echoed from the hangar, "I need to make sure it's over, I'll be back in a minute... promise."

There was only a mumble and a half hearted grab of his sleeve from Jake. Adam jumped to his feet, picked up the gun and steadied himself. He took a deep breath and headed for the hangar door.

* * *

"Well, well, well, if it isn't Mickey Finn... come to try and finish Mr G off have you, come to cement your place in gangland folklore." Mr G stood over the critically injured Mickey. Mr G had blasted a gaping hole in his right leg, the femoral artery had ruptured and it now bled profusely. Nausea and pain engulfed Mickey, who was still able to register shock at discovering Mr G in the hangar.

"What the fuck are you doing here?" Mickey spoke as if he had no air in his lungs, "You're supposed to be back in London...grateful I busted this up..."

Mr G let out a sigh and a shrug of the shoulders,

354

"Another one? Another pawn in the game…sorry about your leg Mickey, but to be fair you did bust in here and kill my people." Mr G let his gun dangle down to the side of his, now no more than ten feet from Mickey.

"Tell me something Mr G, is it true that Barry was doing deals behind your back…behind my back?" Mr G nodded, Mickey didn't have long to live, the colour and life was draining from his face.

"Who with?" he asked.

"I thought he had drugs deals going with these Winchester boys…I was wrong."

"He had no deal with them…" panted Mickey.

"The Winchester boys said Barry was using the Petrovs to distribute coke in London…turns out that the Petrovs were actually supplying the drugs…"

Mickey nodded. "Makes sense…"

"What you doing here Mickey?"

"Came to take out the Petrovs – Adam told me he had taken over Barry's role on the deal, but that the Petrovs were making threats and needed sorting out. All I had to do was turn up and hit them as they left."

Mr G nodded. "You deliver me the Petrovs and reveal Barry's other London connection…."

"You're supposed to be so grateful you let me run the manor." Mickey coughed a mouthful of blood onto his chest.

"Jesus – Adam, he played everyone off didn't he…"

355

"Seems so…he called me to hit the hangar, not the planned ambush. So you found out the truth then."

Mr G sighed and looked around at the chaos and bodies in the hangar, "Something like that, yeah."

Mickey coughed again and slumped a little deeper toward death.

"Mickey, do you know who killed Gregor Bartok? It's been bugging me for a long time."

Mickey let out little chuckle that ended in a rasping cough.

"Yeah… I know who it was" he paused, Mr G leaned in a little closer to hear more clearly.

"It was the Petrovs."

"Oh man," said Mr G.

"When Bartok ripped you off he ripped them off, they got to him before me. Barry didn't know."

Mr G shrugged his shoulders, in a "of course" manner.

"I have one last bit of information for you…." Mickey beckoned Mr G in. He bent forward to hear the fading voice and as he did so, the click of an old fashioned revolver hammer made him look down. Mickey had drawn a vintage Smith and Wesson revolver, he had it aimed straight at Mr G's chest.

"What you thinking Mickey, you going to kill me?"

"I had given it some thought yeah….no G-Men left to protect you now are there?"

"Why now Mickey?"

"Coz -You would never have let me take over Barry's manor would you…"

Mr G didn't say anything, his silence speaking volumes. Mickey shut his eyes, nodded, a lifetime of service, giving his all for lost causes in and out of the ring, he felt the light around him darken. His once great strength finally ebbing away, with his last breath he pulled the trigger. He didn't hear the body fall or see the large red stain grow centimetre by centimetre on Mr G's white Fila tracksuit.

Adam popped his head over the bonnet and cocked it to one side like a nervous prey, listening for any more sounds. The hangar was in ruins, half the roof had caved in and giant open wound-like holes adorned the walls.

He'd heard Mickey and Mr G talking and he'd heard a final shot but nothing since. He sneaked along the wreckage of the Defender, stepping over and around the bodies as he went, his eyes scanning the debris, searching for any sign of Melissa. He moved to the other side of the wrecked Defender and saw Mr G lying face down in heap on the floor. He scanned left then right and noticed Mickey, prostrate on his back, seemingly frozen in the last position of their fatal showdown, a faint disturbing smile etched on his lips.

Adam turned back towards the door, bodies and limbs littered the floor, the nausea induced by the carnage about to get the better of him. Then he noticed a pair of delicate feet, protruding from the body of Irena Petrov and a headless G-Man. He kicked at the decapitated body pushing it inefficiently off the unconscious body of Melissa. He bent down and grabbed the younger Petrov sister by an ankle and slowly dragged her limp, bloodied corpse away from Melissa.

Once he had cleared her of the bodies, Adam tried to scoop her up in his arms, his knees buckling as he did so. He staggered towards the door, his biceps burning with the dead weight. As he reached the door a metallic glint caught his eye. It was the aluminium suitcase. Adam eyed it hungrily.

Dismissing the notion that he could carry both, he continued out of the door. They emerged into the full glare of the daylight and Adam immediately set out for the nearest trees, carrying Melissa to the left side of the airfield, the western edge. It had at least an acre of heavy woodland beyond the perimeter. He reached the long grass, about fifty yards from the hangar and gently laid her down. He wiped his hand across her face and checked her for injuries, she had a nasty gash on the head but seemed to be otherwise OK.

He cupped her small face in his hands and pulled her lips to his own and kissed her, she didn't respond, "I'm here baby…Adam's here…I'm sorry." He kissed her again and held her face to his for a moment, then he lay her gently back down on the grass.

He sprang to his feet and raced back to the hangar. Reaching inside the door he grabbed the handle of the aluminium suitcase and tugged. It put up only minor resistance. When it was safely in his hands, he fumbled clumsily with the latches and eventually the lid popped open and the brightly coloured notes beamed back at him. Momentarily he moved his hand across the money…then pulled his hand back clenching it into a fist, almost as if hot to the touch. Suitcase in hand he trundled back to where he had left Melissa. He looked down bewildered at the now empty spot of flattened grass.

"ADAM…ADAM" the bleary cry forced him to turn, he looked across the airstrip to where Jake began stirring, trying to get to his feet. Adam stared at the empty space only moments ago occupied by a seemingly unconscious Melissa, his eyes tracking her likely route into the dense woodland beyond. He stared into the trees and undergrowth, scanning left and right, trying to catch a glimpse of where she might be. A twinge of adrenalin lurched in his stomach, and he took a step towards the trees, reaching out with his arm to push branches aside.

"ADAM… ADAM, where are you." He stopped in his tracks as he heard the mournful calling of his name and with his head slightly bowed he looked into the wood again.

He made a decision.

He filled his lungs and called out.

"IF YOU CAN HEAR ME…if you can hear, YOU NEED TO KNOW, I LIED, I lied when I said that it was in the past tense, …YES I DO STILL MEAN IT, I DO STILL LOVE YOU…" He waited, longing for a response, but he heard only the faint sound of the gentle breeze through the trees.

When nothing came he yelled, "I'M SORRY TO..."

"ADAM...!" Jake's call jolted him back to the present once again. He turned his head and listened hard, squinting as he did so. There in the distance, the sound of the rustling trees had been joined by the faint wail of sirens, clearly drawing nearer. Adam took one last lingering look into the wood, then he turned and raced back to his friend.

Jake stumbled, trying to stand, his legs disobeyed him and he couldn't manage it alone.

"Give me your arm Jake." Adam hauled his friend to his feet and tucked his shoulder under Jake's arm and heaved. He teetered under the weight for a moment and stepped forward. Stumbling short steps at first that grew into more confident strides, he set off towards the northern end of the airstrip, back to where Adam had been hiding at the beginning of the day.

Adam grunted under the weight, the sirens rising in volume as they drew nearer. "Come on mate, you've got to help me," he said, "we've to get to the trees before the police get here." Adam chanced a look over his shoulder, still nothing to see, but the sirens grew louder. He tried to imagine how far away that made them and came up only with 'too close'.

Adam began to trot, his breath exhaling in powerful bursts. He staggered past the point where the runway meets the grass, the point he had nose dived earlier. The long grass and molehill-riddled grass tripped him, he stumbled, but stayed upright and in control of Jake. The sweat gathered on his brow and his shoulder screamed its displeasure at the dead weight it supported. The sirens sounded deafening, they were all Adam could hear. Now he was just thirty feet from the sanctuary of the trees.

The police car roared into the airfield, its view of the far end obscured by the hangar, two more cars followed in quick succession, their squealing tyres announcing their arrival. Adam urged his legs for one final push and as the trees approached he dived head first, launching the semi-conscious Jake into the woods just as the first car rounded the hangar.

He tumbled into the undergrowth and landed on his knees beside his prostrate friend. He turned his head, looking over his shoulder to see the police cars gather at the hangar entrance.

Dragging Jake behind him, he scrambled further into the wood.

"Adam…" Jake, still groggy, tried to pull himself up.

"We've got to get to the car, have to get on a normal road before any helicopters arrive…"

Adam, panting from the run to the woods, only had the breath to utter, "Righto".

Five minutes later Adam unceremoniously shoved Jake head-first into the car. He hopped in to the driver's seat and started the engine.

Pull away slowly and calmly, he repeated to himself.

He drove along the dried mud lane and out of the wood surrounding the airfield. Adam kept checking for a helicopter but heard and saw nothing. He followed the track by the field, taking them away from the scene of the crime, before entering a second spinney. This small half mile of wood concealed them from both road and air, and led them to a tarmac road, again partially hidden by overhanging trees and to what he hoped would be sanctuary.

Chapter Twenty Eight

Adam dropped the newspaper down on the table with a slap and scattered his car keys across the kitchen counter. The newspaper headline read,

"MASSACRE AT AIRFIELD: LATEST GANGLAND KILLINGS..."

He sipped at the Café Nero grande latte he had bought in town, getting that unsatisfying mouthful of foam before the scolding hot liquid hit his lips. He stared at the title, maybe for the fifth time. He couldn't relate the story and headline to the events of the last week or so. Nothing seemed real.

It had been an unremarkable three days, compared to the previous week. Adam had tried to return to normal, he'd even managed the odd work meeting, he had tried to engage in as normal a life as possible.

That normally involved Jake.

Jake had demanded he be left alone, refusing to accept Adam's plea for a get-together. Adam understood he needed to physically heal, but it was the mental scars of the battle that Adam would never be able to relate to. Adam had recovered from the grazes and scratches, his own wounds centred on emotional rather than physical pain.

The conversation had been brief .

"Adam leave me alone – I don't want to talk about it."

"Please Jake, I need to talk it through with someone. There isn't anyone else but you."

"Not my problem… go away. Please." The words were firm, the desire clear, but Jake didn't put the phone down in the intervening silence.

"I found the case. I have the £100,000 from the handover."

Jake said nothing.

"We've the full £200,000 Mr G gave us as well." Adam wanted to keep the thrill out of his voice but he didn't succeed.

"I don't care Adam…" Jake's voice sounded drawn.

"We're in the clear, I checked the hangar. Everyone is dead…" he lied.

Adam could hear the receiver at the other end move, it clicked and banged and sounded like Jake had put the phone down and walked away. He hadn't.

"That isn't something to celebrate Adam…a lot of people died because of you." The statement came out like a missile, locked on target and focused.

"They all came to kill."

"Did we Adam?" Jake asked.

Adam didn't reply, the phone crackled during the lull in conversation.

"We aren't the bad guys in this Jake."

"No? Then what are we. Tell me what we are?"

Adam bit his lip, he'd never heard his friend so down, so lacking in his customary verve. It unnerved him, but Adam knew he was hiding from the truth of his friends words.

"We were in the wrong place at the wrong time…innocents caught up in the cross-fire." Trying to convince himself more.

"Don't make me laugh. Innocents!" Jake spat the word out like it was poison.

" I was in that hangar. I heard it all. No one had to be there, none of it had to happen. It happened because you…no, we made it so."

Adam noted that Jake included himself. Adam accepted the guilt of getting his friend involved, but said nothing.

"Blood on our hands eh Adam. Covered in it we are. Responsible, totally fucking responsible"

Adam didn't know how to respond, like consoling a bereaved friend, he had nothing left but platitudes and clichés.

"I want you to leave me alone.."Jake said again.

"And the money…"

The phone went dead. The dial tone sounded like the loudest alarm Adam had ever heard. Adam hadn't tried to call Jake again.

Adam had also ignored the calls from his mother, he knew he wouldn't be able to do it indefinitely, but for now, he couldn't face the questions and gentle prying. She would have read the papers and seen the news report. Beano and Mr G's faces would soon be plastered across the media, he knew he might have some explaining to do.

He checked his phone again. Maybe for the tenth or eleventh time that morning, still no message from Melissa. He poured the remains of the coffee down the sink, it tasted vile, insipid and over brewed as always. He thought about what he had paid for it, thought again that he simply didn't need a pint of coffee...who did?

"You shouldn't waste coffee," the voice cut through him like a knife. He wheeled around dropping the cardboard mug on the floor. Sitting, crossed legged on his easy chair, looking radiant and alive, more alive than he had ever seen her, was Melissa Henderson.

"I hate the stuff...I buy it out of habit."

He moved toward her, dropping to his knees so his face met hers, their faces leaned together and their lips touched. A slow gentle kiss, his hands grasping her face throughout. She pulled away first, self-conscious, but never taking her eyes from his. He eyed the elastoplast that secured a swab of cotton wool across the gash on her forehead. He went to touch it but she jerked her head away.

"Why did you run?" he whispered gently.

"I came to and heard the sirens…no one was around, I just ran."

Adam nodded unconcerned; relieved she was well and had made contact.

"Was it you that pulled me out of the hangar?" she asked.

Adam nodded yes. Their heads came together and they sat forehead to forehead as they spoke.

"You didn't hear me shout then...I had to go back for Jake. He was injured, but I yelled..." His words tailed off.

He felt guilty about leaving her and he didn't know why.

"I think so…but I was worried about the sirens and the cars...Tell me something Adam, why was Barry at the handover? He shouldn't have been involved."

"The plans got changed… you shouldn't have been there either." A small boy's grin broke out on his face.

"I know, I hadn't planned on being… it seems all our plans were messed up... I don't understand why Barry was there as Mr G's prisoner."

"It's a long story Mel and not my finest hour…"

"I have the time…"

Adam took in a big breath and sighed it out. He had hoped to see Melissa again, but was not keen on having to explain his actions.

"You have to understand Mel, that a lot of decisions were taken as a result of subsequent actions… all a bit cause and effect I'm afraid." He looked at her expecting a response. When none was forthcoming he carried on.

"Remind me what we agreed," he said trying to look flippant.

"You were supposed to hold the cash and begin the launder process and I would make contact with the Petrovs," Melissa said.

Adam nodded and chimed in a sing-song way..."to undermine Barry and set up a new drug deal – then once that was done we could sell the information to Mr G."

"Because he would pay handsomely for the information..." Melissa interjected.

"You weren't wrong on that front," added Adam.

Melissa patted her palms on her thighs in agitation, "Barry...what about Barry?" she persisted.

"Well you went out for a walk that morning and while you were away I was attacked by Mickey, who was hell bent on breaking my fingers and finding you...that seemed a little aggressive."

"I arrived back in time to see them...I did as you said. I ran. Straight to the Petrovs and set the plan in motion. We texted, we agreed." Melissa added.

Adam swayed his head, weighing up what he would say next. "Well Jake came to the rescue, beat up Mickey and the other one – it made him an accomplice."

"Sounds a bit handy your friend Jake."

"He is. Mickey was less keen to get physical after that..." She looked at him hard, "So..?"

"I had to think on my feet Melissa. They weren't supposed to find me, you said they wouldn't, remember?" Adam rubbed his hand over his face and focused his mind on the story.

"I had to make a new plan, Jake decided that we should give the money back to Barry – so we arranged the handover."

"How did that happen?"

"Jake wasn't party to the bigger picture was he, if Barry got the cash then you and I would miss out. So I filled the bag with paper and spread £10,000 across the top and thought I could bluff out the handover – you know put the bag down and run like hell."

Melissa gently shook her head, surprised at Adam's audacity.

"Well Barry acted like such a moron, shot his mouth off and his bloody gun…Jake dealt with the situation and him…Barry shot his own man, not us."

Adam almost seemed proud of the point, ensuring Melissa understood the emphasis.

"Sorry for coming back to this point – how come Barry ended up at the Petrov handover?"

"Well the other guard was run over by one of Jake's cars and we ended up kidnapping Barry." Adam and Melissa slowly separated as they chatted, the events of the recent past driving an invisible wedge between them.

"I figured his disappearing would help you and speed up the process with the Petrovs, all I had to do was keep him safe until the rest of the plan was done…"

Adam stood up and moved back across the room. Melissa had an edge to her voice and her usually welcoming eyes now looked cold and grey.

"You shouldn't have imprisoned him Adam"

"Why does Barry and what happened to him matter…you don't owe him anything…do you? Without the money, he would have had nothing to pay Mr G and it would have made your job easier and our take bigger. I thought it was the right thing to do."

Melissa ignored him, she got to her feet and looked out of the window, out through the off white net curtains. "How much did Mr G pay for the information about the Petrov deal in the end?"

"A lot more than you thought… He paid £200k," Adam said.

"Wow." She was genuinely surprised…. "That's double what we expected."

"Yeah well my deal with Mr G had an added component, something you hadn't banked on."

"You said you could deliver Barry as well as the Petrovs. Neat, very neat Adam".

"We have to recognise that Jake is now fully involved. He became part of the whole deal because he discovered the bag wasn't full at the handover and I gave him an edited version of the truth." Adam moved towards her, but something about her manner held him back.

Melissa moved around the room so that her back was to the door.

"So is all the money here, my original £100k and the £200k from Mr G…you have it right?"

"No…" Adam felt uneasy, he couldn't see any love in Melissa's face, and recent events had made him cautious.

"I have half and Jake has half of the Mr G money," he lied. Half of it he had actually hidden in the new house over the road. Jake had pushed him away when he had taken the rest to him, shutting the door in his face. It sat in the same black holdall under the stairs.

"Your original money, minus the £10,000 is in a safety deposit box in town."

"Why is £10,000 missing?"

"Jesus Mel – we're discussing £300k and the death of a lot of people and you're pissed at £10,000 missing. If you must know it's at Jake's storage depot, where we left it after the stupid handover. Frankly I figured he could keep it and use it to cover a few expenses he has incurred."

"It,s not your money to give away Adam."

Incredulous at the statement he had just heard, it felt like a light had come on and all that was blurred and indistinct now came into sharp focus.

"You don't want to share any of it …do you?"

No response.

"You never intended to…did you?" He said.

Melissa did a little clap.

"Well done speedy Gonzalez, you should also know that I never stole a penny from Barry. He gave it to me, he knew I needed to have something to tempt you with…."

Adam looked puzzled, made some calculations and deductions, a realisation of the truth beginning to dawn on him.

Then a voice from the grave filled the room.

"Hello boy."

The disembodied voice cut through Adam. From behind Melissa Barry Hunt limped into the room, his face bore the scars of the airfield catastrophe, his limp the result of the collapsed roof, an automatic pistol in his hand.

"That's right boy…Barry's back." He levelled the gun at waist height and pointed at Adam.

"Fuck it," said Adam.

"What she says is true, she never took a penny."

Adam did his best to stay calm and show as little emotion as possible.

"I should thank you, your little fun and games meant we got twice what we expected from Mr G."

"With the added bonus, that all of them that wanted you dead, ending up as stiffs themselves…" Adam offered.

"You played a blinder boy….Melissa said you were a smart lad… she also said you'd do anything for her."

"She knows me too well."

"Yeah, seems like it," Melissa said, " people rarely change." A vindictive smile etched on her face.

"Where's the money?" Barry kept the pistol low and pointed at Adam's stomach. Adam eyed it carefully.

If you tackle him, you need to get within the killing zone, he thought to himself, recalling Jake's once seemingly glib advice.

"My half is under the stairs in the cupboard." Melissa didn't need to be told twice, she trotted out of the room to retrieve it.

"Jake has the rest."

"Jake – the partner in crime, yeah he was an unwelcome addition to the plan, that one. His idea was it, to sell me as well as the information to Mr G?"

"I never planned for him to be involved, not this much anyway. He saved me from Mickey. They seemed very intent on busting my fingers, anyway Jake pulled me out of there…I had to improvise after that."

"He's not lying about the money, there really is only £90k in here." Melissa pulled open the bag to emphasise the point.

Adam remembered the look on Jake's face several days earlier when he had looked in the same bag.

He retreated back into the living room, anxious to draw them both further into the room. He posed a question, knowing that by a quirk of nature, they would approach nearer to him as they answered.

"Can I ask Barry, why you didn't just take the bag at the handover, I mean you knew I didn't have a clue about your involvement.. take the bag, you'd have the money?"

Barry moved forward, arm outstretched, pistol still trained on Adam's stomach.

"I planned to take it, though I wanted to find Mel as well. I figured you might have done something to her... but in the heat of the moment I got over excited, felt I needed to make a point, make your friends shit their pants. I hadn't expected old army boy and his merry men to be on hand did I?"

Melissa rolled her eyes. "Only you could decide to scare a group of ex-soldiers and professional killers."

"Mr G had turned up the heat on me. It meant everything had to be bought forward. I needed to get out of London fast. No time to see our full scam of you through. I was planning to disappear as soon as I had the cash from the handover – I'd just shoot Leon and Bobby, collect what I had syphoned from the manor and vanish with Mel."

Adam joined the dots, the full picture was becoming clear. "I'd fed Mr G a line about Mickey's little deal in Winchester and how it had gone all tits up," Barry said as he moved deeper into the room. Melissa stayed where she was.

"He knew I was coming south to sort it, if I vanished, then he would have gone to Mickey for answers and of course the missing money the manor owed."

"And Mickey and us would have have gotten the blame?" He wanted to keep Barry talking and lull him into a false sense of security. Barry hitched his trousers; he found it tough with one hand holding a gun, his gut got in the way.

"You put me through a lot boy, locking me up like that. No honour amongst thieves is there?"

"I haven't seen a lot so far."

"You turned me over to Mr G without a second thought, lucky for me he likes his theatrics or I might be dead."

"What did I care? Don't get me wrong. I understand it all now…but I thought the more money we got for you and the information, the more Melissa and I could share. But then I had no idea about your own scheme together did I." Adam tried to lace his voice with contempt.

"Why did I believe you and your plan Mel?" Adam shook his head in self disgust.

"Enough with the self pity," interjected Barry, "you did what you had to do."

"Really?"

"You saw the situation and ran with it…part of me admires you. Maybe you remind me of myself at the same age."

Adam shook his head, "Jesus that's some compliment."

Barry laughed, his face turning red with the effort. He turned to see if Melissa was joining in. He came to an abrupt halt when he saw her expression unchanged.

"Careful Barry," she said, "you'll rupture the scabs."

Barry dabbed at the mess of welts, scars and bruising on his face and his jollity receded.

"Tell me about the Petrovs boy."

"Well it seems Mel did too good a job convincing them that they could take over your old manor…the Petrovs got greedy."

"You offered me to them as well didn't you? They saw me as a golden ticket to get well in with Mr G."

Adam nodded, taking a tiny step forward.

Melissa now chuckled. "So Adam, you set up the meeting to trade Barry off to the Petrovs and had Mr G waiting in the wings to take them down for their dealings with the missing Barry…who you had already sold back to Mr G."

Barry stepped up to her and threw his free arm around her and gave her sloppy kiss. Adam jerked involuntarily, part of him wanted to lunge at the vile old man in front him. But he knew he would never cover the distance before Barry fired a shot off

"What I don't get..." Barry asked, unaware of Adam's intent,

"... is who the hell hit the hangar and took out the G-Men?"

Adam looked at Melissa, "Didn't she fill you in, you seem to have all the answers between you."

"Adam, how would I know about that, it was chaos in there, a pitch battle."

"Well Mr G was supposed to simply kill the Petrov at the handover," Adam began, "… and you of course, Barry."

Adam waited a moment, Barry waved the pistol at him to continue. He stepped forward a little to hear the response.

"He was supposed to make his point, collect souvenirs and drive away with the Petrov drugs and his reputation restored. Trouble was we knew that our little scam would come unravelled if Mickey ever told him the real nature of how we met…so it was too dangerous for us to have Mickey in charge of your old manor Barry..."

"So you went and set poor old Mickey up as well…" Melissa showed a sense of pride for Adam's plan.

"Yeah…we simply told him that if he hit the Petrovs at the drug deal he would be able to go to Mr G as the hero. He'd deliver some dodgy drug dealers and wipe out a threat to his existence in one fell swoop."

"And of course you just happened to know when the Petrovs would be conducting an illicit deal that Mr G would be very grateful to have stopped." Barry said.

"So Mickey was prepared to ambush the group at the airfield on your say so." Melissa also pieced together Adam's jigsaw of events.

"Correct, only Mickey thought he would be hitting the Petrovs when in fact we knew he would of course be hitting Mr G."

"Mr G would fire back at Mickey because he would assume Mickey had been part of Barry's double cross all along and that it was a hit…" Melissa added.

Adam applauded them both. "Simple hey?"

Barry nodded his appreciation, "clever stuff... but how could you be certain that everyone would kill each other in the gun fight?"

"It all went tits up when she pitched up." Adam pointed at Melissa, "she shouldn't have been there. Without her, no one at the handover would have known the truth."

"I get that…so you called Mickey to hit the hangar instead of the ambush…to start the gun fight…you tried to save her didn't you?" Barry said, a condescending smirk on his face.

Adam bowed his head, his cheeks flushed a little with embarrassment.

"BUT…what if someone ended up alive after all that mayhem, you couldn't leave anyone alive," Melissa added.

"Right. I would simply finish off anyone left."

"You would have killed anyone left?... right I'll believe that when I see it." Barry laughed smugly.

"Needs must when the devil drives Barry... I missed you in the rubble though. I thought you were dead…"

"I managed to scramble away, hide... but you saved the girl…what a hero!"

Adam breathed heavily, "Yeah… well I thought things were different. So you went in and got him?" he asked Melissa.

"That I did, he was near the big hole in the wall anyway…" she said without emotion.

"I also saved Jake," Adam said. He bowed his head but moved forward a step.

"No more talk sunshine. We're off to say hello to Jake, and find this safety deposit box to get the rest of my cash."

"Look you have £90k, take it, leave…leave Jake out of this. Leave me out of this…take her, I'll give you the details for the deposit box, it's not a bank one, you just need the key. Take it all, the cash, her and just get out of my life." Adam's voice sounded tired, but a sense of controlled venom lurked in the background. His love for Melissa evaporated by the second, the space left in his heart being rapidly filled with hate and revenge.

"I can't believe you lied to me again…I am such a loser…I did all this. I did all those things for you…"

"Fuck me Adam, you are a gullible twat. I flash my baby blues, do a bit of cooking and wiggle my arse and I get you to do anything I want…don't make out your greed is any different to ours, you wanted the money as well."

Adam shrugged, he knew she was right.

"Did the sex mean nothing, do I mean nothing? Tell me honestly was every word you said a lie?" His voice had no trace of pleading, no hint of desperation. His eyes cold and dead looked right through her.

"Every word."

"And you love this balding old twat." Adam sneered.

"This 'balding twat' as you call him, took me off the streets Adam, helped me stand tall.."

"Bullshit. Stop it Melissa. Do you even know when you're lying anymore? You saved him from the hangar and are with him now for one reason only. MONEY."

"Watch your mouth." Barry pointed the gun once more.

379

"Money Barry, not love. You've got what, close to a million quid syphoned from the manors profits. That's a million reasons Mel is hanging around." He was shouting now, but Melissa just smiled.

"Don't worry Barry babes, you know how I feel about you."

"Same old Mel... you cooked up this plan for Barry, it's your idea isn't it? All of this just to get another few hundred grand out of Mr G so you could ride off into the sunset... and then dump him somewhere down the road."

"SHUT IT BOY" Barry forced the gun to Adam's face.

"OR WHAT?" Adam shouted. "I sat and watched you snivelling and crying in that cell. Without Mickey to protect you you're nothing but a fat old loser..."

Barry raised the gun and aimed.

"Are you going to shoot me Barry?...after what I have seen and done in the last few days...you don't fucking scare me, not one fucking bit."

Adam sized up to Barry, pressing his chest against the barrel of the pistol, moving into the killing zone.

"Pull the trigger...come on Barry," Adam whispered, "blow me away, show her how hard you are, impress the lady, show her what a big man you are..."

Adam's face hovered no more than six inches from Barry's, they could taste the other's breath.

"Don't push me boy...I can get my hands dirty all right..." he leant back slightly from Adam's jutting head.

Melissa stood, amused at the scene playing out in front of her, the black holdall slung over one shoulder. "Boys...easy, what do you think, settle it with an arm wrestle?"

The men didn't move.

"Tell you what. I'll suck the winners cock."

Barry turned and let out a little laugh.

"Who's your money on?" Adam asked.

"Jesus, come on... one of you does this for a living the other is playing at it. You work it out."

Barry guffawed, his head lolled back as he did so.

It created a pause, what Jake would call a deadly moment. Adam had moved in for the kill and he didn't hesitate. He brought his left hand up from below, hitting Barry's gun holding arm, grabbing the wrist and forcing the gun into the air. The speed and accuracy confused Barry. He leaned back to avoid the fast rising pistol.

Adam thrust out his right hand, creating a rigid V with his thumb and palm. It shot out, as fast as he could manage. Three feet covered in a hundredth of a second. With Barry's head back his neck sat exposed, the Adam's apple protruding invitingly.

Adam's hand hit it flush.

He extended his arm straight through the crunch of flesh and tissue. A sickening sound ensued as the neck collapsed. It folded as if all the air had been sucked out of it.

Barry fell to his knees, eyes bulging at the sudden lack of oxygen, Adam twisted his arm and relieved Barry completely of the gun. Barry raised his hands to his throat as if clutching at some invisible device constricting his air.

Adam dropped to one knee and swivelled to face Melissa, the gun raised, but he found only an empty space. His eyes tracked through the house to the kitchen and the swinging, open back door. He rose, sneaked forward through the house to the door and peered out, just in time to see a figure of a woman sprint round the corner at the far end of the alley, carrying a black holdall.

For the most fleeting of moments he contemplated giving chase, but instead he simply pulled the door to and walked back to his living room.

Barry Hunt sat fighting for breath and Adam kneeled in front of him and spoke, barely above a whisper.

"Jake tells me the victim of this injury has about a minute from point of impact to death, if you do it right. It was my first time…maybe you'll last two…"

Barry's eyes searched the room for salvation, some kind of hope. Adam followed his gaze, understanding he was trying to look to the door.

"She's gone Barry. She didn't even pause, took the bag and went."

He knew she had no intention of staying with Barry.

"Tell me something?" Adam patted the dying man on the shoulder in mock solidarity.

"Do you know any Aesop fables?"

Barry sagged forward, Adam propped him back up so he cold look him in the eye. The last effort of life was running out of Barry's body. Adam settled into the seat and made himself comfortable.

"A friend told me this fable…I didn't understand it at first…but I think I do now."

"You see, there was a frog and a scorpion…"

The End

Printed in the United States
209557BV00002B/103-108/P